The
Husband
Checklist

ALSO BY JASMIN MILLER

Brooksville Series

Baking With A Rockstar - A Single Parent Romance

Tempted By My Roommate - A Friends to Lovers Romance

The Best Kind Series

The Best Kind Of Mistake - A Workplace Romantic Comedy

The Best Kind Of Surprise - A Surprise Pregnancy Romantic Comedy

---

Standalone

The Husband Checklist - A Brother's Best Friend Romance

Kings Of The Water Series

Secret Plunge - A Surprise Pregnancy Sports Romance

Fresh Meet - A Single Dad Sports Romance

The Husband Checklist

JASMIN MILLER

The Husband Checklist

Copyright © 2019 by Jasmin Miller

Published: Jasmin Miller 2019
jasmin@jasminmiller.com
www.jasminmiller.com
Editing: Marion Archer, Making Manuscripts
Proofreading: Judy Zweifel, Judy's Proofreading
Cover Art: Najla Qamber, Qamber Designs & Media

To my husband,
The man who matched my own checklist perfectly.

Chapter One

JULIA

*M*y shoes squeak as I make my way up the porch steps, banging on the white door with the heel of my hand. "Come on, Ollie."

The puddle at my feet grows as I wait. I want nothing more than to get out of my soaked clothes, jump under the hot shower, and curl up in bed. After alternating between knocking and ringing the bell, the door finally opens, and I let out a sigh of relief as I look up.

But, holy moly. This is most definitely *not* my brother standing in front of me.

My vision is filled with none other than his best friend, Carter.

The same one I grew up with, at least once both he and my brother finally accepted I wasn't going to leave them alone, even though I was two years younger.

"Jules? What the hell happened to you?" He gives me a once-over, his eyes going wide as he takes in my appearance and the suitcase behind me.

My stomach rolls, his question bringing back today's

events. Events I'd rather not think about. Instead, I force the fresh memory back into a box in my mind, not planning on going there anytime soon.

"What are *you* doing here? Are you rooming with Ollie?" The second the words leave my mouth, I vaguely remember my brother mentioning something about it the last time we talked.

That's what happens when you don't pay enough attention.

"I am."

Two words, and I'm pulled into all things Carter. So much easier to focus on him, letting him distract me from this shitshow my life has turned into.

The tepid temperatures of the rain have slowly turned my skin cold under my soaked clothes, but I'm not a hundred percent positive that's the reason for the goose bumps that appeared out of nowhere. When I saw him a few months ago, he definitely didn't greet me like this.

Suppressing a shiver, another question tumbles out of my mouth. "And why on earth are you half-naked? Do you usually open the door like this?"

He looks down his body as if it would answer for him, which doesn't take very long given he only has a towel wrapped around his waist. Not that there isn't a lot to check out with his well-over-six-foot frame. But that's more for me, of course.

Despite the messy state I'm in—both physically and emotionally—I can't help but roam over the fine contours of his upper body while he's not looking.

I guess old habits die hard. It feels a little bad, like looking at him is taboo.

He's the forbidden fruit, per my brother's demand at least. But Ollie isn't here, and since I'm newly single, it's really no one's business who or what I'm looking at.

Large parts of Carter's upper body are covered in tattoos —chest, biceps—and if memory serves right, there are a few on his back too. Most of them are abstract—beautiful black drawings I wanted to trace a time or two when I was younger.

Carter clears his throat, and I snap out of my trance. No one can fault me for being fascinated by all those tattoos and muscles.

The embarrassment of getting caught still flames my cheeks, and I refrain from covering them with my hands. I only walked a few feet from my car to the front door in the rain, but I know it was enough for my mascara to run down my face. I'm probably only making it worse the more I try to wipe it away.

But I shouldn't be ogling Carter so soon after my boyfriend broke up with me. Then again, Carter has always been hard to ignore—all male with wide shoulders, narrow hips, longish, messy dark-blond hair, a slight scruff on his face. Not to mention the most hypnotizing blue-gray eyes I've ever seen.

"I'd just turned off the shower when I heard the bell ringing. After the tenth ring—not to mention the incessant banging—I thought it might be urgent, so I didn't waste any more time by putting on clothes." He crosses his arms in front of his chest, and I close my eyes for a moment, hoping like hell his towel will stay put. I couldn't live through that sort of mortification tonight, even though Carter would probably find it hilarious.

He's never been shy.

Stepping to the side, his hand goes back to the door. "Are you planning on coming inside or what?"

Right. I mentally facepalm myself, probably looking like a total idiot.

Just when I'm about to step over the threshold, I'm reminded of my messy state. "Could you get me a towel first, please? I don't want to drip all over the floor."

"Sure thing." But before he turns to walk away, a grin appears on his face. "Or do you want this towel, Jules?" He points at his hips, and I'm yet again happy for my zombie look.

This is the Carter I know. Carefree, goofy, flirtatious, and silly as heck.

Normally, I enjoy his lighthearted demeanor, but right now, it pushes all the wrong buttons. "Not now, Carter. I've had a shitty day and really don't feel like jokes, okay?"

There's no gusto in my voice, but the tone says it all. It's thick and shaky, cracking near the end.

My finger is poised to poke his chest to make my point clear, but I pull it back when I remember all the naked skin in front of me.

The smile falls as quickly from his face as it appeared. "Shit. Sorry. I'll get that towel. Be right back."

Turning around, he walks off toward the bedrooms. I use that moment to take off my hoodie and let it drop to the ground, somehow managing to bump into my suitcase that tips over, landing on the welcome mat with a loud *thud*. I stare at it for a moment, briefly wondering if kicking it would make me feel better, before continuing with my task. I'm in the middle of taking off my sneakers when Carter reappears, this time dressed in tan cargo shorts and a black T-shirt.

After setting both shoes on the ground, I take the towel from his outstretched hand and rub it over my hair. "Thank you."

"Why don't you take a shower while I get your things?"

I nod absentmindedly and look back up at him to thank him once more, just to find him staring at my chest. This time I *do* poke him. "What are you staring at?"

"Sorry, but . . ." He doesn't finish his sentence, pointing at my top instead. Following his gaze, I groan when I realize my black lace bra shows through my wet tank top, nipples on show and all.

Throwing my hands in the air, I probably give him an even better show. "Gosh, you're twenty-five, not fifteen."

"They're boobs." He shrugs, like that explanation clears up everything.

On second thought, it probably does for him. Or maybe every guy? I wouldn't be surprised.

I sigh and push past him. "I'll go take that shower now."

The face that greets me in the mirror after my shower still looks a bit scary, but at least more human. I traded off the runny-mascara zombie face for red, puffy eyes.

My messy reflection is a true representation of today's events. I walk out of the en-suite bathroom into the bedroom, wondering if Carter would ignore me if I just slipped into bed and pulled the blanket over my head to hide for a while. I'm not sure I can play pretend tonight. I'm too raw. *We're no longer right for each other, Julia. Surely you understand why.*

No, it still makes very little sense at all. Much like why Carter is here and not Ollie.

So I put on my big girl pants and walk into the living room. Carter's in the kitchen, facing away from me. The high ceilings of the open floor plan have always been one of my favorite things about my childhood home.

My brother has updated a few things over the years, giving the whole place a definite male touch, with lots of dark colors, leather, and chrome. I like it. The only thing he didn't change is my old bedroom, the one my mom and I redid my senior year.

Carter looks over his shoulder, watching me approach the kitchen. Looking around the room, I admire Ollie's great taste in furnishings.

"I made you some tea with honey. We don't want you to get sick." I turn toward Carter and wonder when he became so thoughtful.

"Thank you." I take the steaming mug from him, noticing the words on it. *Better late than ugly.* I raise my eyebrows and look back at Carter, but he's nonchalant as always. Things don't shake Carter easily.

"It's your brother's, not mine."

"Well, that explains a lot. Speaking of Ollie, is he still at work?"

He cocks his head to the side and studies me for a moment. "He didn't tell you he went on a vacation with his girlfriend? Last-minute trip to Hawaii."

"He did *what* and with *who*?" I move my hands without thinking, forgetting about the hot tea I'm holding.

The *very* hot tea.

"Dang it." Some of the liquid spills over my hands, and I almost drop the mug.

Before I can react, Carter takes it from my hands while leading me to the kitchen sink. The faucet is on a second later, and he pushes my hands under the water before I can protest.

His hands are under the water with mine, gently rubbing my skin. "Are you okay?"

My eyes are trained on our hands, and my mind goes momentarily blank as I stare at our connected fingers. My skin tingles while my heart skips a beat, and I close my eyes to take a calming breath. It doesn't happen every day that I pour hot tea over myself, which is the only reason I can come up with why my body is reacting like this.

A minute later, Carter turns off the water and gently dries my hands with a kitchen towel. His touch is careful, like he's afraid to hurt me. My hands look so small in his considerably larger hands, and I watch with an odd fascination as he slowly turns them back and forth to examine them.

"Your skin's a little red, but it looks okay. You good?" His voice is gentle, making me look at him.

His eyebrows furrow, pulling together tightly across his forehead.

Carter and I haven't had a lot of contact over the last few years, only occasionally seeing each other in passing and mostly sticking to small talk. Nothing significant happened to make us spend less time together, even though I think it was my fault, at least partially. I've always written it off as being a part of growing up, as going after different things.

When he looks up from my hands and our gazes meet,

there are a million questions in his eyes. So, now I wonder. Just in the last few hours alone, I've come to realize that I like to live in denial, apparently not seeing what's right in front of me, or rather brushing it under the rug like it doesn't exist. I'm not sure I'm ready to face all the reasons for that yet. My brain is too muddled to think clearly, and to be honest, I don't want to think about anything anymore tonight.

I just want to forget.

If there was ever a moment for Carter to have one of his carefree, everything-is-so-much-fun moments to cheer me up, this would be it.

Instead, the worried look in his eyes does the opposite. After all the crying—first at my boyfriend's apartment, or rather ex-boyfriend now, and then on the way to my brother's —I promised myself to not shed another tear, at least not today. Yet here I am, my eyes all hot again as they get ready for what I expect to be a long night of wallowing and self-pity.

"Come here." Carter pulls me in for a hug before I have a chance to say anything, the big lump in my throat blocking anything to get by.

Being in his arms feels good. The familiarity returns like it was never gone, this moment giving me more comfort than I could have hoped for, especially with my brother not here.

After a few minutes of tears and sobbing—so much about my plan to not shed another tear—I finally feel like I might be able to speak. I take a deep breath, trying to calm my still shaky insides. Carter stays silent, continuously rubbing my back in soothing circles.

I force the next words up my throat as fast as I can,

somehow wanting to get them out in the open. "I'm homeless. Nate broke up with me."

Carter pushes me back in one swift move, looking at me wide-eyed. His grip on my arms tightens for a fraction of a second before he lets go. "He did what? Weren't you supposed to move in with him?"

"Yup. He had a last-minute change of heart." I sniffle, trying my best to wipe away any remaining evidence of my meltdown, the word diarrhea in full progress now. "Apparently, he had a *moment* when I was on my way over to him with all my stuff and realized we shouldn't take this next step but should break up instead. He said I've put on too many pounds, have an embarrassing job, and my personality is lacking. So generally speaking, I guess I . . . just suck."

He stares at me with his mouth hanging slightly open, his nostrils flaring, just as the doorbell rings.

When Carter doesn't move, and the doorbell rings again, I jab my thumb in the general vicinity of the front door. "Are you expecting someone?"

"Crap. I totally forgot." He snaps out of his trance, looking back and forth between the door and me in a frenzy before holding up a finger. "One sec. Let me take care of this quick."

"I didn't mean to ruin your night. Sorry." And I do feel bad. As much as I like having Carter around, I know he wasn't sitting here waiting for me tonight.

His posture stiffens. "What? No. I mean, yes, it's my date, but no, you're not ruining anything. Let me tell her we won't hang out tonight. I'm sure she'll understand."

I stare at him, suddenly having the strong sense to shake

him while also wanting to hug him. I think my feelings are already in Crazytown. "Why would you do that?"

He scratches his forehead, his voice louder than before. "Because of you, obviously. Why else?"

"Me?" I point my index finger at my chest, my voice suddenly an octave or two higher, and maybe slightly shrill too. "Don't be ridiculous. I'm fine. Totally fine. You hang out with your . . . friend, and I'll see you later or tomorrow."

His eyes roam over my face, but I keep what I hope is a believable smile plastered on it. It's so big, it hurts a little.

"Are you sure? I'll take her out for dinner instead."

I nod almost manically, surely matching my crazy smile. "Yes, absolutely. I'm sure I can find something sugary in the kitchen that will help me smother my sorrows."

What I really want to yell is "No, please stay" and get another reassuring hug, but I won't invade his life like this. Instead, I give him a push toward the door.

He still looks unsure but nods slowly. "All right. But call me if you need anything, okay? My number's still the same."

"Yes, Dad. Now go."

A moment later my fake smile slips as I lock the door behind him before sinking to the floor, refusing to let the tears fall down my cheeks.

Time for step one of my solo recovery phase: sugar treatment.

Chapter Two

CARTER

I lasted less than an hour with Jody. After making up a lame-ass excuse halfway through dinner, I hurried back to the house.

As soon as I open the door and step inside, I realize even an hour was probably too long.

Stupid.

"Carter, you're back," Julia yells across the room, a happy smile on her face.

At least this one's real, not like the fake one she gave me before I left. I knew she was putting on a show for me, and I let her. I thought she might need some alone time, but I should have listened to my gut and stayed with her.

Shit.

"Why are you standing there? Come join me. Now the party can really start." She still hollers, most of her words a slurry mess.

A quick scan of the coffee table in front of her confirms my suspicions that Julia was busy while I was gone. Not only has she found every imaginable sugar source that could possibly be in this house, but she also found the wine stash. Looks like she almost made it through a whole bottle.

Despite the situation, I have to laugh, making her smile even wider.

"What are you doing, Jules?" I walk over to the couch and sit next to her.

I try to take away the sizeable wine glass in her hand, but it doesn't go unnoticed, and she snags it right back, giving my hand a soft slap.

"Get your own glass, Carter." She sticks out her tongue, and I roll my eyes. She's so damn cute like this.

Most of our time growing up, the three of us—Ollie, Jules, and I—were a tight-knit group, which made it easy to keep watch over her alcohol consumption at parties in her teenage years.

I guess I have a drunken Julia for tonight, which is okay since she's usually a happy drunk. A bit silly sometimes and too impulsive but in a good mood.

"Have you talked to your brother?" I hope the change of subject might sober her up some, or at least make her put down the glass.

She nods and her whole body moves with the simple gesture. Wine sloshes dangerously close to the edge of the glass, but of course, Miss Tipsy doesn't notice. She might make an even bigger mess by dumping the whole glass on herself.

"Yup. He told me all about his awesome girlfriend and their last-minute trip. Apparently, he was going to call me tomorrow to update me on everything. I explained my sudden homeless situation to him and that I'd be staying here for a while. I think he said something about calling you soon about it too. Not sure what you have to do with any of it, but yeah." She finally takes a breath, but her mouth opens again a second later. "So how was your date?"

I'm still stuck on the part where Ollie is about to call me to talk about his sister staying here. It will undoubtedly be all about taking good care of his sister and making sure her stupid ex doesn't come anywhere near her while also keeping my hands off her. It's been a while since we've had *that* conversation.

Ollie used to give the keep-your-hands-off-my-sister speech all the time to our friends. I never told him, but so did I, imitating his big-brother persona. In hindsight, I wonder if there was more to it than I thought back then.

Not that I really know why he feels the need to remind *me* of that every so often.

"Carter, you keep zoning out." Julia punches me in the arm, successfully spilling half her wine on both of us in the process. "Oops. Sorry," she mutters to herself while putting the glass on the table.

Finally.

Nope. I take that back. Looks like she put it down so she can take off her wet shirt.

Oh, for the love of . . .

That leaves her in a thin tank top and nothing else.

Nothing, as in no bra.

Shit. Where the hell is her bra? And when have I ever wondered that about a girl?

Before I stare at her boobs again like a moron, I quickly get up to walk to my room. "Let me get new shirts." After switching my own shirt, I go back to the living room with an extra T-shirt for my new roommate.

My roommate. How things have changed in the matter of a few hours.

My childhood-bestie-turned-total-hottie—drunk off her ass, apparently not caring that I can see the outline of her hardened nipples—is now my new roommate, in her brother's place, who also happens to be my best friend and business partner. That about sums it up.

Crap.

I want to turn around so I can shove my fist in my mouth and bite on it to relieve some tension, but I hand her the shirt instead.

Of course, she shakes her head at my outstretched hand.

"I'm fine. I'm already wearing a shirt, see." She pulls the top away from her body, exposing even more skin in the process.

Somebody, please save me.

"Jules, that's barely a shirt." I give her a pointed look, hoping to convey a whole lot of things I don't want to say out loud. She does not need to know that I think she's hot as hell, even while sloppy drunk and sad. Nope.

We have a silent staring contest, and just when I'm about to say something, her expression turns grim and she snatches the T-shirt out of my hand, roughly pulling it over her head. "Right. Too much skin. Especially this body." She points to herself with disdain. "Nothing like the girls I've seen you with."

What the hell?

Before I can react, she grabs the wine glass and chugs down the content in one big gulp.

Why do I feel like I just did something wrong?

I sit back down and rub the back of my neck while Jules

silently finishes the rest of the wine bottle before focusing her attention on the goodies on the table. I'm not sure where she found all that food, but it looks like half the candy aisle puked all over the coffee table.

Drawing in a breath and releasing it, I look at her out of the corner of my eye, wondering if she's still mad. "So, what are we watching?"

She shrugs one shoulder. "Not sure. Looks like some reality show."

"Ah." I look at the TV, the *muted* TV. "You don't like listening to it, though?"

I look at her when I feel her gaze on me, or more so her glare.

One thing's for sure: she's got that down pat. It's mean, and my balls might have just shriveled a little.

Retreat, Carter. Retreat. We're in the middle of a damn minefield.

After a few more minutes of staring at the silent TV—watching a couple fight at the grocery store—I turn to the side when I hear quiet sniffles.

"Oh, Jules." I sigh. "Please don't cry."

"Why did he say those awful things, Carter?" Her voice breaks, and my chest aches for her.

Her stare is distant, tear after tear spilling over the rim of her lower eyelids. It's probably the saddest I've ever seen her, and it makes me want to hunt down Nate right now.

"Because he's a fucking moron, that's why." I shake my head in disgust and open my arms. "Come here."

Julia leaps into them, and I cradle her on my lap, slowly smoothing my hand over her hair and down her back until the loud sobs finally subside. I absolutely loathe seeing her like this.

I wish I could take away her pain. Julia is one of the sweetest, funniest girls I know, and she shouldn't believe the lies that asswipe said to her. How does she not know that?

We stay like this for a long time, and I know I'm probably enjoying her nearness more than I should. Oliver would kill me if he found us like this.

"It's going to be okay." I've repeated the same words so many times, they're almost like a mantra. "He doesn't deserve you, never did and never will."

Her fingers brush over her face, probably trying to wipe away the remnants of her little meltdown. Somehow, I expect her to move away, but instead, she snuggles closer into my chest, pulling her knees up to her body, forming a little ball.

Maybe I should be the one pulling away, but I can't bring myself to do so. A few minutes later, her breathing steadies.

It's as though the only place she feels safe is in my arms, and I'm sitting here smiling like an idiot.

Clearly, there's something wrong with me.

I sigh, keeping my voice down. "Oh, Jules."

When I stand up with her in my arms, careful not to jostle her too much, I'm reminded of when I was ten. She was eight and fell out of a tree, and since there was no one else around that day, I had to carry her back to the house. Back then, to my scrawny little self, it felt like she weighed a million pounds. Now, she feels light and tiny in my arms, definitely not like a burden. It's like she belongs there, and I like that.

I walk to her room she's already managed to make a mess

of and gently put her down on the bed. "Things will be better in the morning."

After covering her with the blanket, I look at her for a few moments. Just as I'm about to turn and leave, she grabs my arm and pulls on it.

"Please don't leave me alone, Freddy."

My body freezes instantly at her pleading words. She hasn't called me that in a *very* long time. She gave me the silly nickname forever ago when we had our little Scooby Doo obsession. It was our thing since Oliver refused to be named after the characters.

Hearing the name leave her lips does weird things to my stomach.

Maybe I ate something wrong earlier.

"Don't worry, Daphne. I'm right here." I'm not even sure she can hear my whispered reply, but I don't care. I climb into bed and lie down beside her.

After a minute, her breathing evens out again, her hand still holding my arm tightly.

Maybe I should leave. If I was worried about Oliver seeing her on my lap, this would be way, way worse.

Despite that, I relax next to her and close my eyes, because, quite frankly, this feels incredibly right.

Chapter Three
JULIA

My head. Painkillers. I need a painkiller in the worst way. Like yesterday.

Even though my eyes feel like they have fifty-pound weights on them, I somehow manage to open them slowly, relieved it's still dark outside, and I don't have to deal with the bright sun shining in my face. A quick glance at the digital clock on the bedside table tells me it's five in the morning. Good enough to get up and make some coffee. I have a feeling I might need a lot today.

Pushing the blanket aside, I try to lift my upper body as slowly as possible. I freeze when I'm held back by a weight on my belly, making it impossible for me to move any farther.

What the heck?

There's an arm slung across my midsection, and I'm trying hard to boot up my brain. I need to know what happened. But, I draw a complete blank. Most of last night is fuzzy at best.

I finally manage to lift my head enough to peek past the

fluffed-up pillow next to me and stare straight into Carter's sleeping face.

A quick double take of our bodies assures me we're both fully dressed—thank goodness—even though I'm not entirely sure why I'm wearing his shirt. Not that I think I'd forget having sex with Carter.

I don't even want to think about that though since the thought alone would be a disaster on way too many levels. The pounding in my head gets louder, clearing my brain from all other thoughts.

"Carter." I keep my voice down, mostly for my own benefit, and push at his arm as hard as I can muster.

Instead of waking up, he only grunts and turns his head to the other side, his arm still firm around my middle.

Somehow, I manage to wiggle out from under his embrace, and after a quick bathroom break and taking some painkillers, I head to the kitchen for a much-needed caffeine fix.

Before I know it, I'm a few cups in, cuddled up on the couch with the sun shining brightly outside, closing my favorite photo album of my parents—the one from their college years. Where they met and fell head over heels in love with each other, inseparable from that moment on. I always wondered, and maybe even hoped, if I'd find my other half that young too.

Instead, all this crap happened, and I'm probably as far away from the love of my life as I could be.

I blow out a loud breath, suddenly bothered by that thought.

Even though my brain still feels a little fuzzy, it works

enough to attempt and analyze my life and how I got to this point.

Dumped by my boyfriend of two and a half years and somewhat homeless, because I'm not planning on *really* moving in with my brother *and* Carter.

Getting embarrassingly drenched in the rain, followed by the most awful entrance back into Carter's life I could have imagined. Getting high on sugar and drunk off my ass.

The weirdest thing is, I'm not heartbroken. Yes, Nate's words hurt me, but I feel like I'm done crying over him. I want to say I'm surprised, but I think I secretly knew I never fully gave him my heart. Maybe not even more than a teeny tiny bit as it turns out. It was nice with him, but maybe it turned more into a convenience over time than anything else.

What screams the loudest in my head is probably the disappointment, the way my stomach clenches thinking about the last few years and how I let myself go. It's as if I've been . . . complacent. Things with Nate were okay, so everything else in my life was okay as well. I've lacked . . . luster.

Turns out, Nate might have had some good points after all, and a sudden determination to change my life for the better hits me, filling me with a new kind of high.

Since my laptop is still on the coffee table from last night, I snatch it and open a new Word document. After staring at the blinking cursor for a while, my fingers start flying over the keyboard like they're on fire, the constant flow of caffeine keeping my mind awake and going, despite my slight hungover state. Before I know it, the page is filled with random notes and a small list at the bottom. I stare at it for a moment before jumping into action.

Two minutes later, I speed-walk across the living room back to my bedroom, armed with two coffees in hand, and my laptop tucked under my arm.

Ready to go to war.

Well, something like that.

It feels good to be productive and active, and I'm hyped up on life. Okay, it's probably more the caffeine talking, but still.

I march into the room and plop down on the bed beside sleeping beauty.

Growing up with him, I got to watch him change from a cute, gangly kid to a flirty and cheeky teenager. But grown-up Carter, he's something else entirely.

Without a doubt, he's all man now. Tall and filled out in all the right places, a confident air about him that makes people take notice of him.

He's handsome and deliciously *sexy*, even I have to admit that.

Without overthinking it, I use the next few minutes to study him silently. His dark-blond hair has gotten longer since the last time I saw him a few months ago, now unruly falling over his eyes. If he doesn't brush it out of his face, it covers up his beautiful blue-gray eyes. To some they might seem boring, but to me they represent the ocean he loves so much, the ocean we *all* love so much.

They're my favorite part of him, and every time they zoom in on me, I want to let out a little sigh. Not just for me, but for all women across the world, and surely plenty of men too.

Watching him, being this close to him, brings back memories. From a time where I was happier, where life didn't seem so dull and sad. A life where the people I loved the most hadn't left me yet, and I didn't have to figure out how to manage life without losing myself in the process.

Now, Carter represents everything good that happened before then, and I enjoy basking in the joy he brings me with his presence. After my parents died in that awful accident, it hurt too much to think about them, to think about anything from the past. Getting to this point where I'm able to think about them and setting foot in their house again didn't happen overnight and took a lot of therapy sessions, but the pain has subsided some and is now mostly linked to positive memories.

"You don't think it's creepy to stare at me while I'm sleeping?" Carter's voice is raspy and full of sleep, immediately snapping me out of my thoughts.

I huff out a breath, letting myself fall back on the bed to stare at the white ceiling instead of him, biting the inside of my cheek to refrain from smiling. "I think it's rude to pretend to be asleep when you're not."

I missed this banter with him. I missed *him*, plain and simple.

The truth that I made a mess of my life these past few years hits me hard, and I know it will take me a while to work through this.

I met Nate shortly after my parents' death, and the years I spent with him, I can now see I virtually disappeared from my old life. My best friend, Michelle, is the only one who was able to stick with me, and it was anything but easy to say goodbye to my roommate and confidante of so long last week when she left to be an au pair in Australia for the next year.

My brother was a whole different entity, and I only saw

him on occasion, mostly when we had our combined therapy sessions. Once those ended, we started meeting up in places I deemed safe. This house, our parents' house, didn't feel safe. Not for a very long time. It was too much for me. Still is sometimes, but I can handle it.

Most of the year surrounding my parents' death is a blur. I spent it mostly at the apartment I shared with Michelle for a few years and the therapist's office. I took a year off school, and once I went back for my sophomore year, I met Nate. He was nice, and for some reason, he felt safe, maybe because he didn't know the old me. With him I could pretend everything was okay.

Now, I feel like everything I avoided those years—this house, my brother at large, and Carter—were actually missing pieces of me.

Maybe that's why it feels like old times with Carter because everything is clicking back in place.

He clears his throat, and when he speaks, the smile is easy to detect in his voice. "Color me surprised, but you're a lot more chipper this morning than I thought you'd be."

It's so easy to smile with him, his company effortless. "I might have had some coffee."

"Define some."

"I didn't really count, but I think I'm somewhere halfway through the second pot." The words flow out of my mouth in a rush before I look over at him.

He shakes his head as much as he can with his head still smushed into the pillow. "Of course. You and your brother both have an affinity for caffeine."

"Anyway. I got some for you too." We both sit up, and I

grab one of the mugs from the nightstand to hand it to him before grabbing my laptop. "And I need your help."

After leaning against the headboard, he sends me a look over the rim of his coffee, the corners of his eyes crinkling. "Uh-oh. Is it something I'm going to get in trouble for?"

I can't help but laugh at the expression on his face. Both wariness and amusement seem to battle his facial muscles, and I'm not sure which one is actually winning.

"No trouble." I shake my head. "At least I don't think so."

He slowly rubs a hand over his face before focusing on his coffee. Somehow he manages to look like a model, even though he just woke up a few minutes ago in his rumpled clothes from last night.

Totally unfair.

I'm sure I still look like a homeless person, maybe even like I'm on drugs with the way my hands are shaking from the caffeine. But since Carter has seen me in worse conditions— puke and flu incidents included—he's going to endure my . . . au naturel state at the moment.

"Well?" He raises his eyebrows. "Are you going to enlighten me about what you need help with?"

I clear my throat and open my laptop. "Yes. Of course."

He chuckles while I drum my fingertips on the keyboard, waiting for it to refresh. I peek at him over the screen. "By the way, what are you doing in my bed?"

His mug stops halfway to his mouth as he stares at me. After clearing his throat, he chugs down what must be most of the coffee. "Well . . . you were pretty drunk and passed out on my lap, so I wanted to make sure you were okay."

I vaguely remember him comforting me after I had

another major meltdown, but I fell asleep on his lap? Man, I was really out of it. How embarrassing.

"Thank you." My response is mostly mumbled, and I'm relieved when the document finally pops up on the screen. I pretend like it didn't happen and focus on my new project instead. "So, since we just established my drunken status from last night, I can't remember what I told you, but my ex-boyfriend—on top of some epiphanies I had this morning—has given me plenty of reasons to think about myself and my future. Even though his parting reasons weren't delivered in the best way, a bit assholish really, I can't deny he had a point. So I made a plan for myself, a checklist of sorts."

Carter looks at me like I've lost my marbles. "Firstly, I disagree completely with what your idiot ex said about you. And secondly, you made a checklist? For what?"

I nod, fresh pain shooting through my temples. Dang it. "Yes. You know how some people make lists for a project, personal goals, et cetera?"

For a brief moment I wonder if he's the right person to talk to about this, but since it's the middle of the night for Michelle on the other side of the world, Carter will have to do before my brain explodes.

Even though, my eyes ping-pong around everywhere but on him. "Well, I thought I could make a checklist to find a husband."

Once the words are out, I look up and see his eyebrows raised as he chokes on his drink.

"You want to do what?" *Cough.* "Find a husband?" *Cough.* "And make a checklist for that?"

"A husband checklist, yes." My head bobs up and down robotically.

Carter is a very fun-loving and carefree guy, but he can also be incredibly analytical, so I give him time to absorb the info I just threw at him.

"Explain."

I try to ignore his expression and focus on my laptop screen instead. "Mmm, let's see. Since my brain isn't working at full capacity yet, I'll keep it simple for now. I can always come up with a more elaborate list later if I feel like it. For now, I've mainly focused on the things Nate pointed out."

Carter grimaces and groans. "Please tell me you aren't listening to anything that jerk said."

"He might be right though." I hold up a finger to stop him from interrupting me. "Let me finish first, okay?"

He frowns but nods. "Fine."

"As much as I hate to admit it, I think I understand where he came from. A little bit."

Carter's jaw tenses as he quietly takes in my words, and I'm pretty sure I just heard him grind his teeth.

"Nate's a businessman first. We met in business school, after all. He wants to be this top-notch lawyer, and his public image is very important to him. I might not have tried my best to fit into that world."

"You shouldn't have to try to fit in anywhere." Carter's outburst startles me for a moment. "It's like he didn't even know you if he thought you'd change for him."

I can't help a sigh slip past my lips. "It took me a while to tell him what my business was, and I realize now that he thought I wasn't serious about my career. Maybe he was hoping it was just a hobby, and I'd find something better and more respectable to do in the business world."

He rubs his forehead, looking more confused than before.

"I thought you got your business degree to help build your jewelry business?"

"Yes."

His gaze is laser sharp, one hundred percent focused on me. "And why is a jewelry business not good enough?"

"Because it's kids' jewelry." The words come out mumbled, and I throw my hands in the air.

Carter stares at me for a moment before he chuckles, shaking his head. "That guy is such a moron, I swear."

More chuckles, my own mouth twitching in response.

Hearing him laugh has always lifted my spirits, no matter what mood I've been in, and it doesn't fail me right now either.

"Stop it already." Unable to hold my own laugh in any longer, I push at his chest a little but regret it the second I feel his hard muscles flex underneath my fingers.

The contact makes him snap out of his laughter, making him stare at me with a serious expression instead.

"Sorry, Jules. You sure know how to pick 'em. He's obviously the idiot in this whole scenario, especially with your family background. Your dad and uncle are business moguls, and Ollie and I aren't doing bad with our investment company either." He grins again and shakes his head. "And then there's you, rebel Jules. Ollie mentioned the business is doing well though, right?"

"It is. I got lucky and had some high-profile moms buy some items from me. Once they started posting about it on social media, word spread like wildfire. The rest is history, so to speak." I sigh. "Nate never even wanted to hear about the business. He said I was wasting both of our times and I should find a real job."

He pinches his lips together. "Why did you stay with him if he treated you like that?"

Running a hand through my messy hair, I feel the frustration build in my stomach. "I don't know. I guess I hoped it would go back to how it was at the beginning when we first met. We were a great couple back then. I think. Maybe we never were. I don't know. It was just after Mom and Dad died, and I actually felt . . . content, something I hadn't felt for some time, as you know."

Carter points a finger at me. "I get that, Jules, but that's mistake number one. Don't ever compare your later relationship to your honeymoon phase."

The laugh erupts out of me without a warning. "Where did you learn that, Dr. Love?"

"I think my mom told me."

"Ah, that explains it. She's on her what . . . sixth marriage now?"

Over the years, Carter has learned to take his mother's marital adventures with a good dose of humor. Ever since she divorced his dad when we were younger, she's been trying to find true love wherever it hit her. Her words, not mine.

To my surprise, he shakes his head and smiles. "Nope. Still number five. Fingers crossed this time."

"Wow, that's impressive." I smile, genuinely hoping this marriage will last for her. She might have always been a bit delusional when it came to love and marriage, but her heart is in the right place.

We're silent for a moment before I focus back on my laptop. "Anyway. I'm definitely not changing my job. I love what I do, and it pays more money than any other job I could get right now."

His eyes widen. "It does? Really?"

"Yup." I give him a huge smile, my lungs expanding on a deep inhale. "If things continue the way they have, I should be able to crack six figures this year."

His jaw drops an inch or two, and I can't deny that I don't enjoy this moment. I also can't help myself leaning forward and gently pushing his chin back up.

"Wow." One word. That's all he gets out.

When it stays quiet, I decide distraction is the best tactic. "I have to agree with Nate that I have put on a few extra pounds over the years, and even though I hate eating healthy and working out, I can't say I'm happy with the way I look either."

"Jules, you look absolutely fine." He almost rolls his eyes.

"*Fine.*" I snort. "Has no one ever told you that fine basically equals crap?"

His eyebrows pull together, and I decide to not even bother with this right now.

Instead, I tap my screen that's already covered in about a million fingerprints.

"Anyway, so the list is long and will probably still get longer. But when it comes down to it, I want to lose weight, become more interesting, a better cook, and dress nicer. I need to learn more about men and what they like and don't like. Oh, and become a sex goddess."

He clears his throat. "*That's* your husband checklist?"

"Well, kind of. I mean, I looked up what men look for in women they want to marry and all that. And based on that info, I started my list. If I get through it all, I should have no issues finding a suitable husband, right?" My tone sounds a lot more confident than I feel right now.

Nothing. Not a word.

His mouth opens and closes a few times but still absolute silence.

"I really think a male perspective is necessary to succeed though." I stare at him, still waiting. "So . . . are you going to help me, Carter?"

Chapter Four

*W*ithout a doubt, I must have the most stupid expression on my face after everything Julia just dumped on me. My brain still has a hard time processing her words.

Especially the sex goddess part.

Yeah, I'm definitely still stuck on that.

I mean, what the hell is she thinking? That I'd help her get better at that too?

That's probably it. She *isn't* thinking. Not one bit.

She nudges me, sending an electric shock up my entire arm, and I feel like I'm in some alternative universe today. "Carter, stop overthinking this. I can see the wheels turning from over here."

Her chuckle is melodic, a smile automatically forming on my face.

"Jules, I . . ." I swallow. "What exactly do you need help with?"

"Well, you know . . . nothing crazy. I need a workout partner to kick my butt and someone to go shopping with to make myself a bit more presentable. You know, stuff like that." She looks down her body as if she has no idea what she's actually wearing. "I might have overdone the whole leggings and yoga pants phase a bit. I think I should save that for later on when I'm a mom. Isn't that what moms are known for?" She brushes a hand over her black leggings.

I shrug. What the hell is she talking about?

To me, she looks like Julia.

The girl I've known ever since I became best friends with her brother. I can't even remember a life when Julia wasn't with us. When we were younger, she felt a bit like a pest, because what ten-year-old wants his best friend's little sister to shadow their every move? But as we grew older, it became normal to hang out together, up until her brother and I left for college.

We tried to stay in touch and somewhat succeeded, even though we definitely didn't see each other that often. But when their parents got into a boating accident a few years later, everything broke. That's when we really drifted apart, no matter how hard I tried to get through to her. And I did try. Fuck, I loved her parents. They were always there for me, for their kids.

In the small moments when I did see Julia though, she'd looked so . . . hollow. So, lacking in vitality, which had been her default nature. I hated it. I hated that she didn't turn to me to console and comfort her. But she had the dickhead. Now? Chatting as if no time has passed, it feels good. Really good. But why the hell does she think she needs a list? A marriage list?

"What are you thinking about? You keep going somewhere else." She crosses her arms over her chest, making me once again aware that she's still braless. I'm pretty sure I saw the outline of her nipples for a moment before she covered them with her arms.

Wrong thing to think about. Especially given that I'm in her bed.

"Sorry." I give myself a stern warning and try to get my head back in the game. "I guess I'm still trying to wake up. How about we take a shower and get ready, and then we'll go have breakfast at that little beach café you like so much. The rain has stopped, so it looks like it's going to be a nice day."

She stares at me with wide eyes. "You want to take a shower with me? Together?"

"What?" My voice comes out a lot higher than it ever should, and Julia is already cracking up. "Very funny, Jules."

"Sorry, you're just too easy this morning. You should have seen your face. Priceless." She's still laughing when I finally get off the bed.

"Half an hour or I'll leave without you." When I'm almost out the door, I look at her over my shoulder. "And please, Jules, put a damn bra on." I slip out of the room before the pillow she throws reaches me, hitting the door with a *thud* instead.

Forty-five minutes later, we're finally out the door.

To Julia's delight, it's actually my fault we're late. Ollie *had* to call right when I got out of the shower, keeping me on the phone forever. As I suspected, he's concerned about his sister and asked me a million questions, mixed with threats of doing some serious harm to that asshole Nate. Can't blame him there. That douchebag better not show his face around here. All bets are off where he's concerned.

I also had to repeatedly promise Ollie I'd take good care of Julia, which is easier said than done with this wild firecracker. At least, she's wearing a bra now. I've got to count the little blessings with this one.

"I missed the ocean air." She sighs as we walk, the beach café only a few streets away.

"You haven't been out here much, have you?"

She doesn't answer right away, and I give her the time she needs, knowing exactly how hard it hit both her and Oliver when they lost their parents. Julia was almost done with her first year of college, while Ollie and I were finishing up our third. It was such a shock for everyone.

One moment they were there, and then they were gone. Just like that. The nicest parents anyone could ask for. They always treated me like I was part of the family.

Her gaze is off in the distance, her voice somber. "I'm okay now. I couldn't stand being here at the beginning. Wherever I looked, I saw Mom and Dad, and I didn't have a clue how to handle it. It's gotten easier over the years though. I still miss them like crazy, but now I can appreciate the memories we made here."

The small smile on her face makes me stop in my tracks. It's a special smile, one not a lot of people get to see, reserved for when she talks about the people she truly loves—her family. I wish I could have helped her more when it happened, but even Oliver couldn't get through to her until she was ready to go to therapy with him. She's never been the same, but who can blame her for that? I'm not the same either.

Tom and Mary Bradford were not only funny and warm, but they were knowledgeable about starting and running businesses too. There have been moments over the last few years that I've wished I could reach out to Tom.

"Can we sit outside?" Her gaze is fixated on the small café ahead of us. It's situated at the end of the narrow street, the sand starting right behind it. The ocean's just a few hundred feet away, and the owners set up small metal tables and brown wicker chairs out back.

"Of course."

We make our way to the sand where Julia takes of her shoes before walking to one of the tables on the large patio.

The waiter arrives quickly, and we both order their special breakfast plate, not finding it odd in the slightest that we still eat the same thing after so many years. I guess that comes with familiarity.

It also reminds me of the fact that Julia is so different than a lot of the girls I've dated who would have been repelled at ordering anything but a miniscule meal. So many get small and healthy meals, just to stare longingly at my food throughout the evening. I don't think I'll ever understand that kind of behavior, even though I guess I can blame the Southern California lifestyle for that and the beauty standard that comes with living so close to Hollywood.

Regardless, Julia feels like a breath of fresh air, making me realize how much I've missed her. How easy it's always been with her to just be. No expectations. Simple and easy.

Julia clicks her fingernails on the table, amusement dancing in her eyes. "So . . . I think you've had enough time to fully wake up. Are you going to help me?"

I take her in, her almost makeup-free face—except for

mascara from the looks of it, not that she needs it. The eyelashes framing her brown eyes have always been incredibly long and thick. I blew my fair share of them off her fingers when we were young—all for good luck of course. This natural look suits her. It can be fun to see women dolled up for a night out, but I prefer her like this. The same goes for her brown hair. It's twisted in some bun on top of her head. It might resemble a bird's nest a little, but it looks good on her.

Clearing my throat, I will my brain to focus on her question, even though it's far more interested in reacquainting itself with every little facet of her. "I don't think you should change anything about yourself. At least not for the reasons you told me. Don't you think you should find someone who loves you exactly the way you are?"

She regards me for a moment with her gorgeous eyes before she leans back in her chair. "You're right, but I still want all those things."

I can't hide my surprise. "Really?"

Pausing for a moment, she looks away from me, her gaze immediately finding the ocean. "I changed a lot after Mom and Dad died. It took me a really long time until I finally felt somewhat okay again. But by that time, I was different. I was quiet and barely left our apartment. I was living a safe and comfortable life, and I'd gotten used to being that person. Don't get me wrong, I like this side of me, the lazy yoga-pants-wearing, good-girl type. But I also realized I miss my old self. I miss feeling good about myself and just having fun."

Her eyes shimmer with unshed tears, and my heart struggles to pump for a few moments.

"You're not having fun?" My throat feels constricted, and I wonder if Ollie knows about any of this.

"I know this sounds super lame, but I think this"—she points her finger at herself and then at me—"is the most fun I've had in a while. Just thinking about the list I made makes me all giddy and excited. I think it's going to be good for me to focus on myself before I tackle a real husband checklist."

"Wow." I grab my water and gulp down the contents of it, trying to wrap my head around what she just said.

Julia mimics my motion, downing her water too. "The more I think about it, the more certain I am that I've been hiding from life as much as possible over the past few years. Apparently, it took Nate to kick me to the curb to realize that. Looks like he actually did me a favor there on several levels, not that I'd seen much of him lately anyway, but I was blocking that out too."

Just the mention of his name makes my blood boil.

"So, you want me to help you get back to your old self then?" I ask tentatively, still not a hundred percent on board with this.

"Kind of. I don't think I can be the person I was before, so I guess what I really want is to find out who I actually am now? The new me, so to speak. And while I work on that, I'll whip up a real husband checklist too. You know, all the things I look for in a guy. And all the other things will be my 'New Julia list.' That makes more sense, doesn't it?"

She leans across the table, and I'm wrapped up in her sweet scent.

I still have a bad feeling about this list, but what else am I going to do but help her? Can't say no to her, that's for sure. "I guess."

Man, I sound like a total idiot this morning.

"We should probably try and make the most of it while

Ollie's gone. I don't think he'll understand and will just complain about it, or try and take over. He still thinks I'm a child sometimes and has to be the one in control. I know he means well, but that's the last thing I need right now. What I do need is some support and help." She gives me a sweet smile. "So, Carter, are you in or out?"

"Definitely in." I'm about to send a search party to look for my brain cells, because clearly they're absent given the words that just left my mouth.

Julia claps her hands in pure delight at my answer, and with a huge smile on her face, she jumps out of her chair, runs around the table, and throws herself at me. "Thank you so much, Carter. I knew you'd help. It'll be fun, I promise."

I can't get rid of the feeling that I just shot myself in the foot by saying yes, but despite that, I smile and hug her back.

Chapter Five

JULIA

y stomach growls loudly just as Carter strolls through the front door, full takeout bags in both hands.

Thank goodness.

Since work has been busy for him, I've barely seen him the last two days, and I'm glad he's back home. Between relaxing and working on some jewelry orders, I stayed busy enough, but I'd rather have company than be alone.

My cheeks hurt from smiling widely. "You're an angel for bringing me food."

He laughs at my statement and walks past me to the kitchen, placing the bags on the kitchen counter. He's dressed in a suit, looking like he just walked for the latest fashion show. Nate wore suits whenever he could—I think it made him feel important—and I'm glad to see it didn't put me off men in suits.

Because, whoa.

Carter in a suit . . . what a sight for my sore eyes.

Yesterday's was black, and today's is a deep navy blue that works beautifully with his eyes. Definitely my favorite so far.

The sound of his shoes is loud on the hardwood floor, his stride confident as he makes his way over to me. "Sorry about leaving you alone so much. I was planning on working from home, but a new client needed my attention."

He looks around the dining room table that's filled with my supplies, the only place large enough for me to set up shop at the moment. "Looks like you've been busy, though."

"Yeah, I had some orders waiting, and someone's got to do them. Sorry about the mess though, I'll clean it up once I'm done."

He shakes his head, his hand landing on my shoulder. "No worries. We'll just eat over at the breakfast bar or on the couch. Whatever you feel like."

Whatever you feel like?

I'm momentarily stunned, wondering how Carter can be so accommodating. Nate would have rolled his eyes and grumbled something about my inane career path before stomping away. And I accepted that and apologized for my thoughtlessness . . . "Couch sounds perfect. I'll be done in a few minutes. I just want to finish up this necklace." I hold up the string and beads in my hand and he nods.

"I still have to get changed too, so no rush."

His hand leaves my shoulder, the spot feeling oddly empty, and I watch him as he walks toward his room, his broad shoulders and dominant stride screaming confidence and strength.

One thing's for sure, Carter Kennedy has changed, filled out in all the right places, and has turned into one sexy man.

Then I sigh. I actually sigh out loud. Thankfully, he's too far away to hear it though, at least I hope so.

Less than half an hour later, we're settled on the couch, both of us with a decent plateful of food on our laps.

I swallow the food greedily, trying to savor the taste as much as I can. "Gosh, this is so dang delicious."

He nods around a mouthful of food.

"Is it from a new place?"

He wipes his mouth on a napkin. "Yes, this Chinese restaurant opened a few months ago. They better stay around for a long time."

After spearing some broccoli on my fork, I nod. "Heck, I'll stay forever if they will."

He pauses and looks at me. "You will?"

"Well, not in this house. I mean, I know it's half mine, but Ollie's been making it his, and I'm okay with that. He can handle it better living here than I can." My shoulders drop with a sigh before I focus back on him. "How about you? Why are you living here anyway?"

He grins at me, and I'm instantly reminded of the boy I grew up with. No matter what was going on, Carter always has an easy smile to share. "It's convenient and I'm lazy."

A chuckle slips out, and I look at my food. "You've always been lazy."

The impact of not having him in my life the last few years hits me once more, this time with a force that makes the breath hitch in my throat. My therapist mentioned once that everyone deals differently with grief. My first instinct was to pull away from everyone who reminded me of my loss. In hindsight, it seems silly, but our minds and hearts have strange ways to handle emotional challenges.

I couldn't avoid Ollie, especially once he and my uncle talked me into family therapy. But that was all I could manage at that time, and then it became my new normal. Once I started dating Nate, I focused on him.

He elbows me gently in the side. "You okay?"

"Yeah." I swallow and nod. Leave it up to Carter to see right through me. "So, this is temporary then?"

"Definitely not forever. The lease on my apartment in LA ran out a few weeks ago, so your brother offered to let me stay with him until I find something permanent. The two-hour commute here to Malibu was killer, and we've been super busy with our company downtown. And you know, time is money and all that."

"Makes sense. I'm surprised Ollie didn't mention it more." I wonder if there's a reason for it.

"He's been more forgetful than usual about things since he started seeing Cora. She's been preoccupying his mind." He chuckles once.

I let that sink in, placing my fork on my plate. "Sounds like it. He's mentioned her before, but I didn't realize they were that serious. I mean, you don't just go on a two-week vacation with anyone."

Carter shrugs his shoulders. "He likes her, and she seems nice, so we'll see."

"Nice, like the one you went on a date with?" The words are out of my mouth before I can stop them, and I want to groan in frustration. I'm not even sure why I brought it up, it just kind of slipped out.

He puts his empty plate on the coffee table, keeping his

gaze in front of him. "You know I'm not looking for anything serious, Jules. Nothing's really changed for me in that aspect."

I nod, silently acknowledging his statement. But as usual, I can't keep quiet for long, my tone gentle. "You know you're not your parents, right?"

That gets his attention, and he turns to fix me with his gaze. "Don't. You know I don't believe in relationships, so I don't see the point in even trying. Why should I set myself and another person up for something that will only fail and end in heartbreak anyway? We don't need to discuss that and you know it."

He doesn't sound mad, maybe a little irritated, but I hold up my hands in surrender anyway. "All right, all right."

"Sorry. You know I hate talking about this topic. I love my parents, but talking about this crap makes me feel like I'm in therapy again, and we all know how much I enjoyed that time in my life." He's turned away again, focused on cleaning up the table.

I touch his shoulder. "Sorry I brought it up."

He shrugs, the muscles effortlessly moving under my hand, and I let go, not wanting this to be awkward.

"No worries." His shoulders rise and fall before he finally faces me. At least, he sounds normal again. "So, have you thought some more about your plans for the week? Do you think you'll be okay here by yourself? I have to fly to Vegas for the weekend. One of our clients has a new deal he wants to talk about. He's rather old-fashioned and refuses to do video chats, which means I have to see him in person."

"Vegas?"

He rakes his hand through his hair, brushing it out of his face. "Yeah, just for a night. You'll be fine here, right?"

"Well . . ." I chew on my bottom lip. "I'm sure I would be, but can I come with you? Before you say anything, I know you'll be busy with work, but I could explore the city by myself. I still haven't been there."

He looks at me like I have a third eye. I'm actually contemplating for a moment if I should check my forehead when he finally snaps out of it. "You want to come to Vegas? With me? Ollie would kill me."

Ollie can be a bit overprotective, especially after losing our parents. I'm the only close family he has left—apart from Carter . . . and maybe Cora—and if he could, he'd pack me up in cotton, and I'd never leave the house. I'm not the only one who changed after the accident. That's been Ollie's way of dealing with things. And as much as I don't want to disrespect my brother and hide something from him, what should it really matter if he's away? He deserves to have his own life and live it freely without fearing for me and mine. "We just won't tell him then."

Carter harrumphs, and I nudge him. "Come on, Freddy. It'll be fun, and I'll stay out of your way."

"I don't know, Jules." The indecision is written loud and clear on his face.

"Pretty please, Carter. You won't even know I'm there." I'm literally begging now, my hands clasped together in front of me, hanging on to this thought of doing something new.

He huffs out in frustration, raking his hand through his hair several more times. "I know I'll regret it, but fine. Just don't get drunk and disappear on me."

"I'll try my best not to, I promise." I hold up two fingers and say, "Scout's honor."

"Jules, you were never a Girl Scout." He shakes his head, but I can see the corners of his mouth twitch.

I barely stop myself from clapping excitedly but can't hold back the triumphant chuckle. "I know."

He points a finger at me. "Let's talk about something else before I change my mind. Tell me about your plans for the rest of the week."

"Okie dokie. I was thinking of going to the gym tomorrow and then do some shopping after. That's probably all we can fit into this week if we fly out to Vegas on Friday and still need to pack. That's less than three days. Speaking of, I need to get a ticket." I sit up straight. "Oh crap, do you think I can still get one?"

"Calm down, Jules." He puts his hand on my arm, and I sink back into the comfy couch cushions. "I don't think we'll have issues getting you one. Let me check." He grabs his laptop from the side table and starts it up.

I nod, peeking over his shoulder. "Thank you."

"Of course."

"Oooh, when we go shopping, maybe we can look at some books too. I thought it would be nice to get some on self-improvement and relationships." I grab my phone to see what the book world has to offer.

He glances at me. "Do you really think that's necessary?"

I put my phone down. "Please, Carter, just let me do this. You might not agree with me and my list, but I think this is good for me. Maybe even necessary to finally move on with my life." And not just from Nate, but from feeling the need for such strict boundaries that have done nothing but promote isolation. It's time to be me. I hate the term moving on with life because that's not what healing from grief means. It's about exploring the new me with this new permanent hole in my heart. I can't change the fact that I lost my parents, but I can still live and fulfill my dreams.

His gaze is intense, like he's trying to look inside my head. "Gym and shopping it is."

"And Vegas, baby." I throw my hands up in the air, while Carter drags his hand over his face.

"Why do I feel like this has bad idea written all over it?"

Placing my hand on my chest, I give him my most innocent look. "I have absolutely no clue. You know I'm practically an angel."

"I'll believe it when I see it." He gives me an I've-known-you-for-too-long-to-get-away-with-this look, and I bite the inside of my cheek to keep from laughing.

Chapter Six

CARTER

*U*sually, I enjoy my time at the gym. It's really the only time in my life where I can completely let go. I don't have to think about anything but pushing my body to its limits and reaping the benefits from all the hard work. It's invigorating, and after the initial exhaustion, also incredibly uplifting and energizing.

But not today.

Today, it's hell.

Pure, torturous hell.

I'm on the treadmill after my strength training, which is usually the more relaxing portion of my gym visit. My mind is unable to quiet down, utterly focused on Julia, who's on the elliptical in front of me—particularly her ass in those tight pants. And because that's not distraction enough, she's been chatting with the guy next to her for a good ten minutes. It looks like I might leave the gym in worse condition than before, at least mentally.

Why do I even care?

The same question that's been preoccupying my mind for the past few days. The only explanation I can come up with is that Julia turned into a gorgeous woman.

And I'm a guy who likes beautiful women. Simple.

Maybe I shouldn't think about her that way, but my body seems to have a different agenda, growing more obsessed with her by the minute.

Obviously, I won't act on my attraction, so there shouldn't be a problem.

I'm sure it'll go away soon. End of story.

"Carter." Julia's voice penetrates my thoughts as she pulls out one of my earbuds.

I'm so startled I miss a step and almost fall off the treadmill.

Definitely not my normal gym day.

"Are you already done?" I try to act nonchalant after my almost faceplant, but it's easy to tell she's having a hard time holding back her laughter.

An impish smile makes her mouth twitch. "Yes. The twenty minutes you told me to do are over."

A quick glance on my own machine confirms her statement. "You're right. I didn't notice the time."

"Well, I guess I'm gonna head to the shower then. I'm exhausted. I'm sure I'll feel it tomorrow if not tonight. You worked me way too hard, Mr. Overachiever."

My machine comes to a halt when I push the stop button. "I don't think I did."

She smiles at me. "I'm just kidding. I'm fine. I actually really enjoyed it. I'm glad I did some yoga yesterday before working the weights with you today. I think it helped some."

The guy she talked to on the elliptical walks past us, and they smile at each other. He lifts a hand and waves at her. "See you next week, Julia."

"Can't wait." She waves back before facing me again.

"Who was that?" My curiosity is impossible to ignore, burning through my veins like a wildfire on a mission to destroy as much as possible.

"Oh, that was Chad." Her eyes are wide, making her look almost innocent.

"Chad?"

"Yes, Carter. His name is Chad and he asked me out."

"And he fits your husband checklist?"

"I still have to make one, okay? Any other questions that can't wait until later, or can I finally go shower?" She puts her hands on her hips and looks up at me expectantly.

Looks like the little firecracker has come out to play.

When she wrinkles her nose at me, I can't hold back a chuckle, trying to ignore the mention of her already having a date set up. But like she said, we can talk about that later.

"All right, Daph, calm your horses." I wink at her and gather my things. "Hurry. I'll meet you in the lobby when you're done."

She gives me a huge grin. "Oh, don't worry, I won't take long. I'm too excited to go shopping."

I groan, and she laughs, clearly enjoying my misery.

She points her finger at me. "You promised."

"Yeah, yeah, I know. Now go." I wave her off and watch as she makes her way through the maze of equipment to the changing rooms.

What a way to get in over my head.

Two hours later, I'm fully convinced someone has carefully planned my death for today.

"How about this one?" Julia spins in front of me. Left, then right, before doing it all over again outside her changing room.

We're still at the first store she dragged me into, and at this point, I'm not entirely sure we'll ever leave. It's like a black hole in here, and the enormous pile of clothes she stacked on the chair next to me doesn't seem to get any smaller.

At the moment, she's wearing a red dress that fits her like a glove. It looks stunning on her, the color of the dress working wonders with her dark hair she left down after her shower. I didn't realize clothes shopping with her would be this difficult. It's a lot harder to look at her without . . . well, *really* looking at her. How does anyone expect me to give her an objective opinion if all I see is accentuated body parts?

And hell, does this red number make both her boobs and ass look spectacular.

She waves her hands in front of me, her eyebrows pulled together. "Carter? You're doing this weird staring thing again. Are you sure you're all right? We can go home and finish up another day if you don't feel well. Or I can just come back tomorrow while you're at work."

I shake my head, feeling a little guilty. "No, no. Sorry. I just have a lot on my mind."

"If you're sure." She doesn't look convinced but lets it go. It doesn't escape my notice that she's a little quieter, the light in her eyes a little dimmer. I hate even the slightest possibility that I did that. "So, what do you think?"

Focusing on helping her as much as I can, I scan her body again, trying my best not to linger in certain places. "I think it's great. It suits you. Are you sure you need all these fancy dresses, though? I mean, you're not going to work in them when you're home, right?"

She brushes her hands over the material, keeping her eyes downcast. "Of course not. But hopefully, they'll come in handy when I go out, you know, on dates and that sort of thing, maybe some business meetings. And I'll buy more casual clothes too. I was just in the mood to try on the pretty dresses first."

Well, lucky me.

"For your dates, huh?" The filter between my brain and mouth seems to be out of order.

She lets out a long breath and walks over to me, letting herself fall into the seat next to me that's not occupied by clothes. "You don't think I should go on dates?"

I push my hand through my hair. "I don't know, Jules. I obviously can't tell you what to do, but you've only been out of your relationship for less than a week. Don't you think you should wait for a while? You might not even be ready for anything new yet, I don't know. Isn't there usually a certain amount of time that should pass? Like a mourning phase for your old relationship or some shit like that?"

One look at her, and I know she's going to burst out laughing in a second. And she does.

A snort-like noise escapes her mouth, making her eyes go wide. "Carter, if I didn't know any better, I'd think you're showing signs of PMS with the mood swings you've been having the past few days." She still chuckles as she continues. "I think most relationships do have a natural phase of alone time in between, some longer than others. But I've already realized something, and I know it's going to sound strange, but I don't think I really loved Nate."

"Huh?" My eyes open wide, and I force myself to close my mouth that fell open at her admission.

Her face turns serious and she drops her head, visibly shrinking in front of my eyes. "When Mom and Dad died, I felt incredibly lonely, even when I was in a room full of people, and I had no clue what to do with my life. I kind of lost my path there for a while and barely went anywhere. School got so bad I had to drop my classes and take some time off. I did the bare minimum to live. When I started going back to school, I ran into Nate. He was a nice guy, and the best thing was, he didn't remind me of my old life. He didn't know anything about me or what happened. Before I knew it, I clung to him like he was my lifeline. Since he never complained about it, I suspect he enjoyed the fact I needed him like that."

"Mmm." What the hell am I supposed to say to something like that? Grief is such a difficult thing to manage, and standing by the sidelines unable to help sucks too. Ollie didn't do well after his parents' deaths either, but at least, he seemed to deal with it. I automatically assumed Jules did too.

"Nate did help me to get out of my deep hole, I can't deny that. I'm definitely grateful for that, and I think that's exactly what happened. I confused gratefulness and friendship with love. One thing led to another with us, and I never really looked much deeper than that. I slowly started living my life again, but this time with Nate by my side. It wasn't like my old life but a ton better than all the months following the accident. I can't blame him for things not working out. It was mostly me putting on my blinders, not wanting to analyze anything too closely. We should have never stayed together, or maybe even gotten together in the first place."

She sniffles and wipes at her nose with the back of her hand, turning away from me as much as possible.

"I still think he's an asshole." Leave it up to me to say the first thing that's on my mind. Thankfully, she looks at me and laughs.

"He's absolutely an ass for dumping me the way he did. But I'm over it already. I'm more upset with myself for wasting so much time than anything else, but I don't want to think about it anymore." She slaps me lightly on the knee and gets up from the chair. "I still have a few things I want to try on, but you really don't have to stay here with me. I can do the rest by myself."

"Are you kidding me? I can't *wait* to see the other outfits." I put on my best smile for her, wanting nothing more than to see her happy again. "Seriously, I promised you I'd do this, so I'm going to stay right here in this incredibly uncomfortable chair, waiting for the rest of the fashion show to take place. So, are we doing this or what?"

Her eyes are still a little watery, but at least I can see a spark of the previous amusement back in them. For a moment, I thought I saw something else too, but it was gone before I could work out what it was.

She bends down, pressing a kiss to my cheek. "Thanks, Carter. I really appreciate it. You're a good guy."

I nod, trying to smile but unable to pull it off. "Don't

mention it. That's what friends are for, right? I mean, I obviously can't take you to Vegas in your yoga pants and oversized T-shirts, can I?"

If the twitching corners of her mouth are any indication, she sees straight through my shit.

Please, may there be no bathing suits in this pile. I will not cope with that.

I'm not sure why anyone would call this tight space an airplane seat. I call BS, because my butt barely fits, and it's not *that* big. It also reminds me of why I haven't been to Las Vegas yet, or any other place you usually travel to via airplane.

"You hanging in there, Jules? We should have talked about this before. Damn it." Carter's voice is low, maybe even a little frantic, and he looks at me like I'm a puppy that just got stepped on, his brows raised high.

"I'm fine." I'm not sure I say it for his benefit or mine, but I repeat it several more times in my head like it's a mantra. It can't hurt, and maybe I'll actually start to believe it.

"You're as white as a ghost, and I'm afraid you might rip the armrests off any second now, or at least leave some claw marks." He leans closer, his breath tickling my face. "Not my definition of fine."

He's right. Shoot.

I slowly pry my fingers off the armrest and clench my fists

tightly on my lap instead. "I knew I should have taken a parachute with me."

He chuckles beside me, and I glare at him.

His hands immediately go up in surrender, and he stops laughing. "Sorry, I thought you were joking."

"Do I look like I'm joking about anything right now?" Leaning my head on the headrest, I close my eyes and take a deep breath in through my nose and out of my mouth.

In and out.

In and out.

The total chaos that's trying to take over my body slows down a little, my breathing still too quick and shallow, my skin still sweaty and flushed. "I'm sorry."

"Hey, there's nothing you need to apologize for. It's my fault. I didn't realize it's still this bad. Somehow, I just assumed you've gotten over your fear of flying over the years." Carter's arm nudges my shoulder and slowly moves around my back for a side hug. He pulls me as close to him as possible in this tight space with our seat belts buckled.

I lean into him, his soothing voice and the comfort of his closeness making this already more bearable. "To be honest, that's kind of what I was hoping for too. I *was* totally fine until we sat down. Ugh, I hate feeling like this. It's so stupid, but I just can't control it."

"Stop worrying about it, please. We're totally safe, I promise, and the statistics are definitely in our favor." The tone in his voice has changed; it's stronger now, more matter-of-fact. I'm not sure it helps, but it does make me feel marginally better.

Leaning closer, I get a good sniff of his cologne. It's a mix of citrus and musk, something he's used for years, a scent I associate with him. "I'm not sure if numbers will make me feel any better right now. They also wouldn't change the fact that we're sitting in a small metal tube that's loaded with flammable liquid. And don't quote me on this, but if the media is anything to go by, the person I'm supposed to trust the most on this airplane might as well have an alcohol problem."

An involuntary shudder runs through me at the thought alone, and Carter squeezes my shoulder.

The low rumble and quivers of his laughter shake his body, and therefore, mine too, and I can't help but grin a little as well. "Okay. That might have been a little dramatic."

The look he gives me is filled with amusement. The laugh lines at the corners of his eyes oddly fascinating. "Definitely entertaining though."

His hand tightens on my arm and he squeezes my whole frame into his side once more.

When the flight attendant walks around to check the seat belts, he pulls back his arm but stays close with his face. "Just take a few deep breaths. I'm right here to help you however I can. If you want to, we can play games to distract you."

"Thank you." The words barely slip out of my mouth as I focus on my breathing.

"Anytime."

I'm not sure if the deep breathing helps with my anxiety, but at least his cologne distracts me every time I inhale. It keeps my mind occupied for the time being, and I'm grateful for it as the crew gets ready for takeoff, checking the overhead bins before getting settled in their own seats.

When the plane starts moving, I desperately try to find

something to hold on to that's sturdy enough when Carter offers his hand.

"Just don't break it, please." He flexes his fingers as if he's getting ready to battle.

"I promise." Not even wasting a thought on the scenario, I grasp his hand tightly in mine.

He immediately interlaces our fingers and rubs his thumb over the back of my hand in soothing circles.

Feeling the sensation combined with watching the movement, finally quiets my mind, at least momentarily. It's almost hypnotic and makes my skin buzz in a weird way, like it's hypersensitive and doesn't know what to do with this new sensation.

Before I can ponder on it any more, we speed down the runway, my eyes wide as the tremors of the airplane jolt through me, my stomach getting that weird drop feeling I hate so much. The same one I get on roller-coaster rides. Not only does my heartbeat increase from it but my breathing as well, making me slightly dizzy.

Carter squeezes my hand repeatedly before bending forward to retrieve something from his backpack. A moment later, he offers me a small bottle of orange juice. Since I don't want to let go of his hand under any circumstances, I open it while he holds it. The corners of his eyes crinkle in amusement when I take it, gulping down the sugary sweetness as fast as I can.

"Thank you." I give him a small smile, trying to focus on his face instead of the fact that we're quickly gaining height, already several thousand feet in the air.

"Of course. Just look at me, and we'll get through this together."

I nod, thankful he's so sweet and helpful. Other people would probably be annoyed with me.

"Eyes on me, Jules." He reminds me once more as my gaze sways to the side. "All right, time for a game. If you could see the future, what would it be like in five years?"

"Huh?" I feel like I missed something.

"We're going to ask each other questions."

"Just anything?"

He grins. "Yup."

I swallow loudly, realizing how quickly this could take an embarrassing turn if he decides to ask the wrong or rather right questions.

"Okay, let's see." I take a moment to actually think, knowing he's chosen a good question for me. "It's nothing exciting really. I'd love to expand my business over the next few years, maybe hire a person or two to help. That sort of thing."

"That's a great goal, and very reasonable too." He studies me intently, his voice lower than before. "How about your private life?"

For some reason, my gaze flicks to our still intertwined hands before answering him. "Well, I guess you kind of know the answer to that already. I'd like to be married and if possible, have a baby at that point."

He grimaces, and I laugh. "You really want to be a mom that young?"

"Carter, I'm twenty-three. You can hardly call becoming a mom in your late twenties young."

He tilts his head to the left, his eyebrows drawn together. "I thought it was the new thing to wait until you're in your thirties."

I shrug. "For some probably, others are perfectly happy to get married at eighteen and get started with a family right away. I don't think the age matters as much as finding the right partner and being ready for it."

He thinks about that for a moment. "I guess."

My body freezes momentarily at his response before something dawns on me. "You don't want to have kids, do you?"

I still feel like someone pulled the rug out from under my feet when he shakes his head.

"You know how I feel about marriage, and children kind of belong in the same category for me. Don't get me wrong, I don't have anything against children, I actually like them. But what's the point of having a child with someone when you know you won't stay together? And to have a child just for the sake of having one so you can pass it around for the rest of their life seems selfish and wrong in my eyes."

The slightly harsh tone of his voice and the hard, distinctive line of his jaw throws me for a moment, so contrary to the fun and carefree version of Carter from mere minutes ago.

If I'm honest, it's hard for me to wrap my head around this. On one side, I see where he's coming from, but on the other side, I'm sad to hear him say something like that, especially since it means so much to me. Also, the possibility of his parents screwing him up majorly in that aspect, not to mention irreversibly, makes me incredibly mad.

He touches my nose with his finger, the negative emotion wiped off his face. "Stop worrying about it. This wasn't supposed to get you all depressed. I'm fine, I promise. Besides, just think how lucky your kids will be to have me as their uncle. It's your turn to ask a question." He pauses for a moment before the corners of his mouth turn upward. "And make it interesting."

I'll probably ponder over the fact that he doesn't want to be a dad some more later on. But for now, I'm distracted enough to think of what embarrassing thing I could ask him.

"Oh," I finally exclaim, smiling broadly. "What's the worst thing anyone's walked in on you doing?"

Carter throws his head back and laughs. I not only feel but also see several eyes from other passengers snap our way, quite a few appreciative gazes among them when they see who the noisemaker is.

He wiggles his eyebrows, the humor still dancing in his eyes. "Easy answer. Stacy."

"Stacy?" I cock my head to the side, curious to hear more.

"Yeah. Do you remember her from high school? We were kind of dating for a while, if you can call it that."

I groan in response, having a good idea where this might be going, or at least what's going to be involved. "Well, spill it already."

He rubs his free hand on his thigh, chuckling to himself. "All right. So, we finally started to have sex after seeing each other for a while, and you can imagine how stoked my high school self was. One day, I took her back to my place and we were in the middle of doing . . . you know . . . when the door burst open and my mom waltzed in. She shielded her eyes with her hand, saying she just needs to get the laundry quickly, or it would be too late to start it. Then she added that she hoped I was smarter than my dad and was using protection. She gathered what she needed and left again. Needless to say, the moment was ruined, and Stacy wasn't so forthcoming with her affection afterward."

"No way." I stare at him for several seconds before I burst into laughter. "Oh my gosh, that totally sounds like your mom. No wonder Stacy was acting so weird all of a sudden whenever you were around."

We laugh together for several minutes, before I get a tissue to wipe at the corners of my eyes.

"Yup. I never brought another girl home after that. Who knows what else my mom would have come up with."

I snort, still shaking my head at the absurdity of his story. "I don't blame you. Your mom has always had her own way of doing things."

"She really has." The smile lingers on his face. "Your turn. Worst pickup line you've ever heard."

I roll my eyes at him, not even having to think about that one. "Easy. No wonder the sky is gray today, as all the blue is in your eyes." I look up at him and flutter my eyelids dramatically until we both clutch our stomachs.

"That's the stupidest thing ever." Carter's gasping for air while I wipe away more tears.

I nod. "I know."

I can't even remember the last time I laughed this hard.

"I mean, not only is it completely unoriginal, but your eyes are pretty obviously brown." He squeezes my hand as more laughter rolls through him.

The movement makes me stop in my tracks, my laughter quickly turning into quiet chuckles. In the midst of this fun, I forgot our hands were still connected, the contact suddenly feeling more intimate.

Awareness spreads through me. We're obviously

comfortable together, holding hands and sitting closely, but how does this look to the people around us?

"No one can be that blind or unoriginal." He shakes his head, his gaze momentarily focused on our hands before he lifts it up to mine.

I have to stop my mind from putting its own spin on things, wondering about things that aren't there. We might look like a couple to those around us, but I have to keep focused on the truth. I promised myself years ago to never cross the line and want more from Carter again. We're friends, and I know he'll never see me any differently. I just have to ignore the sting that causes too.

Chapter Eight

CARTER

he lobby of the Bellagio Hotel buzzes with noise. There are people everywhere—families, business people, couples decked out to the nines, college kids, groups of friends, seniors—most of them poised to take pictures with their cameras or phones. Above all, they're directed at the opulent ceiling. The wonder about the colorful ceiling sculpture made of glass-blown flowers is audible all around me.

Only in Vegas can hotel-hopping be popular. But, most of the hotels are either plain stunning or so ridiculous they're cool again.

A quick glance at the clock confirms that Julia should be here any minute. Thankfully, she did okay for the rest of the flight, besides the landing, where she shrieked and nearly broke my hand. After getting situated at the hotel, we agreed to go for an early dinner before I meet up with my client for drinks.

My gaze sweeps over the bank of elevators, just as she steps out of one.

Oh for fuck's sake. Not *that* dress.

How on earth am I supposed to survive this evening when she's wearing the red number that clings to all her curves like it was handmade for her? She's so fucking beautiful. It ends an inch above her knees, with the barest hint of cleavage visible when I stand above her. Her black heels are shiny and click rhythmically on the marble floor, giving her an even more impressive entrance.

She stops right in front of me, her hands brushing over the smooth fabric on her thighs. "Sorry I kept you waiting."

Getting up from the bench, I let my eyes slowly wander up her body until I finally get to her face. She went above and beyond to get ready. Her makeup is bolder than usual but without being too much, her hair in soft curls around her face. I prefer the natural look on her, but she's breathtaking like this.

"Jules, you're beautiful."

Her cheeks turn pink, and I briefly wonder if Nate ever complimented her. Since that douchebag is the last person I want to think about though, I push all thoughts of him aside, not wanting anything or anyone to ruin my time with her.

"Thank you." She pushes a strand of hair behind her ear, meeting my gaze for only a moment. "Now, let's go. I'm starving."

"That's my girl."

The second the words are out, I regret them. So much.

We shouldn't cross that line of our friendship or all hell will break loose, not just with Julia but also with Ollie. And those two have always been my second family, and I wouldn't want anything to get in the middle of that.

She looks up at me expectantly. "So, where are we going?"

Either she didn't hear what I said, or she chooses to disregard it, so I do the same, holding out my arm for her. She wraps her hand around my bicep, and I try to ignore how right she feels on my arm, like she belongs there.

We walk deeper into the hotel, the crowds thinning out marginally. "They have an Italian restaurant here that's to die for. Quite possibly the best food I've ever eaten."

Her fingers tighten around my arm, her mouth morphing into a wide grin. From the looks of it, she's about a minute away from bouncing in place. "You know Italian is my favorite, so please lead the way."

I chuckle at her excitement. She's too cute for her own good. And of course, I know Italian is her favorite. It's impossible to forget all the nights I spent at the Bradford house eating mountains of it, and the reason I made some last-minute phone calls to secure us a reservation.

Since I've been here several times before, I have no trouble maneuvering us through the crowd to the restaurant where we get seated immediately.

Once our waiter has taken our order and leaves us with the drinks the hostess ordered for us, I look at Julia across the small table that's nestled into the corner of the restaurant.

It's a little secluded, almost intimate, and I immediately wonder if this was a mistake. The last thing I want to do is give her the wrong impression, or worse, make her uncomfortable.

"I hope this table is okay."

She gazes at me over the floral centerpiece. "Of course. It's perfect."

Tension I was unaware of releases in my body, and I tell myself to get it together. This busyness of work, especially with this last-minute trip, and balancing time with Julia in her quest has thrown me off more than I thought this week.

I nod. "I'm sorry I have to leave right after dinner. Our client is very social, so whenever we have a business meeting with him, we usually get together for drinks the night before. He's very peculiar about that."

She brushes her hand over the tablecloth in front of her, absentmindedly repeating the motion. "Don't be silly. I tagged along on this trip last minute. You're here for work, not to babysit me, so there's really no need to worry. I'll go watch the show you got me a ticket for, and then tomorrow I'll explore the city during the day. That's probably a lot safer, not to mention less crowded."

Since she doesn't look upset, I nod.

Not everyone understands when the business calls for weird hours, but this is Julia we're talking about. She grew up with her dad and uncle building their insurance business from scratch. Their uncle took over the business since Ollie wasn't interested in the insurance market. Instead, he teamed up with me to build our investment company. Oftentimes, that requires us to put in long hours, especially during the first few years when most of the foundation is constructed and giving it your all is most crucial.

I give her a smile, truly appreciating her understanding. "Thanks, Jules. I'll definitely be able to squeeze in some time for you tomorrow, I promise. My meeting won't be until noon, so we can have breakfast together and then explore the strip after if you want to."

"Sounds perfect."

"Is there anything specific you'd like to see?" I lean back in my chair, waiting for her answer.

She shakes her head. "I don't really know what's out there to be honest. Since we seem to be smack in the middle of it all though, maybe just walking up and down the strip and sneak into some of the cool hotels to check them out? I saw some casino brochures in the room and more in the lobby too, so I'm sure we'll have no problem staying busy."

"Very true. It's hard to get bored in Vegas."

She takes a sip of her wine, her gaze momentarily averted while mine stays on her, taking in her soft features and those plump lips on the rim of her glass.

Before I can take that thought any further and imagine that mouth around something else—my mind playing more and more tricks on me—I clear my throat and focus back on our conversation. "But you'll go back to your room after the show, right?"

Her long curls bounce as she nods. "I might go to the bar for a drink after the show, but that's probably it."

I'm relieved to hear that, not wanting her to wander around the city by herself, especially not the way she's dressed. It wouldn't take a minute before someone tried to pick her up. "Good. I'm not sure how I would explain to your brother that you're out by yourself having a crazy night. Especially since he doesn't even know you're here with me."

It still doesn't sit well to withhold that little detail from my best friend, but I'm not sure the alternative is much better.

The restaurant noise disappears around us for a moment when she leans in, exposing the top swell of her breasts. "He doesn't need to know everything. It's already enough that you worry and freak out over everything I do."

There's a gleam in her eyes that makes my stomach uneasy.

Thankfully, the waiter arrives with our food, and we drop the subject of the impending big-brother drama, at least for now. I'm sure it'll come back eventually since situations like this tend to bite you in the ass, but I'm trying to stay optimistic and choose ignorance at this point.

A few hours later, I part ways with my client for the night, glad we only met a hotel over. I briskly walk back to the Bellagio, checking my phone to see if Julia's messaged. I try calling her, but she doesn't answer.

A look at the time tells me her show ended about an hour ago, so she should be back in her hotel room. Even with a drink at the bar, she shouldn't be out and about anymore.

I try calling again but it keeps ringing until her voicemail kicks in.

This time I wait for the beep. "Jules, where are you? You said you'd text me when you got back to your hotel room. Please let me know you're okay, so I know you made it back in one piece. I'm on my way to the hotel. Call me." I push the end button.

I was hoping that leaving her a message would make me feel better, but the opposite is true. The hairs on the back of my neck stand up, a strange mixture of concern and fear starting to build up in my body, the feeling of uneasiness strong enough for me to start pushing through the crowd as fast as I can.

The sun set while I was inside, the sunset gradually morphing into twilight, leaving the sky a beautiful shade of pink. The bright lights of the casinos stand out more against the darkening backdrop, and getting around people turns out to be harder than I thought since a lot of them are already highly intoxicated or on their way there.

I'm still clutching the phone in my hand when it vibrates, Julia's name flashing on the screen. I'm so relieved, I almost drop it.

"Jules. Where the hell are you?"

For a few seconds, all I hear from the other side of the line is loud noise before she finally starts talking. "Carter? Are you there? Oh my gosh. Vegas is *soooooo* much fun."

And then the phone call drops.

I stare at my phone screen in disbelief. What the fuck just happened?

When I call her back, the voicemail kicks in right away.

Shit.

Our hotel comes into view, and I practically run inside. Since Julia was clearly *not* in her hotel room, I rush through the bars on the lower level, having more than just a few curious—and some annoyed—looks thrown my way.

Just as I was afraid of, the search is fruitless. I'm off to the elevators to check her room anyway, even though I'm positive the chances are incredibly slim she's there. The elevator ride takes forever, and I'm ready to rip my hair out when I finally make it to our floor.

"Come on, Julia. Please open the damn door." I pound on it over and over, still hoping she'll magically appear.

Two seconds later, I'm ready to punch a hole in the wall, knowing what the possibilities are of actually finding her in a city like this.

My phone vibrates again, this time alerting me of a new text message.

From Julia.

Thank fuck.

I'm not sure I still feel the same though when I read it, certain the little bit of color I had left on my face is now gone.

Julia: Come meet me at the Wedding Chapels on the first floor. Wear your suit. Hurry up.

Oh shit.

Chapter Nine

JULIA

Leaning back in one of the chairs, I check the clock on the wall. Again. I sent Carter the text about ten minutes ago, right before my phone died for good. It shouldn't take him this long to get here, contrary to us, but we stopped several times for drinks and to look at the fun promenade shops that led us to the luxurious waiting room in front of the Wedding Chapels. It's beautiful with elegant seating arrangements, creme-colored chairs, and intricate wall and ceiling patterns alongside lavish chandeliers.

Who would have thought Vegas is so much fun? I mean, I've heard a lot of stories about this place, both good and bad, but it's different to experience it yourself. I definitely should have come here sooner, because it's been absolutely exhilarating so far.

"Jules?" Carter's voice carries across the expansive room before he comes in my line of vision, sprinting over to me.

He stops in front of me a moment later, putting his hands on his knees to catch his breath.

"Took you long enough." I lean forward to get a better

look at his face, a laugh breaking from my chest when I see his frown. Teasing Carter is so much fun. Then I clap my hands together and yell, "Now we can get started."

"Can we finally do this, babe?" The tall figure that was slouched over one of the other chairs pushes himself up, his speech slurred. I think. It's hard to fully think past my own buzz.

"Yes." I beam at him, until I take in the expression on his face. He looks different than before. Not as happy and smiley anymore. I thought we were having so much fun. Or maybe my alcohol levels have dropped. "Is everything okay?"

"What?" His eyebrows are furrowed, and he looks at me like he's seeing me for the first time. "Yeah. Sure, sure. I just really want to do this already."

"Jules." Carter's sharp tone snaps me out of my maybe-blissful conversation—I haven't decided yet. "Can we talk for a moment, please?" He grabs my elbow and pulls me over to the side, away from the seating area. "What the hell is going on here?"

"It's wonderful. Marc and I are getting married." I smile widely, the corners of my mouth slightly achy from the motion.

His head flinches back before he rubs his forehead. "I'm afraid I already know the answer, but who's Marc?"

I point at the man we just walked away from. "Obviously him. We met at the show tonight. Neither one of us really enjoyed it, so we skipped it after a little while and went to the bar instead. We had a few drinks, talked, and decided to have some fun. Somehow, we ended up here."

Carter looks at me like I'm speaking Chinese, so I keep

talking, "Marc just split up with his girlfriend and needed a little cheering up, just like me."

"So you guys thought that getting married would cheer up both of you? Please tell me you're kidding." He lifts a single eyebrow and cocks his head.

"You don't think it's a great idea?" My smile falters a little, but I keep going. "It's something new and exciting, and it seemed like we were meant to meet tonight. And in Las Vegas of all places. What are the odds?"

He shoves his hand roughly through his hair. Usually, he does that when he's frustrated.

I take a step closer, tripping over my own feet and halfway stumbling into him, holding on to his arm for dear life. "Carter? Are you okay? Did the meeting not go well?"

He looks down to where my hands tightly clasp his forearm. "Why are you asking?"

"You're clearly upset about something."

He throws his head back and laughs, loudly, causing Marc to grunt behind us. When I turn around, he isn't sitting like he was a few minutes ago, but instead, he's lying down on one of the benches.

Wait. Is he *sleeping*?

I gasp just as Carter stops laughing.

"Jules, you don't think there's anything else I could be upset about?" He points around the room before throwing his hands in the air. "How many drinks have you had?"

I look at him, this conversation sobering me up more and more by the minute. Then I shrug. "Not too many. Just a few Long Island Iced Teas. Marc got me started on them since I'd never had one before. They're really good."

He groans in response, but I'm having trouble understanding why.

"Is something wrong with that drink?" I ask him.

"Nothing wrong per se, but they're very strong. And you"—he points his finger at me—"are not a heavy drinker."

"Nope, I'm not." I giggle, enjoying this light buzz more than the heavier one I had when Marc and I left the bar earlier. The delicious dinner I had with Carter has probably helped soak up a lot of the alcohol too by now. I look around the room once more. The beautiful room that serves as a gateway to several chapels and is now adorned with a snoring man—random dude-slash-new friend-slash-almost husband? I bite my lip as my brain is busy firing up again, the fog slowly clearing in my head. "They were delicious, but maybe I should stay away from them in the future."

"You think?" He lets out a loud breath. "Oh, Jules, what am I gonna do with you?"

I shrug.

"What exactly did you want me here for tonight anyway?"

I grimace and avoid his gaze as the reality of what I was about to do crashes down on me. Covering my face with my fingers, I peek through my fingertips at him sheepishly. "Be my best man?"

He takes a step closer, his presence pushing away the remnants of my muddled brain. "In case we aren't clear on this yet, in no way are you getting married to Brad."

"Marc."

"What?"

"His name is Marc, not Brad."

"I honestly don't give a shit what his name is." Once

more, he points his finger at me, his words almost resembling a growl. "You're not getting married to Marc, or anyone else for that matter. You're clearly not thinking straight."

I put my hands on my hips and pout. When I realize what I'm doing, I chuckle.

Carter, on the other side, is frowning at me again. "What is it now?"

"Nothing. I just think this is all so much fun, that's all. I haven't felt this alive in years."

He pinches the bridge between his eyes, briefly closing them. When he opens them, his gaze is softer, the tension leaving his face as he grabs my hand. "Come on, Jules. Let's get you back to your room so you can sleep this off."

I look over my shoulder at my almost husband, and so does Carter. "Looks like he's out for the night anyway. We better tell someone on the way. Oh well, I had a fun evening with him."

"I don't think spending a few hours with someone fun qualifies them as spouse material. I'm afraid we have to talk some more about your sudden urge to find a husband. But that will have to wait until tomorrow."

I'm not sure I like where this is going. That feels like a serious talk, and I've had enough seriousness in my life for the past few years. "It's not *that* bad."

He suddenly spins me around to face Marc who is now snoring loudly on the bench. Carter's breath is on my neck, the smell of his aftershave infiltrating my senses. I let out a little sigh of appreciation, and Carter stiffens behind me.

After drawing a breath, he releases it before speaking, making me shiver involuntarily. "Does this guy," he murmurs into my ear, unmistakably talking about the sleeping person on the other side of the large room, "look like someone you want to spend the rest of your life with? At least I always assumed you wanted to be married for a long time and not end up like my mom."

My mouth falls open, the statement clearing the last remnants of the fuzziness straight from my mind. Even though I'm still a little distracted by Carter's close proximity, I suddenly see everything in front of me with a shocking clarity.

Gone is the cheery, funny guy I met earlier this evening who I was laughing with nonstop. In his place, is a guy who looks exhausted and very sad, deep frown lines etched into his forehead even when he's passed out.

I shake my head. "You're right. Let's go. He probably would have been bad in bed anyway."

Turning around, I walk out of the room, and down the long corridor.

It takes Carter a few seconds before he starts running after me, falling in step next to me. "Just like that?"

"Yup, just like that. I can be reasonable sometimes." I raise my chin as he eyes me curiously. "Plus, I've sobered up, so I'd appreciate it if we could just pretend this never happened. Now, I need some fresh air before we head back inside."

After telling an employee about Marc, and Carter practically forcing an entire bottle of water down my throat, we walk through the busy hotel in silence until we finally find an exit. It happens to be perfect timing too since the water fountain show is about to start.

I rush to one of the balconies, trying to avoid all the people coming from every direction. Carter's on my heels, following me wordlessly until we're both pressed into the balcony landing as more people join us, *oohing* and *aahing* with us throughout the whole show.

Once the show is done—absolutely magical, and way better live—the crowd dissipates around us.

Carter clears his throat next to me. "So . . . What did you mean earlier when you said that guy would have been bad in bed?"

His sole focus is on me, his body tilted my way.

I snort as I think about my best friend and lean in conspiratorially. "It's really more Michelle's doing than mine."

"How so?" Crap. Impatient Carter has returned. He has this twitchy eye thing happening when he's like this.

"Well, she's convinced it's possible to tell if someone is good or bad in bed by really looking at them. Something about paying attention to the details like intense eye contact, being confident and attentive. There was more, but I can't remember what else she said." My eyes are wide as I stare at him, expecting him to laugh.

Instead, he frowns at me. He's been doing that an awful lot tonight, and it's something I'm not used to seeing much. Of course, he isn't always happy, but his bad moods usually don't stay for long.

"That's absurd, but Michelle's always been a bit crazy. I mean, I'm sure it's a lucky guess sometimes—the chances are fifty-fifty after all—but she can't possibly pick guys that way." His brows furrow as he seems to seriously contemplate this.

I smile at him, trying to bring this conversation back to the happier side. "So far she's been right every single time, both good and bad."

He shakes his head in exasperation. "There's so much I want to say about this, but I don't need to know anything about Michelle's sex life, please. Not to mention, I'd rather not spend our one night in Vegas talking about her."

I tip my head in his direction. "Fair enough."

He grabs my arm and pulls me closer to him when a rowdy group of guys walks past us. "Seriously though, Jules. Please don't put too much into that theory."

I stare at him, just stare at him, while the synapses in my brain are trying to figure out which way to take this conversation. I have a response on the tip of my tongue, but the civilized part of my mind is trying to reason with me.

I'm not sure if this is the last bit of alcohol speaking, or if I might just have had enough of doing the right thing after the way I've lived the last few years, but . . . Unable to contain my smirk, I watch his face, not wanting to miss his reaction to my next words. "So, that means you're not good in bed then?"

Chapter Ten

CARTER

 hooosh.

That's all I can hear right now, a strange whooshing sound in my ears.

Jules is staring at me with her expressive brown eyes, waiting for a response. There's also something else in her gaze. *Is she testing me?* Daring me? If anything has proven how much she's changed over the past few years, it's tonight's behavior. Right now, I don't think anything about this woman would surprise me anymore.

Whenever I talked to Ollie about his sister, he suggested everything was still the same with her. Very odd.

Which I'm pretty sure was either a load of bullshit, or Jules put on a happy front for her brother.

Now, I'm staring at one of my oldest friends who seems to be silently challenging me.

To do what exactly?

Simply answer her question or something more than that?

"What do you want from me right now, Jules?" Holding

on to her arm, I spin us around so we switch places. People kept bumping into her, so now she's safely standing on the side, leaning against the rough balcony while I block the crowd around us.

She shrugs, her voice lower than before. "I don't know. I can't say I'm not curious."

She mentioned earlier she isn't drunk anymore, and I believe her, even though it's hard to wrap my head around what she just said. This bold and direct Jules—someone I've seen several times over this last week—is extremely hard to ignore. She's becoming bolder . . . more daring. But, what the fuck?

I narrow my eyes at her. "Curious about what exactly?"

She lifts her chin, exposing her neck some more, and I'm momentarily distracted by it, almost missing her answer. "*You*, Carter."

The way she looks at me makes me feel like I'm a freaking wonder of the world. I don't realize I've taken a step closer to her until I see the reaction on her face. Her sharp intake of breath as she glances at me with wide eyes.

"What about me?" My nose fills with the smell of her perfume. It's subtle, the same one she's been using for as long as I can remember. This time, it's mixed with something I can't identify though, something unique to just her.

"I've always wondered about you, I suppose."

Even though her reply wasn't anything special, it does something to me. A strong awareness of my heartbeat overcomes me, and I feel breathless. Despite that, I smirk at her, momentarily wondering if I'm losing my mind. "You've wondered if I'm good in bed?"

At that, she averts her eyes from me.

But I won't have it. "Look at me and answer my question, Jules." I know I'm pushing her right now, but something inside me needs to know. "Is that what you've been wondering about?"

She throws her hands up in defeat. "Yes, okay? Are you happy now? Goodness, Carter. I mean, look at you. You look like a freaking model, and you're a good guy on top of it. We've all wondered. I can't think of a girl in high school who didn't have a crush on you at some point."

Her statement, mixed with her red cheeks, makes me stop for a second, my mind going completely blank before it reboots. "*You*," I say, "had a crush on *me?*"

"Oh, please. Don't act like you don't know. I'm pretty sure Ollie told you all about it and you guys had a good laugh about his silly little sister." She purses her lips, and I see that sass returning.

"Wait, wait. Your brother *knew?*" Wow. This keeps getting better and better. I'm floored, to say the least. "He never said a thing. Not once."

Now, she looks as shocked as I feel. "He didn't?"

I shake my head before shoving my hand through my hair.

"Oh," is all she says in response.

We're quiet for a moment, both of us lost in our own thoughts.

This revelation is *huge*. For me at least.

"So . . . you had a crush on me, huh?" I can't help myself but feel a little cocky about it, wanting to dig deeper. No way can I let this go easily. Thankfully, the crowd has mostly disappeared, and the commotion around us has turned into white noise.

"I think we just established that, Carter. Can we move on from that now? I've already embarrassed myself enough." Her head dips, and I instantly miss the connection.

Since I'm not sure what else to do, I keep pushing. "Do you regret having a crush on me?"

She frowns at me. "No. Just talking about it feels weird and humiliating, especially since I thought you knew all these years and just ignored it."

I still can't believe my best friend kept this from me. Somehow, I'll have to figure out why.

My hand goes to my chest. "I swear I had no clue."

She smooths out her dress even though it looks flawless. "Well, now you know and we can stop talking about it, all right?"

In a twisted way, her obvious discomfort is amusing. She looks fucking cute, all flustered and discombobulated. Like I'm getting under her skin. "Okay. Let's get back to the 'being good in bed' part then."

Her mouth drops open at my words. It takes her a moment to compose herself, but I give her whatever time she needs. When she gives me a small smirk that's sexy as hell, I wonder if I'm playing with fire, and suddenly, I wouldn't mind getting a little burnt.

This whole conversation is a game-changer.

She leans in closer like she's about to whisper a secret to me. "Does that mean you're ready to tell me then?"

Knowing she had a crush on me when we were younger has fueled something inside me. Something forbidden, a fire that's tormenting me, begging me to take what it wants, what it has desired for so long but has always been denied.

The taboo of it all has somehow vanished. Even though I

can think clearly enough to know there'll be consequences, I don't care.

Something inside me snaps, and I take another small step toward her.

Bending down, I move closer to her face, barely missing her cheek as I move my mouth to her ear. "If you're so curious about it, why don't you find out yourself?"

Silence.

Even though we're in the middle of a busy public place, it feels like only the two of us exist.

Then she lets out the tiniest yet most potent moan I've ever heard. Not sure I was supposed to hear it, but I did. Despite knowing exactly what's right and what isn't—making a move on my best friend's sister is definitely not on the right side—I turn my head slightly to the side and take her earlobe between my teeth.

After a soft tug on it, I move further down and give her throat a gentle kiss.

"Carter, what . . . what—" The rest of her sentence disappears into thin air as I suck on her skin.

After a moment, I move back a few inches to look at her. Her eyes are closed, the lights around us bright enough to show her flushed cheeks. When she opens her eyes, they're pure fire. It's potent and draws me in like nothing else. She licks her lips absentmindedly as her gaze flickers to mine.

A brief moment of doubt hits me. "Jules, I don't know what to say."

"Then don't say anything."

Instead, I can't help myself and gaze at her mouth too, making it pretty obvious what I want.

When I look back up at her, the fire seems to burn even

brighter in her eyes.

"Just kiss me already, Carter." Her voice is steady, and I know those words will forever change our relationship.

So I do.

Any willpower I had left vanishes the second my mouth makes contact with hers. Her lips are like a whole new world, begging to be explored, urging me on to learn everything there is about them.

This feels good. So damn good. Maybe even too good.

I can't think clearly anymore, my mind completely taken over by everything Julia.

She keeps making little noises in the back of her throat that spur me on even more. Our lips and tongues fight for dominance, unable to get enough of each other fast enough.

Grabbing my shirt, she pulls me even closer, not that I'm complaining. This gets me exactly where I want to be, pressed as close to her as possible.

My hard body pushing into her soft one.

Her hands find their way into my hair, around my neck, and down my back, until it feels like she's touching me everywhere. I know we're both in trouble when she squeezes my ass, and I'm close to pulling her legs up around my waist.

Loud catcalls around us snap me out of the fog, clearing my muddled brain enough to pull back.

"Jules," I whisper, waiting for her to open her eyes.

When she finally does, a small smirk forms, her eyes shining with mirth.

She takes my hand and starts pulling me away from the balcony. "Let's go back to the hotel bar, Carter. I might need another drink."

How am I going to survive this woman?

Chapter Eleven

JULIA

*T*he bar is more crowded than it was during my earlier visit with Marc, which makes sense. It's now close to 10 p.m., meaning prime time is just starting in Vegas. People are everywhere, most bodies showing more skin than they're hiding. Displaying your best attributes loud and proud definitely seems to be the theme in this city, even more so when the sun is down.

By some luck, a couple leaves their spot at the bar just as we make it there, and we conveniently slip into the smooth leather chairs.

Thankfully, the bartender spots us right away, and Carter orders two Long Island Iced Teas and some orange juice.

What the heck?

He looks at me and shrugs. "If there's one thing you do even worse than drinking alcohol, it's mixing alcohol. I'd rather have you drunk again than hanging over the toilet half the night."

"That only happened once years ago. How do you know all this stuff? You weren't even at that party." I give him a look, still more shaken up about that kiss than I'd like to admit.

Because . . . Carter Kennedy just kissed me.

Kissed. Me.

Holy.

Shit.

He doesn't answer immediately. Instead, he looks at his hands, giving me a chance to study him without interruption. His jaw is clenched and his mouth is drawn into a tight line, making my body tingle. It's hard to focus on much else at this point when I can still taste him on my lips. Even forming a coherent thought proves to be difficult with our kissing scene imprinted in my mind and on endless repeat.

"I just do." The words are barely a whisper as his gaze flicks back to me. Even in the dimmed light of the bar, his eyes flash brightly, the hunger I saw earlier easier to recognize now.

Hunger *for me.*

The thought alone makes me press my legs together and squirm in my seat.

He's watching me so intently I'm certain he knows exactly what's going on with me.

Reaching out, he brushes a lock of hair from my face. "What are you thinking about, Jules?"

"You."

It's official: my brain's on vacation.

What is it about this man?

I've never been this bold. With anyone. *Ever.*

Somehow I like it. A lot actually.

"What about me?"

The drinks arrive and after taking a sip of the orange

juice—much to Carter's delight—he plays with the rim of his glass, clearly toying with me.

His eyes shine with amusement, and the smirk he gives me turns my mind into a buzzing mess of static. Looks like he's challenging me just as much as I challenged him earlier.

"Oh, Carter." Usually, I'm not one for playing games, but doing this with him is a thrill I've never experienced before. It's incredibly exciting, not to mention a major turn-on.

Moving to the edge of the barstool, I conveniently wedge myself between his open legs. Leaning forward, I keep track of his eyes as they move away from my face down to the neckline of my dress. "I think you know exactly what I mean."

The corners of my mouth twitch when I watch him swallow several times.

He takes another sip. "Are we going to talk about what happened?"

I shrug, the sheer thought of Carter and me together giving me sharp palpitations. "I don't know. What's there to talk about?"

"I don't know, Jules. Maybe the fact that you could start a small fire with the tension between us. This will be hard to hide from anyone, especially Ollie when he gets back from his vacation."

I stare at him for a while, my thoughts racing a mile a minute. Thankfully, he lets me be, probably knowing the wheels are turning in my head.

There really are only two options in this situation.

Option one: forget about the kiss we shared and pretend it never happened. I'm not sure how realistic the chances are of going back to the way we used to be before though because

Carter is right, the chemistry between us is insane. It's undeniable, and I can easily spot it in his gaze now that I know what it looks like. Seems like we're a walking billboard of sexual tension.

Option two: give in and provide our bodies with what they so clearly want. I mean, we're both adults, so it shouldn't be hard, right? Isn't that what some people do? To get it *out of their system*? I know how Carter feels about relationships, so I wouldn't run into any issues with him afterward either since we're on the same page. Both of us knowing this wouldn't go anywhere.

We can just have a wild night in Vegas and that's it.

Nothing else.

No old crush coming back to haunt me and no broken hearts, right?

Easy peasy.

I clear my throat. "As I see it, there are two choices. The aftermath of both will more than likely include some level of awkwardness, but I think at this point, that will happen regardless."

He cocks his head to the side, listening intently. "Go on."

"I suppose the question is, which kind of awkward do you want?"

His voice is steady, his gaze alert. "I'm good with whatever you decide. I'll deal either way."

I'm not sure I'm happy he's putting the ball back in my court. It's thoughtful he leaves the decision up to me, yet at the same time, I'd like to get a better read on him too.

He must sense my indecision and leans closer. Like whatever he has to say next should stay only between the two of us.

Grabbing me by the waist, he rubs his thumbs over my hip bones. "Don't doubt for a second how much I want you. I'm close to losing it right here and taking what I want. But I also know this is a line we can't re-establish once we cross it. I like to live on the edge though, and there's no one else I'd rather take there with me than you."

My heart races like crazy, skipping beats as the sweetest buzz of excitement and anticipation rushes through my body. Those sensations make me even more aware of his eyes on me and his touch as one of his hands slowly makes a descent down my hip.

I silently will that hand to move a few more inches to the hemline of my dress, both my body and mind already yearning for his hands on my skin.

Looks like I found my answer.

The aftermath of it definitely scares me a little, but the feeling of not taking this to the next level, and quite possibly missing out on the best night of my life, is even more frustrating.

I take a sip of my Long Island Iced Tea, the warmth of the alcohol rushing down my throat. The smallest buzz in my system gives me the final boost in confidence I need.

Closing the last bit of distance between us, I brush a finger across his lower lip. "I think we should put out this fire we started. Together."

He grabs my hand and brings the back of it to his mouth, pressing a soft kiss to my knuckles. "Fuck. Yes. Lead the way, gorgeous."

I close my eyes and take a deep breath, ready to melt into a pile of liquid lust.

Carter chuckles quietly, clearly enjoying my state of

desperation. I finally turn around and make my way out of the bar and toward the elevators as fast as I can, his hand still tightly clutched in mine.

The ride upstairs seems to take forever, and I feel like ripping my hair out. We stop on almost every level, people filing in and out of the small enclosure, unaware of the need boiling inside me that's threatening to make me go up in flames at any moment.

Carter isn't helping either, his fingers continuously playing with mine. The tension is intense, and by the time the doors open to our level, I'm ready to cry out loud because I'm so relieved.

Luckily, we're the only ones to leave on our floor and the hallways are deserted.

"Finally." I let out a deep breath, desperately wanting to shake off some of this tension.

"You can say that again."

Carter's voice seems off, and when I look at him, I'm stunned by the intensity of his gaze.

Before I can think about it, I'm pressed to the wall by his body as he leans in to give me a kiss that tastes of sweet promises and an unforgettable night.

Chapter Twelve

CARTER

I groan when the light on the card reader *finally* switches to green and the door opens. We stumble into my room, still attached in as many spots as possible. My lips are on Julia's neck, since I can't get enough of her skin. It's soft and warm, and smells amazing. Our hands roam over our bodies like it's a competition—squeezing, testing, and touching body parts I've been dreaming of exploring for a long time. And she has no clue.

Julia arches into me while I kick the door shut. We definitely don't need an audience for anything going down inside this suite.

Pulling back, I look straight into her lust-induced face. Her eyes are half-closed and she's wearing this small smile that's sexy as hell.

Everything about her is sexy.

"Jules, are you absolutely sure you want this?" It would kill me if she said no, but it would be worse if she regretted it later on.

We both know there's no going back from having sex with someone, as much as some people like to pretend there is.

Sex changes things; it changes people.

"Oh, hell yes." Her voice is raspy, her smile turning into that sexy smirk from earlier.

I'm a total goner.

"Thank fuck." I let go of her to take off my suit jacket before throwing it carelessly over the couch. My tie is next, followed by my shirt while I step out of my shoes too.

All the while, Julia watches me, and I get a kick out of that. When I'm about to unbutton my pants, she swats my hands away, trailing her fingers from my waistband to my chest. She's teasing me, leaning in to bite one of my nipples.

"Jules." The warning is a growl, my need for her so strong, I want nothing more than to throw her on the bed and put my hands on her.

Thankfully, she takes pity on me, her hands wandering back to my pants. She unbuttons and unzips them, putting her hands into the front before they even hit the floor. At this point, I'm not sure who's more desperate between the two of us.

She cups me, eliciting a loud groan out of me when she squeezes gently. There isn't much I want more than her hands on me, maybe her mouth too, but I know I wouldn't last long. We'll have plenty of time for that later.

"Enough." My voice is rough and laced with need as I spin her around and pull her body into mine, my throbbing hard-on pressing into her ass.

My hands are firmly clasped around her midsection, holding her by the waist before they wander to her breasts, exploring them. I sigh, loving the fullness in my hands before kissing my way up her neck, to her ear, and finally around to her mouth.

Her head is tilted back, and she captures my lips hungrily, wrapping her hands around my neck to pull my face closer.

"Carter," she moans breathlessly when we pull apart a few minutes later. "I'm all for foreplay and taking things slowly, but I can't wait much longer."

I couldn't possibly want this woman any more than I do right now, and I remind myself that we have plenty more time to slow things down later.

My hands move away from her breasts and under her dress. Pushing her underwear to the side, I sink my fingers into her wet heat. "Is this what you want, Jules?"

"Yes . . . please." She pushes her body against mine, circling her hips in an almost hypnotic motion. "That feels so good." Her voice is barely more than a whisper as her breathing picks up.

"Fuck, you're hot." I'm about to lose it at any second just from watching her. I don't think I've ever seen anything more sexy in my entire life. Her full lips are parted, her eyes closed. Her head rests on my shoulder, and I cherish the contact.

Since we never bothered to turn on the light, the room is only lit by the city below us, the vast floor-to-ceiling windows giving us a perfect view of the buildings outside while no one can see inside.

It almost pains me to take my fingers away from her slick skin, but I don't want any more layers between us. By sheer luck, I manage to unzip the dress in one swift move. Less than a minute later, not only is her dress on the floor but her underwear and the rest of my clothes too, and I managed to put protection on.

"Wow." She turns around, and we stare at each other for a moment before we both spring into action. We're a blur of lips, teeth, and hands as our bodies hungrily rub against each other, the room filled with our moans and groans.

Just when I think I can't take it any longer, Julia grabs my hard-on and pulls me even closer to her, almost painfully so. Standing on her toes, she wraps one of her legs around my waist while she guides me toward her entrance.

I pick up her other leg and carry her to the window.

"Now, Carter. I need you inside me. I can't wait another second."

The words almost do me in as I press her against the cool glass, making her gasp out loud.

When I sink into her a moment later, I pause for a breath, wanting to make this last for as long as possible.

"Oh my gosh. This is . . . you . . . can you—" Her whimpers get more desperate by the second as she presses her head back into the glass.

Her whole body arches back with the movement, her breasts on full display right in front of me. Leaning down, I greedily take one nipple into my mouth. The moans get louder, the breathing more desperate, and soon I'm pumping in and out of her at a frantic pace.

My body is on fire, and if Julia's flushed face is anything to go by, so is hers.

"I need to touch you, Jules." Without waiting for a reply, I carry her to the bed as she crushes her lips to mine, sucking and nibbling so hard, I'm going to go crazy soon.

I lay her on the bed as gently as I'm capable of, squeezing

her ass once more for good measure. The second she's on the mattress, my hands move to the front of her body, touching and rubbing every inch I can reach, resuming my thrusts until I'm convinced I might never recover. While my one hand is still busy playing with those gorgeous breasts, my other one moves lower.

"You're so fucking beautiful," I groan as my movement speeds up, getting a little sloppy when she starts clenching around me.

Her head thrashes back and forth on the bed, her parted lips swollen from kissing. "I'm so close."

I increase the pressure on her sensitive nub with my thumb while stealing a few more hungry kisses.

When she tightens around me, I pull back enough to see her, not wanting to miss the look on her face when she comes. It's a sight to behold just like I thought it would be. Her moans still fill the room when I follow her over the edge, unable to hold on to my control for another second.

Endless waves of pleasure shoot through my body during one of the most intense orgasms I've ever had, until I collapse on her, our sweaty bodies fitting perfectly together in more than just one way.

A moment later she giggles into my ear. "Can't breathe."

Shifting back, I put some of my weight on my elbows.

Looking down, her eyes hold me hostage as I play with the silky tendrils of her hair. I stare at her like she's a freaking miracle because, right now, she absolutely is.

"Hi." Her voice is all husky, the smile on her face huge.

And so damn gorgeous.

"Hi yourself."

"I'm hungry."

Only Julia would say something like that right after having sex. "Oh yeah? Hungry for what exactly?" I wiggle my eyebrows, teasing her as I run my hand down her body.

"Food." She giggles and squeezes my butt. "And then some more of you, of course."

I chuckle, my body high on endorphins. "How about a shower, food, and then some dessert?" I wink at her and she laughs.

The sight of her so close to me, not to mention under me, is pretty damn perfect. We're still connected in the most intimate way, and Julia looks so beautiful with her hair fanned out around her and her face still flushed.

Regret works its way into my chest at this being only one night, but I push it away.

I slide out of her, and after depositing the condom in the trash, I lift her up and carry her to the adjacent bathroom.

"Maybe we should have more dessert first after all." Her mouth attaches to mine hungrily as I put her down in the big shower and turn on the spray.

"Hell. Yes."

"*Y*ou don't think it's creepy to stare at me while I'm sleeping?" I ask the same question Carter asked me last week, the corners of my mouth twitching.

Since it's completely silent, I know he hasn't moved since I last peeked. After a moment, my curiosity wins and I open my eyes. Just a teeny tiny bit.

He's still standing at the foot of the bed, a huge, cocky grin on his face as he watches me, his fingers busy putting the cufflink on his right shirtsleeve. "You're a little brat sometimes, but you already know that."

There's that same sexy undertone in his voice I heard a whole lot of last night, and my body immediately starts to tingle in all the right places. On second thought, I'm actually surprised my body is capable of feeling anything after last night.

After the sex marathon we had, I thought I might be out of shivers and orgasms for the next year or so.

I pull the sheet up and over my head when my cheeks heat from the memories, knowing I'm as red as a tomato.

So much for playing it cool and not letting him know how much this affects me.

Footsteps echo around the room, and a moment later, the bed dips on my side.

"Don't hide from me, Jules. I want to see your pretty face." His voice is gentle as he brushes his fingers over the sheet, all the way from my calves to my shoulder. Tantalizingly slow, raising goose bumps across my skin.

Before I can look over the rim of the sheet, Carter has taken matters into his own hands, giving it a rough tug. Since I was just about to lower it myself, the sheet slithers down my body, pooling around my hips. Which leaves my whole upper body exposed.

My *naked* upper body.

"So beautiful." Carter brushes his fingers over my side, making every skin cell tingle. "I hate that I have to leave."

"Is it that late already?" The words come out a little breathy, talking not at the top of my priority list right now.

My body is on fire, and all I want to do is give in to his touch and pull him down onto me. But I don't want to make him late for his business meeting and screw up the deal.

He nods, his eyes still glued to my body. "I really wish we could have some more time." Then his gaze flicks back up to mine. "I promised you some sightseeing too."

I lift my shoulder in a half shrug. "Don't worry about it. I can always come back another time."

He takes the sheet from around my hips and pulls it back up to my shoulders, an almost tortured look in his eyes. "Or . . ."

Those two little letters make my mind reel, impatiently wondering what he'll say next.

When he stays quiet, I ask "Or?"

"Well, I know we said this would be a one-time thing, or I guess I should say a one-night thing, but we could stay until tomorrow?" He looks at me with an unidentifiable, almost nervous, look in his eyes. "You could sleep in your own room if you prefer that. I'd like to stick to my word though and show you around."

"Carter." I sit up, not caring the sheet just dropped to my hips again.

Somehow I gained some sort of uber-confidence last night, at least when it comes to this man and my body. I've always enjoyed sex, but nothing, absolutely nothing, can compare to what I experienced with Carter. No one has ever taken such good care of me while driving me absolutely crazy at the same time. The desperation and need he brings out in me are both new and oddly thrilling.

I go up on my knees to be eye level with him. "There's nothing I'd rather do than stay another night with you."

He swallows, his Adam's apple bobbing up and down. If the strain in his jaw is anything to go by, I'd guess he not only has a hard time keeping his eyes on my face but also to keep his hands to himself. "I'll take care of the rooms and flights." His gaze flicks toward the nightstand and he groans. "Damn it, I really have to go."

I lean forward and press my lips softly to his before slipping out of bed to slowly saunter toward the bathroom. I still wonder who this new me is when I reach the door and look back over my shoulder. "Hurry back, big guy. You know how to reach me if you need anything."

Maybe I'm enjoying the utter look of disbelief in his eyes, or the slack jaw a little too much, but I'm unable to wipe the grin off my face as I walk out of view and into the bathroom to turn on the shower.

Carter: I'm finally done. Are you still out or already back at the hotel?

Me: Still out. Decided to get some ice cream and enjoy the nice day.

Carter: Sounds yummy. Where are you? I'll come to you.

Me: Just out front by the fountain. Let me know when you get here, and I can meet you at the entrance. Probably easier than trying to find me out here.

Carter: If you lick your ice cream like that one more time in public, I won't be held accountable for my actions.

I gasp, my eyes snapping up from my phone, wildly searching the crowd around me. It doesn't take me long to spot him as he makes his way toward me. His hands are casually tucked into his dark pants, his suit jacket open, the top few buttons of his white shirt unbuttoned. If I'm not careful, I might melt into a puddle. Gosh, that man is sexy.

"Do you realize you ruined the whole meeting for me today?" He stops in front of me but doesn't touch me.

I point toward my chest, not sure what he's talking about. "I did?"

He nods, his eyes scanning my face as if he's forgotten what I look like. "I couldn't get you out of my head and was barely paying any attention. The client called me out several times on it."

"That's awful. I'm sorry." Even though I didn't really do anything, I feel bad about it. I mean, that client is the sole reason he's here. I'm sure my brother wouldn't like the fact that his partner screwed things up because his mind was otherwise occupied either—specifically with me.

Carter winks at me. "No worries. He was more amused by my daydreams than anything."

I let out a sigh of relief. "Good. I'm glad. I was a bit scared there for a second."

His gaze is so intense, the crowd virtually evaporates around me, my brain unable to focus on anything but Carter.

Averting my eyes from him, I focus on my treat for a moment, trying to get a grip on my thoughts. "Soooo, what exactly were you thinking about?"

His eyes bore into mine. "You and me, and the naughty, dirty things I want to do to you." He whispers the last part, causing an involuntary shudder to surge through me despite the blistering heat.

He leans in with a huge grin on his face. When I think he's going to kiss me, he grabs my wrist and lifts it to his face so he can take a giant mouthful of my ice cream. "Delicious. Just like I know you'll taste later."

I blink, unsure if my mouth can hang open any farther as I watch Carter lick his lips. Slowly. Deliberately.

Pressing my legs together to ease the ache, I close my eyes to calm my almost feverish body.

Carter chuckles, knowing exactly what he's doing to me. What a tease.

Being teased by Carter is no hardship. I've always loved his sense of humor, and well, just him really. We've always been compatible. But knowing him sexually? Boy. Talk about *compatible*. In every dang way. This man knows his way around a female body, and I'm fairly sure sex will never be as sensual, as perfect, as sublime with any other man. And nothing feels awkward. Whether that's because he promised another night, I'm not sure, but it's . . . easy.

And I feel insatiable.

Being the epitome of composure, he casually props his elbows on the railing next to me, totally ignoring the fact that he just set my body on fire. "So, what do you want to do for the rest of the afternoon? We still have a few hours before dinner."

I rub the base of my neck where my pulse beats in hard spasms, pulling myself together as much as I can. "Oh. Uh . . . I don't really know. We can just walk around and explore, I guess."

Wow. Very put together, Jules.

Thankfully, Carter doesn't comment on my odd behavior, probably silently enjoying that he's driving me bonkers. "Sounds good to me. What about dinner? Do you feel like eating anything specific? There are a lot of good restaurants out here."

The cold ice cream has started to slide down my hand, and I bend to lick it off.

When I look back at him, the now familiar heat is there. The blue liquid around his pupils is darker than I've ever seen it, silently promising another pleasure-filled night, turning my knees a little weak at the thought alone.

Who knew a look could do that?

But two can play that game.

"I don't know. Right now I'm not even sure I feel like eating out." I take another lick of my ice cream, this time keeping my gaze steady on his as my tongue slowly swirls around the cold delicacy. "How's the room service at the hotel?"

His gaze swings back and forth between my eyes and my mouth as one of his hands goes to his throat to find his already opened shirt. "I've heard it's exquisite, and I can't wait to ravish everything that's on the menu, you included."

"That's exactly what I was hoping for." The desire to erase all distance is too strong to resist, and I lean up on my toes to suck in his lower lip before ending it with a kiss to the corner of his mouth.

He groans, his hands briefly clenching before he releases them. "Sounds like we have a plan then. Let me show you a few sights before I haul you off to the room. I have a feeling we won't emerge until tomorrow."

I link my arm with his and squeeze it once as the lightness in my chest makes me giggle.

Then, I let him whisk me away, because I want everything Carter is willing to give me. This time is ours, and I'm more than ready to make more spectacular memories with this delicious, sexy man.

Chapter Fourteen

CARTER

*A*fter paying the cab driver, I get out of the car and walk around to the other side to help Julia out too. She's been more quiet than usual since we left the hotel in Las Vegas several hours ago. I can't really blame her though, because it does all seem a bit odd.

I think we both expected it to be awkward, but neither one of us could really know how awkward it would be in reality.

It's not regret, because there's no way I'd ever want to undo the time I had with her. It's more that I'm having a hard time looking at her without imagining us walking hand in hand, teasing each other with food, with touches, spooning, screwing raw and hard.

Last night was even more mind-blowing than the night before, and even though I haven't had my fill of her yet, this is what we agreed on. As much as I want to ask her for more time together, I know she's not the girl who does casual relationships. And since that's all I can offer, I'll try my best to be happy with the time I had with her.

"Home sweet home, huh?" We walk up the driveway, the distance between us too big for my liking. Usually, I can read her pretty well, but she's put on a mask that makes it almost impossible to know what's going on in her head. Something's definitely off.

"You okay, Jules?" My mouth feels dry, and I'm really bugged that it takes her several long moments before she finally looks at me.

When she does, she blinks a few times as if to clear the fog in her mind before giving me a small smile. It doesn't completely reach her eyes, but I decide not to press her on it, at least not right now.

Her head dips in a quick nod. "Of course. Just exhausted from the flight."

"I'm sorry." I'm not sure what I'm apologizing for but the words come out nonetheless. All I know is that I hate seeing her like this. It's not like her. She wasn't in the best frame of mind when she came here last week, but at least she wore her emotions on her sleeve. Now, that seems to be the last thing she wants to do, to show me what's going on inside that beautiful mind, and it feels like a punch in the gut.

"You didn't do anything wrong, Carter. I'm sure a relaxed evening and a good night's sleep will do wonders. I'll probably be as good as new tomorrow." She smiles at me wistfully before we walk up the rest of the walkway.

We're almost at the door when it opens and Ollie fills the frame. "Where the hell have you guys been? I've been calling you for hours."

Ollie came back early.

Fucking fantastic.

Because . . . Julia and I haven't talked about what we're telling her brother about our trip.

I rub my chin, hoping we'll get a free pass by some miracle and won't have to answer his question until later. So instead of answering his question . . . "What are you doing here? I thought you were on vacation for another week."

Ollie is close to my six-two and has the same brown hair and brown eyes as Julia. Right now, my best friend's gaze ping-pongs between me and his sister, and the last thing I need is for him to get suspicious. "Cora got a last-minute job offer she couldn't refuse so we came back early."

Julia is the first to jump back into action as she walks over to him and gives him a hug. "Sorry about your vacation, but I'm glad you're home."

He looks at me over her shoulder, a million questions in his eyes.

It's weird to feel this guilt inside my stomach toward Ollie when, at the same time, I know this weekend with Julia was one of the best weekends of my life.

Talk about conflicting thoughts.

Ollie finally looks away from me and gazes at his sister, his gaze softening. "Good to see you, kiddo. It's been too long."

"I know, I know."

The exchange between them makes me realize that nothing much has changed. Even though Julia is only two years younger, Ollie has always felt responsible for her. He's always been a bit overprotective but even more so since their parents' death. We never really talked about it, but I know how agonizing it was for him to see his sister in so much pain.

His eyebrows draw together as he studies her face. "Are you feeling all right? You don't look very good."

She huffs once. "Thanks."

Ollie waves off her reply. "You know what I mean, Jules. You look beautiful, as always, just like you don't feel well. Are you sick?"

She shakes her head at him, and I can tell she's trying to give him a smile. "I'm just pooped, that's all. I talked Carter into taking me to Vegas with him. And well, you know how crazy Vegas can get, and I'm definitely no party animal, so I just need some sleep. Do you mind if we catch up tomorrow?"

It's easy to tell he's unhappy by the way he's pressing his lips together, but he nods regardless. "Of course. Let me know if you need anything."

"Will do, thanks." She kisses him on the cheek and walks into the house without looking back.

My best friend's eyes are back on me the second she's out of sight, trying to bore holes into my head. "You took her to Vegas? What the fuck, CJ?"

Ollie is the only one who still calls me by my old nickname. When we were younger, he envied that Carter James makes cool initials whereas his Oliver Parker doesn't lend itself to any initials worth mentioning, at least not to him.

I exhale loudly, needing to buy some time to think about this whole fiasco. "Let's go inside and I'll explain. But first I need a shower."

"Fair enough. You know where to find me when you're done." The words are barely audible as he turns around to disappear into the house.

Of course, I know he's heading straight for his office. Ollie and I are both workaholics, which is one of the reasons we started our company earlier than we'd initially planned. We knew we could handle the pressure and would put in the necessary hours.

Now, I just need to figure out what to tell him so he won't be suspicious. The last thing I need is him on my ass.

I stay in the shower for much longer than I need to since facing Ollie doesn't sound appealing in the slightest. Not just because I still have no clue what to tell him, but also because it'll be hard to hide my thoughts from him when the memories with his sister are still so fresh. I was supposed to have time to adjust before he got back.

When I walk out of the bathroom and into my bedroom, Julia's standing in front of my bookshelf, looking at the few pictures I have on it. She doesn't turn around as I make my way over to her, even though I'm sure she heard me come in. When I stop a few feet behind her, I'm close enough to smell the scent of her freshly washed hair. It smells tropical, almost like one of those piña coladas she had after dinner last night. The sweet taste of coconut and pineapple on her tongue. Something that will forever remind me of her. Something I'd really love to taste again.

She points to one of the frames before slowly turning around. Her voice is soft, a gentle smile on her face. "I almost forgot about that Halloween."

I frown and put one of my hands on my chest in fake

shock. "How could you possibly forget that? We were the Three Musketeers, for crying out loud."

She swats me lightly on the arm, lingering on my skin for a moment longer before she lets her fingers drop back to her side. "I said *almost*."

Looking past her, I glance at the picture. It's one of my favorites. It was the last year we were all in middle school. We wore giant hats and blue tabards, accompanied by the goofiest smiles on our faces. Once Ollie and I moved on to high school, our little group wasn't the same anymore. Going to different schools was an enormous change for us and our group dynamic but unavoidable.

Julia remains quiet, which enables my brain to go wild, recalling images of her naked on my bed, spread out and eager to be devoured like she was last night. But with Ollie a few doors down, waiting for me, that option isn't in the cards right now. Not that I'm certain she'd be up for it anyway, especially after she practically ran away from me earlier when we got back.

So instead, I snap out of my little fantasy and clear my throat. "So, what's up?"

Her fingers go up to touch her lips as she avoids my gaze. "Just wanted to make sure we're on the same page with our story. From the way Ollie looked, he'll roast both of us."

I nod even though she still isn't looking at me. "He definitely didn't look happy."

"Nope, so we need to be careful. I don't want any fighting, especially since we have to share a house for the time being."

I nod again, starting to feel like a dumbed-down version

of myself that isn't capable of forming clear thoughts or sentences. "Makes sense."

Yup. Point proven.

Let's try this again.

I exhale slowly, and she finally looks at me. "Do you have anything specific in mind you want to tell him?"

"The truth would probably be best. I asked to tag along on your business trip because I didn't want to be alone, and since I hadn't been to Vegas, we stayed an extra day to do some more sightseeing." She chews on her lips, and I clench my hands before I take her spot to nibble on her gorgeous mouth. "We'll just leave out the bit about us, you know?"

Her statement pulls me out of my lust-filled mind. She makes me feel like a damn teenager who can't think about anything other than getting his hands on the pretty girl.

Again.

A smile forms on my face when her tongue darts out to lick her lips and she crosses and uncrosses her arms. The sight of her squirming in front of me does something to me.

Most of all though, I want her close and for her to be okay.

Before I think about it, I open my arms. "Come here, Jules. Let's hug out the awkwardness. I can't stand this nervous tension between us."

It's mostly her, but I keep that to myself.

Uncertainty is written all over her face, in the way her gaze still doesn't connect with mine for more than a second, or the way her forehead wrinkles. But after a moment, she finally steps closer, and I wrap my arms tightly around her before she has a chance to change her mind.

A small sigh escapes her mouth, and I close my eyes, telling myself to keep calm, especially when I feel her breath on my skin, knowing how dangerously close her lips are to my chest.

My *naked* chest, since I'm still standing here in only a towel.

Maybe this wasn't such a good idea. Her sweet scent. Her soft skin. Her hands on my body.

After a few more seconds of her delectable curves pressed to my body, I'm one hundred percent positive this was an awful idea.

Absolutely terrible.

Not even two seconds after my towel starts tightening around my hips, Julia startles in my arms. She felt it too.

Taking a step back, she presses her lips together. "Might be better to put on some clothes."

"Yeah, probably." Since I don't want to make her uncomfortable, or this situation any harder for us—pun not intended—I grab my clothes and make quick work of putting them on, painfully putting away my protesting body part.

Too bad we can't always have what we want.

Julia raises her hand as if to touch me before clasping it with her other one. "So, we're all good then?"

From the looks of it, she's struggling with the no-touching relationship like I am.

I'm sure it'll take a few days before it goes back to normal.

At least that's what I hope, or we'll be screwed when Ollie figures it out.

Speaking of the devil.

His knock barely registers before he pokes his head into the room. He frowns when he sees Julia next to me, and I can't blame him. He wasn't here this last week. The last time he saw us together in more than just passing must have been years ago.

He narrows his eyes, looking back and forth between us before settling on his sister. "What are you doing in here? Everything okay?"

Julia must be the worst actress ever, because she's already struggling to come up with an answer. I inwardly groan, already imagining the major ass-kicking I'll receive from my best friend. But part of me is also a little pissed. Ollie knows I'd never do anything to hurt his sister, and that's why he's always trusted me with her in the past. Just not to sleep with her . . .

Thankfully, she regains her composure and gives him a hopeful smile. It looks a bit shaky to me, but Ollie seems to buy it. "Oh yeah, everything's fine. I was just talking to Carter about the date I have this week. He saw the guy last week when we went to the gym together."

I'm not sure whose eyes are bigger, Ollie's or mine.

"*You* went to the gym?" He looks at me for confirmation and somehow, I manage a nod.

It's funny he reacts to that fact first before inquiring about the date, and it's easy to tell by the pinched expression on Julia's face that she isn't too happy about it either. At least she doesn't look nervous anymore, so that's a good thing.

Ollie starts laughing, and I can't help the chuckle that passes my lips.

Julia shoots us nasty looks before she pulls back her shoulders. "Yes, I went to the gym. And before you ask your next stupid question, yes, I have a date. And I sure as hell will enjoy it."

With another glare aimed at both of us, but definitely remaining longer on me, she storms out of the room. The angry swish of her hips makes her ass look fantastic— Wait, she's *actually* going on a date with the gym douche?

What the hell?

Chapter Fifteen

JULIA

*A*voiding both my brother and Carter for the rest of the night gave me enough time to cool off. It also made one thing crystal clear: the faster I can get this conversation with my brother over with, the better. Which is the reason I'm staring at him first thing in the morning, even though I haven't had a cup of coffee yet. Since that's the only way to catch him before he heads into the office, I'll endure the torture.

The same frown he wore yesterday is still on his face, making me feel like a teenager about to get a lecture.

Shutting his laptop, he clears his throat, and looks up at me from his chair. "Well, I spoke to CJ last night, and he confirmed your Vegas story."

My gaze flicks upward, and I'm moments away from flipping him off. I get that he's protective of me, always has been, even more so since our parents died, but I don't think he actually realizes how bad it is sometimes. "Oh jeez. Thanks a lot, Sherlock. I didn't realize I was being investigated."

He has the decency to look a little awkward after my response, which is something. "Sorry, that came out wrong."

"I think so too, Ollie. You need to get over this. I'm not a little girl anymore. I know you're worried about me and want to make sure nothing bad happens to me, and I really appreciate that. But I'm old enough to make my own decisions, even if they're bad ones sometimes. If I want to go to Vegas and marry a stranger or have wild monkey sex with someone, then that's up to me and not you." I pretty much blurt out the last sentence without taking a breather, or thinking about it, and wish I could take back the words, but it's too late for that now.

Thankfully, he cringes and his face turns slightly red, which might actually be a good thing.

When he opens his mouth to speak, I lift my finger to silence him. "Let me say one more thing before you go off on me. I know you mean well, I really do, probably more than you'll ever know, but you need to trust me to live my life the way I want to. And if I need you, I always know where to find you."

His face still hasn't returned to his normal shade, but the look in his eyes has softened. He lets out a deep breath before getting up from his chair to walk around the glass desk, stopping a few feet in front of me. "I'm sorry for being too invasive and abrasive. Everything that concerns you freaks me out. I know it's often irrational, but the thought alone of you being hurt, or worse, losing you too, is just too much. The fact that I haven't seen much of you since Mom and Dad died probably hasn't helped either."

Guilt pushes heavily on my chest, making me wish I could go back in time and change the way I dealt with things.

But I can't. This conversation has been way overdue for many reasons.

"I know it sounds controlling when I say things like that, but I'd really like to know what's going on with you and what you're up to. Not every minute of course, just in your life in general. You mean the world to me. I want the relationship we once had, because it kills me not to have that anymore."

The back of my throat tightens before he's even done with his last sentence. My stomach rolls like it might get sick, but I close the distance between us and throw myself at him, tears already streaming down my face. "I've missed you too. I'm so incredibly sorry I shut down over the past years. I didn't know how to deal with losing them, and I honestly didn't even realize how bad it's gotten until Nate broke things off and I spent some time with Carter. It was like a light bulb turned on in my head, showcasing how little I actually enjoyed life and how much I'd changed. Carter has been a really big help."

"I'm glad to hear that." Carter's voice comes from the doorway, startling both of us. "What am I missing here, and why was I not invited to this party?"

Despite the mess both my brother and I are—me all snotty with swollen eyes, and my brother with misty eyes too —we chuckle. I can't remember how many years it's been since all three of us have had a moment like this together, which is incredibly sad. The fact I've missed out on so much cannot compare to the happiness I'm feeling right now over having this puzzle put back together in my life. I'm definitely more than ready and excited to get my old self and life back.

"Come here, you big oaf." I open my arms wider so we can turn this into a group hug.

This feels good, just like old times. I've missed this. I've missed *them*.

We pull back after a few moments when both guys start squirming, but we have the same smiles on our faces. Seems like I'm not the only one who missed our trio.

Ollie presses a kiss to my temple. "I'm glad we got that all cleared up. We can talk about it some more later if you want to." Then he turns to Carter. "Did you want anything?"

His eyes widen. "Oh yeah. Cora called me. She said she couldn't reach you, but she got a phone call about yesterday's audition. It looks like the job is hers, so she wants you to pick her up at seven tonight to celebrate."

"Nice." Ollie's lips part in a grin. "I knew she'd get it."

When was the last time I saw him this happy?

Definitely not since we lost Mom and Dad. It's easy to see how much he likes his girlfriend, which makes me happy but also makes my chest hurt. He didn't really tell me about her, but I know I can only blame myself and my withdrawal from life for that. "You really like her, don't you?"

His gaze meets mine, and I'm sure he's fully aware that I know little about her and their relationship. "I do."

"I'm glad. What does she do that she goes to auditions? Is she an actress?" I cringe a little at the idea of my brother dating an actress. Growing up in Southern California has exposed us to a lot of actors and actresses, and we've had more bad run-ins than good ones all together.

Both him and Carter chuckle.

"Nope, not an actress. CJ and I have had our fair share between us, and we figured out quickly they weren't the best fit for us."

The sharp pang in my gut at hearing about Carter's

casual dating life takes me by surprise, but I need to ignore it. There really is no point thinking about it. I know he's a serial dater and not after any sort of commitment.

But I might need a few more days to adjust to hearing about his conquests. And who he'll be sleeping with next.

My brother touches my arm as I will the burning sensation in the back of my eyes to go away. "You okay there, Jules? You're suddenly a little pale."

Man, I need to get my act together.

I wave him away. "Everything's good, sorry. I didn't get a good night's sleep, so I'm a little tired." Pulling at the hem of my shirt, I try and stir the conversation away from me. "So, back to your mystery lady. What kind of job does she have? And why in the world haven't I heard more about her yet?"

His whole demeanor changes, a silly grin curving his mouth. Even his eyes look shinier. "She's a fitness model. She just started out last year, but she'll hit it big because she's amazing."

Suddenly his smile *does* falter though, and I'm sure he's about to answer my second question. "And I'm sorry for not telling you sooner. We haven't been talking a lot, and you barely ever asked questions about my life, so I thought you weren't interested in hearing about her. I would have told you about her eventually but wanted to wait for a bit longer to see how things were going between us."

Carter's hand presses into my lower back, a friendly gesture that's probably meant to comfort me. But the heat of his touch through my shirt has the opposite effect, and my skin buzzes from the contact.

My momentary distraction is gone when my brother's

words finally register, the impact of them making me waver for a second.

There are so many things I want to say right now but don't. I know I'm responsible for most of the distance between us, so I can't blame him for pulling back some too. Even more so if I might have seemed uninterested in hearing about his life.

What a mess.

I tell myself not to dwell on the past, and that there's no better time to turn things around than right now.

Pushing past the lump in my throat, I try and give him the most genuine smile I can muster. "Well, I hope I get to meet her sometime. It's easy to see how special she is to you. Your face lights up like a Christmas tree every time you talk about her."

Ollie throws a quick glance at Carter, who replies, "It's true, dude."

When my brother looks back at me, he shrugs. "You're right. I like her. She's great, really great. And she can't wait to meet you. I've already told her all about you."

I'm flooded with emotions that he told her about me, but I'm also glad he did. "I'm happy for you. Why don't we go out for dinner this weekend?"

He nods. "Sounds great to me. I'd really like that."

Turning to look at Carter, my mouth starts talking without consulting my brain first. "You're coming too, right? I don't want to be the third wheel with those lovebirds."

He glances at my brother before looking at me. "Sure. Why not? It's a date."

I roll my eyes and groan, but at the same time, I'm also unable to ignore the fluttering in my belly.

"Relax, Jules. It'll be just like old times." Carter chuckles and winks at me before looking at his watch and shooting my brother a look. "We better get going if we want to get any work done today."

"I'll be right there."

Carter tips his chin, and after a curious look in my direction, he saunters out of the room.

Ollie goes to his desk and puts his laptop and his notebook in his briefcase. "It seems like you guys really have gotten closer this last week. You're already bickering like you used to."

His comment stuns me, causing me to freeze momentarily. I shake my head to clear my thoughts, knowing I really have to get a grip on my reactions. "I missed both of you. A lot. I didn't realize how much my life had changed until this last week, and I'm truly sorry it took me so long. It's been a bit of a shock, to be honest. Yet, I'm happy I've realized it."

My voice is thick with emotion when Ollie walks back to me to give my forehead a kiss. "I'm glad you feel that way. You're home now, and that's all that matters."

After giving my shoulder a squeeze, he picks up his suit jacket from the hook on the back of the door and drapes it over his arm. "I better get going, but I'll see you later, okay?"

And with that, the two most important men in my life leave me alone to my wacky thoughts. At least, some things never change.

he living room is dark except for the glare of the TV, but I find it oddly comforting. I'm still nursing my first beer, somehow not feeling in the mood to drink. When a certain *someone* left for her date a few hours ago, I thought having a few drinks was exactly what I needed. Guess I was wrong.

Maybe I should go to sleep. She might not be back for a while anyway.

It's not like I'm waiting for her to come home or anything. *Yeah, right.*

Just when I decide to not be sitting here when she gets back, the key turns in the lock before the door opens slowly.

The porch light illuminates Julia from behind, and it's my first glimpse of her today. I've barely seen her since the conversation with her and Ollie two days ago. We've been flooded at work, putting in the necessary extra hours. The little I did see her at home, I'm pretty sure she tried to avoid me as much as possible. Instead of pushing her, like I really wanted to, I gave her some space, hoping this would be the right thing to do.

I can't deny how relieved I am she's not wearing one of the super sexy outfits she got on our shopping trip last week. But the green dress she's wearing is still sexy, highlighting those damn curves of hers, the same ones I can't stop thinking about.

On second thought, I'm starting to think not even a potato sack can hide them. Or maybe I just imagine her naked under me, no matter what clothes she has on.

I groan out loud, annoyed with the direction my thoughts have taken me once again, for about the millionth time this week.

"Carter?" Julia almost stumbles as she inhales sharply, her hand flying to her chest. "You scared me. Why in the world are you sitting here in the dark?"

"I'm not sitting in the dark, I'm watching TV." The words come out a little raspy, my mind still stuck on my previous thoughts of her, when I point to the screen as if she doesn't know where or what the TV is.

Way to go, Carter.

After closing the door, she walks over to me, her eyes focused on the TV. "Since when are you into reality shows?"

A quick check confirms I have obviously no idea what's actually on.

Busted.

I lift my shoulders in a half shrug. "Oh. There wasn't anything else on."

Narrowing her eyes, she gazes at me, and I know she doesn't believe a word I'm saying. She snorts as she sits next to me on the couch but doesn't call me out. Instead, she grabs my beer and downs it.

Less than two seconds later, she swallows hard before pinching her lips together, right before pulling the bottle from her mouth with a loud pop. "Ew, this is warm. How long have you been holding this?"

I roll my neck and stare at the ceiling. "A while?"

"Reality TV *and* warm beer? What's going on with you? Are you okay?" I can hear the smirk in her voice, and I can't help myself and look at her. Her eyes sparkle as she stares at me with a grin.

At that moment, I realize I've actually missed her the past few days. It was so easy to fall back into our old pattern last week that I've gotten used to hanging out with her. Just being around her, laughing with her, it's like sunshine for my body, releasing endorphins left and right. And that was without the sex. Add that on top of it, and my endorphins were on crack.

Since I can't tell her that, I try my best to stay composed. "Sure." I redirect the attention to her, which apparently also turns me into some kind of masochist. "So, how was your date?"

She sighs heavily. "Ugh. Don't ask."

"That good, huh?" The wave of relief that shoots through me shouldn't surprise me, but I have a hard time not pumping my fist in the air. Which I realize is a total dick move, but there's no point in denying I'm happy about the outcome, and I'm afraid it's written all over my face too. I told her I'd help her with her little journey as best as I could, but that guy she went out with was definitely not husband material.

Not that I think anyone is good enough for her.

Also, when I agreed to help her, I hadn't had the

enjoyment of spending countless pleasure-filled hours with her. And that changed things, even though Julia seems to be sticking to her pretense that nothing transpired between us. So I play along, as good as I can.

The least I can do is make sure she doesn't end up with a total jerk.

"I'm not even sure what happened." She kicks off her shoes and puts her legs on the coffee table next to mine.

Her legs. The same ones that were wrapped around my body last week when I was—

"Carter, are you listening?" She snaps her fingers in front of my face to get my attention.

"What?" I blink before my gaze flickers to her face. "Sorry. I just remembered something, but it's not important. Go on."

She eyes me suspiciously for a moment before throwing her hands up. "I don't know. He seemed so nice and funny at the gym last week, didn't he? I mean you saw him too. Didn't you think he was a great guy?"

I cross my arms over my chest, relaxing back into the couch. "I have no clue, Jules. It's not like I talked to him."

"That's true, I guess. Anyway, he was boring as hell. It was so bad I actually drank a ton of water just so I could go to the bathroom more often. He probably thought I have a bladder problem."

Her shoulders shake against mine, and I laugh too. That seems like such a Julia thing to do. She always comes up with the weirdest ideas. But it's something I've always liked about her. It makes her different, unique.

"Only you, Jules. I'm sure there would have been easier ways to escape the evening and your lame company."

The punch in the arm hits me before I can move out of the way, but she chuckles. "Stop it. It still turned out to be a rather productive evening in the end."

My heartbeat increases. *What?*

"Oh yeah?" Does my voice just sound funny to me or can Julia hear it too? I clear my throat, willing whatever is blocking my vocal cords to go away. Neither do I need nor want to feel this *weirdness* around Jules. It only complicates things. "How so?"

She rummages through her purse until she pulls out her phone with a triumphant "Ha" before proudly wiggling it around in front of my face like it's a miracle she found it in the first place. Which might have been the case.

I pretend to give this some serious thought. "Did you play games on your phone to distract yourself?"

She shakes her head.

"Take some funny selfies?"

Another chuckle, this one vibrating through me, reminding me of how much I like to see her happy.

Ugh. Make it stop. Brain, conscious, subconscious, or whatever is feeding me these thoughts. Shut it.

"No, silly. But when Chad was finally done talking about his boring office job, he continued to move on to his even more boring stock adventures he does in his free time. At that point, I couldn't take it anymore and pulled out my phone under the table."

I tip my head in her direction. "Yes, I got that. Just tell me already, Jules. The suspense is killing me."

Not really, but she doesn't need to know that. For all I know, she was planning her next date.

An impish smile makes her mouth twitch. "I finally had the time and inspiration to write my *real* husband checklist."

She looks at me expectantly, clearly wanting a reaction, so I throw my hands up in the worst fake jazz hands performance ever. "Oh, the joy."

She sticks out her tongue. "You're so bad."

"Sorry. Let's hear it."

Her fingers keep pushing on her phone, lighting up her face. It's easy to tell by the remaining smile how excited she is about this.

"Okay. Are you ready?" She turns her body to face me.

Her leg brushes mine in the process, one of her knees firmly pressed against the side of my thigh. I shouldn't react to something completely non-sexual like this but I do. Not to mention the fact that her dress has ridden up with her new sitting position, exposing even more of her gorgeous creamy skin.

I'm so doomed.

So fucking screwed.

After clearing her voice, she holds her phone up. "Here we go. Julia's Husband Checklist:

Number One: Good sense of humor
Number Two: Commitment/Monogamy
Number Three: Family values
Number Four: Steady communication
Number Five: Emotionally stable
Number Six: Confident
Number Seven: Responsible
Number Eight: Respectful (especially to his mom)
Number Nine: Honest

Number Ten: Driven
Number Eleven: Romantic
Number Twelve: Reliable
Number Thirteen: Kind
Number Fourteen: Same life outlook
Number Fifteen: Sexual attraction
Number Sixteen: Good with children."

My brain has tried to keep up with the list, inadvertently comparing myself to every item.

Air is suddenly stalled in my lungs, and my mouth is dry. Since the only thing around is the warm, stale beer, I cough, hoping this feeling will go away. "That's quite the list you got there."

The smile she gives me is dimmer than the previous ones. "The conversations we had since Nate called things off helped a lot. Also, my dinner date gave me lots of additional inspiration of what I *don't* want. The evening obviously didn't exactly turn out the way I wanted, but that's okay. Even though he didn't feel the same way. He actually thought we had a great time and asked if I wanted to come over to his place for another drink. Talk about not being on the same page."

Her words make my skin all prickly. I have to do something about this. It definitely can't continue this way. "Wow, he sounds like a real winner."

I don't say anything else, not wanting the choice words that come to mind to ruin the moment.

"Exactly. Like I said, not who I thought he was at all. But I'm happy anyway. At least now I have my list."

"A very long list."

Julia pushes loose hairs behind her ear. "It is. But I only want to settle for what's best for me and nothing less. Is that so wrong?"

Shit. This whole conversation has put me more on the spot than I liked. "No, it's not. You deserve all that and then some. Hopefully, you can find someone who will be just right for you."

Even if I won't like it.

Even if I will hate seeing her with anyone else, despite knowing how irrational that is.

But of course, I don't mention any of that to her. She seems happy in her world of denial.

"Thank you." The look she gives me is soft, maybe a little hopeful. Shit. I feel like I was just punched in the gut, because it makes me want to be everything on that list just to make her look at me like this every day. Every damn day.

But we both know I'll never fulfill the requirements of her husband checklist. I am many of those things. Most of them really, except the most important one: same life outlook. I can't share that. I can't see marriage in my future, not after my parents have proven me time and time again how foolish love and relationships are, and that nothing good can ever last. And that's what Julia deserves. A love that will stand the test of time and last forever. A marriage like her parents had. A marriage where love is enough.

Julia leans her head on my shoulder and we stay like this for a while, both of us lost in our own thoughts, with one thought especially loud in my head. When she finds her husband, we'll never get to do this again, and a weird scratchy feeling inhabits my chest. How the hell do I get it out?

Chapter Seventeen

JULIA

*T*wo dinner dates in three days.

Well, technically only one since I'm not going on a *real* date tonight. Carter and I are only meeting up with Ollie and his girlfriend.

Staring at my reflection in the full-length mirror, I smooth over the black dress I bought with Carter at the store last week. I love the way it accentuates my hourglass figure. At first, I wasn't sure if it's too much, but I knew I had to have it when I saw Carter's eyes light up the second I came out of the dressing room.

Maybe, just maybe, it played a little role in me choosing it for tonight too. Who am I kidding? It totally did. Watching him drool over me has given me a confidence boost like nothing else has.

Which is a whole other problem.

It shouldn't matter what clothes he likes on me.

It shouldn't matter that I want him to like the way I look.

Yet, it *does*.

This whole going-back-to-our-old-relationship thing has

been a total bust so far, if anyone asks me. Carter has such an undeniable presence—*sensual*—even in everyday tasks. Like . . . putting away groceries.

How is that even remotely sexy?

It shouldn't be.

I mean . . . crap. Crap, crap, crap.

I'm hopeless when it co—

"Jules, are you done in there? We have to leave soon to be on time."

Carter's words, paired with the knock on my bedroom door, snaps me out of my thoughts, the lingering feeling of them making my heart beat faster. If he only knew that he's been invading my mind all week long, starring in some of my late-night fantasies. Okay, maybe not just some, but all of them.

I went out with Chad the other night, even though it was the last thing I wanted to do. Maybe that's why the date was extra bad because he couldn't possibly compare to Carter.

To tell the truth, Carter was on my mind a lot too when I constructed my husband checklist. He ticks off most of the items, probably more than he realizes, but of course, the commitment issue is a real no-no. And that may never change. At least not until he finds the woman he wants to change for. Which stings a little.

Our sexual chemistry isn't enough to forgo something that's really important to me.

With a heavy sigh, I grab my things and open the door.

And oh.

Goodness.

Wow.

Carter looks as sharp as nails in his black suit pants and a blue shirt that's unbuttoned enough for me to see the beginning of the light dusting of chest hair. Knowing his chest tattoo is an inch or two behind the opening doesn't help me stay calm either. I bite my tongue so I don't drool at the sheer sight of it. On second thought, clenching my fists to keep my hands from reaching out to touch the exposed patch of skin might not be a bad idea either.

Just to be on the safe side.

This man really does it for me. And contrary to my belief that a night, or rather two nights, in Vegas would be enough to get him out of my system, I'm not sure how much time would actually be sufficient to get there. The craving for him, the incessant need to be close to him, has only grown since that first kiss.

This is how I imagine addictions start. You get a taste of something you've never had before, something that's incomparable to anything you've ever experienced and might never experience again. You think you can get away with a little taste and stop, but you're lying to yourself from that very first second, knowing the greed will only grow with each passing second.

Addictive part of my brain, meet Carter. Oh wait, we're already past that point.

I'm screwed.

His gaze is so intense, I feel the hair rise on my arms and the nape of my neck. And if his cocky smile is anything to go by, he can read me like a book, knowing all the dirty little things my mind visualizes about him.

I wave my hand in his direction like a total idiot. "You look um . . . nice." The words sound formal coming out of my mouth, and I want to smack my forehead.

A deep chuckle rumbles through his chest. "Thanks. You don't look too bad yourself, Daph."

He follows his statement with a wink, and somehow that irritates me. Maybe it has something to do with the fact that I want to throw myself at him—despite knowing I really shouldn't—but *he* looks completely unaffected by me.

Did you hear that, brain? Carter's not interested. At all. Zero. *Nada.*

"Thanks. Let's go." The words come out more like a low grumble than anything else, and I make my way into the kitchen to open the door to the garage.

Carter trails behind me but stays quiet as we get into his black car and make our short drive to the restaurant.

After a few minutes on the road, he breaks the silence. "I might not have told you the truth at the house."

I turn to him, a weird feeling settling in my belly. I hate lies, and even in these few seconds that pass, my mind goes a mile a minute, wondering what he could mean. "What?"

He scrapes a hand through his thick hair, making a beautiful mess out of it. "When I said you don't look too bad yourself."

I tug at the hem of my dress, suddenly feeling exposed and uncomfortable, wondering if it's too late to turn around and get changed.

We're at a red light when he turns to me. "What I should have said instead, is that you look stunning. The dress looks like it was made specifically for you."

A car honks behind us, and Carter makes a turn into the parking lot of the restaurant, his hand softly brushing against the exposed skin of my leg as he uses the gear stick. My breath catches in my throat at the barest of contact, robbing me of any logical thought. My skin feels like it's on fire.

"Jules, I . . ." He shuts off the engine while my gaze is still fixated on the spot he just touched.

Carter's gaze meets mine for a nanosecond before he shakes his head and springs into action, pulling the key out of the ignition before opening his door. "Please, allow me."

Before I realize what's happening—he thinks I look stunning?—he's at my side, opening my door for me.

I place my hand into his outstretched one, noticing his is trembling. When I look up at him, his eyes brim with heat, periodically flashing to my lips. My hand is still in his, the lingering contact setting my nerve endings aflame. When he leans down, my breath quickens, the intensity of this moment throwing me so far off-balance, I'm not sure how I'm supposed to get through dinner.

Just when I think he might kiss me right here in the parking lot for the world to see, a car door slams close by, and Carter stops. He blinks a few times before dropping my hand and shutting the door behind me.

"Hey, guys." My brother's voice snaps me back to reality, pushing away the rest of my Carter-induced haze as much as anything will tonight.

Thankfully, he's still across the parking lot, giving me time to step away from Carter. Instead, I focus on Ollie's girlfriend, Cora, who has her arm linked with my brother's, both of them wearing matching smiles as they approach us.

Cora's absolutely gorgeous, with her wavy blonde hair and bright blue eyes, but she's far from the typical stick-figure model we expect in the greater Los Angeles area. Instead, she's tall, curvy, and toned, not afraid to show off her assets in the gold dress she's wearing.

Can I be her when I grow up?

They definitely make a stunning couple. No doubt about that.

And she's the type of woman I could see Carter with. Beautiful, athletic, confident, sexy.

All things I'm not.

After being introduced and receiving a heartfelt hug from Cora, we all make our way inside where we're immediately seated in an elegant corner booth with black leather seats. Of course, Ollie and Cora sit on one side while Carter and I sit on the other.

The conversation flows easily. Cora is charismatic, and she fits right in. I actually enjoy her company so much that I push all thoughts of Carter aside. Well, maybe not all of them, but most. Because no matter how hard I try, it's impossible not to react when I feel his gaze on me, our eyes meet, or our hands accidentally brush when we both reach for the bread basket.

We order and our conversation slows down as we devour our food.

When the main dishes are cleared, Cora looks at me expectantly, the corners of her lips quirked into a light smile. "I know we've only just met, and I'm sorry if I'm too nosy, but how long have you guys been dating? I always find it so romantic when people date their childhood friend. And you guys make the cutest couple."

I draw a complete blank, afraid my brain's gone into hiding, and I'm pretty sure my mouth hangs open a little too. I'm not absolutely sure though since I've lost all ability to control or feel my body at the moment. It's not helping that no one else says a word either. My brother's eyes are wide as they go back and forth between Carter and me.

"Did I say something wrong?" Cora turns to Ollie, rubbing the skin at her throat.

A sharp pain in my butt cheek makes me jump, successfully snapping me out of my daze.

What the hell? Did Carter just *pinch* me?

Just when I turn to look at him, he starts to laugh. "You must have gotten something mixed up there, Cora."

Cora glances at Ollie. "Didn't you say they went out on a date the other night?"

"No, honey." My brother shakes his head, reaching out to take Cora's hand. "I said they both went out on dates but not together."

"Ohhhh, I must have misunderstood. Sorry. My bad." Her gaze flickers back to Carter and me, her lips pressing together. "That's too bad though. They look great together."

Ollie laughs so hard, he sounds a little hysterical. "Absolutely not."

I'm still trying to figure out how to feel about his reaction when it hits me what he said about Carter.

Instead of letting it go, which might be the smarter thing to do, I turn to face my bench partner. "You went on a date on Wednesday too?"

Carter shakes his head. "I was going to, but plans changed."

"Oh." My mind is racing, upset over feeling like an idiot for having to ask, even though I have no right to feel like it seeing as I *actually* went on a date. My body doesn't like the visit of the green-eyed monster. The burning sensation in my chest, along with a flash of anger, can both go wherever the hell they came from, because they're certainly not wanted. Not one bit.

I've never been the jealous type, hating how completely irrational it feels, yet I seem to be unable to ward off the ice-cold shiver running down my back or the anxious way my heartbeat has picked up.

I stay quiet after this, feeling Cora's eyes on me for the rest of the time the four of us spend together, and I'm pretty sure she knows something's up. The only positive thing about this whole ordeal is that, thankfully, my brother still seems oblivious. Let's hope it stays that way.

We wrap up the evening and walk out of the restaurant to say our goodbyes.

Cora walks next to me while Ollie and Carter walk ahead of us, deep in conversation.

She lets out the barest of sighs. "This was fun. I wish we could have stayed longer, but I have to get up for work at an indecent hour in the morning, so I need to get as much sleep as possible. But you're just as amazing as your brother said you were."

I easily return her smile, completely at ease with her, on top of being thrilled she's my brother's girlfriend. "Thank you. And likewise. I hope we can do something again soon."

"Me too."

Cora's hand lands on my arm and we both stop walking. She opens and clothes her mouth several times before spitting out whatever seems to be occupying her mind. "Listen. I know it's not really any of my business, and I'm sorry if I'm butting in too much, but I saw you guys in the parking lot when we arrived."

My eyes are as wide as they go, and I slap my hand over my mouth before I even know what I'm doing, my brain thinking back to when Carter almost kissed me.

Cora mirrors my shocked look, shaking her head and waving her hands at the same time. "No, no. Ollie didn't see anything if you're worried about that."

I cover my face with trembling hands before releasing a huge breath.

"I'm so sorry. That was the worst way to start that conversation. I didn't mean to freak you out." She grimaces, and oddly enough, I chuckle.

"If you ever need someone to overreact, you know where to find me." I shake my head at my own inability to keep it together.

Cora reaches out once more, giving me a sympathetic look. "That was my fault. Sorry." She looks over my shoulder before letting go of my arm. "I just wanted to bring it up. And for what it's worth, I think you guys make an incredibly cute couple. I'm sure your brother would come around and get used to the idea too. You know, if you wanted to approach this subject and all, but I won't say anything to him."

Once my nerves have calmed, I flash her a smile, already knowing how much I like her. "Thank you."

Her gaze flickers past me again, and this time I turn too, stiffening when I see Ollie's and Carter's eyes on us.

"Ollie told me your best friend moved to Australia, and I'm known to be a good listener if you ever need one. Or if you want to meet up for coffee." She holds up her hands. "No pressure or anything, I promise."

"I'd like that."

"Perfect, I can't wait." Her gaze flickers to the guys again.

"We probably should go over there before they get too suspicious, huh?"

I chuckle. "Probably."

We all say goodbye, Cora giving me an extra tight hug with a whispered "Good luck" in my ear before Carter and I watch them walk to my brother's car, leaving the parking lot a moment later.

Only once the red taillights have faded into the distance do I dare glance at Carter. Without a word, he takes my hand and pulls me to his car.

Thankfully, the ride home is quick and quiet, and Carter's giving me space, not pressing me to talk. My brain's a busy enough place as it is. Not only with my jealousy over his date that never happened but also my conversation with Cora, both giving me plenty to think about.

Once we're home, I try to get to my room as fast as possible, somehow afraid to have a confrontation with him when I'm still so unsure about everything.

It's undeniable. I'm insanely attracted to him, and he's always had a special place in my heart, which is what scares me the most. If I hadn't known him for so long, and I didn't know what an amazing person he is, this might actually be easier.

But what are the odds of coming out of this unscathed if we continue our little cat and mouse game? For goodness' sake, I've crushed on him for years. Add our insane chemistry and the way he makes not only my body but also my mind sing—like he's made it his life's goal to know every detail of how I tick—and I'm in so much trouble.

So much trouble.

"Not so fast." Carter grabs me by the wrist and spins me

around before I can reach my door, but giving me some room when I face him. "What's going on, Jules? And don't insult me by pretending everything's okay. We both know it's not. Talk to me."

I stare into his beautiful eyes, the connection I have with him already pulling me under like I'm in quicksand.

When it's only the two of us, everything seems so easy. That right there will probably be my downfall, because I don't know how to say no to him. Most of all, I don't *want* to say no to him. Completely losing myself in him for a weekend brought me more happiness than I've had in years.

Then I remember one thing I promised myself after I read one of the self-help books. To be real with the people in my life if I wanted to turn mine around. And I want that. I *deserve* that. Even if this thing with him is only temporary. Or not, depending on how he reacts to my honesty.

Unable to keep my mouth shut, I throw my hands in the air. "I got jealous when Ollie mentioned your date, okay? I obviously didn't know how to deal with it, and it bugs me. Happy now?"

He takes a step closer to me. "Why were you jealous, Jules?"

Warmth flushes my cheeks. "Do I really have to say it? I'm pretty sure you know exactly why."

"Tell me." His voice is low and husky, the mere thought of what it does to me in the bedroom burning a hotspot in the pit of my belly.

He keeps coming closer, so I keep walking backward until my back hits the wall.

"Because it's not as easy to forget what happened

between us as I thought it would be." The words come out in a whisper, and his eyes widen in response.

He's momentarily distracted, so I use the chance and escape into my room, not sure which thought is louder in my head. Or worse for that matter. The one that hopes he won't come after me, or the one that hopes he *does*.

Chapter Eighteen

CARTER

*J*ulia's door is barely closed when I open it again. She's only made it a few steps into the room, putting her purse down on the white desk. When she looks at me over her shoulder, I see the same heat in her gaze that I feel boiling inside me, and I wonder if she expected or even wanted me to follow her.

"What does it mean you can't forget about what happened between us?" My voice sounds raspy, but I don't give a shit. My body, my brain, every last cell is strung tight at the minuscule chance I might have her again. Even though I know I shouldn't, I crave her with my whole being.

There's an almost innate instinct when it comes to this woman that I can't ignore, and I wonder if it has something to do with the fact that she's been in my life for so long.

Despite being surprised at her confession, I'm also incredibly pleased.

Relieved I'm not the only one feeling this pull.

"I honestly don't know, Carter." She grabs a few pieces of clothing from her bed and goes into the bathroom. She leaves the door ajar, and I listen to the faucet turning on and off several times while she brushes her teeth.

The urge to go in there while she changes is almost impossible to resist, but somehow I manage. There's that little voice in my head telling me it wouldn't be the right thing to do. Not at this point when things are still unclear between us.

But shit, do I want to see her naked again.

Now. Tonight. Tomorrow . . .

When she comes back in a pair of sleep shorts and a tank top, looking as cute as ever, I have an idea.

Holding out my hand, I hope like hell she won't refuse me. "Come out to the deck with me?"

She hesitates, the vulnerable look in her eyes almost too much for me to bear, but then she nods.

The tension in my body eases when she takes my hand. Since I don't want to give her any time to change her mind, I pull her after me, out of her room, through the living room and kitchen toward the large glass sliding door.

Julia startles when I unlock it, squeezing my hand like she's trying to crush it. When I turn around, her eyes are shut, her parted lips releasing long breaths.

Pulling my hand out of hers, I place both of mine on her upper arms, giving her a gentle squeeze. "You okay there?"

She swallows and nods. "Yeah. I just haven't . . . It used to be my Mom's favorite spot."

Damn it.

I'm such an idiot.

That was the last thing I thought of tonight. According to Ollie, she's barely set foot in the house over the last few years. If she did, she never stayed long. Usually, they met up in other places or at the apartment she shared with Michelle.

Clearly, she's gotten over the aversion of spending time here, but I didn't realize it might only be the case for certain parts of the house.

Pulling her into my side, I give her forehead a kiss, and even though I've done that hundreds of times over the years, it feels different. Right. "It's a special spot. I remember how much she loved watching the waves and listening to the ocean. It never gets old."

"It really doesn't." Stepping out of my embrace, she links her fingers with mine once more before sliding the door open and leading me outside. When she walks across the expansive second-story wooden deck and over to the rail, I quietly follow her.

This is clearly an important moment for her, and I give her the time she needs, even if we're out here all night long. The more time passes, the more my eyes adjust to the lack of light, the almost full moon offering enough brightness to see her features, at least partially.

Her gaze is still focused on the vast darkness beyond the deck, where the waves hit the shore in a soothing pattern, contrasting her voice that's thick with emotion. "I should have come here more often to cherish my parents' memories instead of grieving in the darkness, trying not to think about them."

Without waiting for a signal from her, I pull her into me. "They loved you so much, Jules. They were the epitome of what parents should be like."

A single tear runs down her face, and I wish for nothing more than being able to alleviate her pain.

All of it. Forever.

But I know that's impossible.

"They were the best." Her voice is quiet, but I can hear the strength in it too. It's something I've always admired in Jules. Her strength. So much like her mom's.

She walks to the oversized lounger, and when she lies down on it, I climb on too, eager to close the distance between us. Because there is no other option. I yearn to be by her side, to be her comfort, the one she turns to. Even if it's only for tonight. Although, I know in my heart I'll always want to be there for her.

"Come here."

Julia moves into my arms, and I tighten them around her. I used to do this sometimes when we were younger and she got hurt. We were always there for each other, all three of us.

Funny how fast things can change. Literally in the blink of an eye.

I have a feeling Oliver wouldn't be okay with this right now though.

But he isn't here, spending the night with Cora.

"I feel so lame and stupid that I allowed my life to slip away from me." Her words are a faint whisper before she pushes her face into my shoulder, her hands clenching my shirt.

"Hey. No crazy talk allowed. You're neither lame nor stupid." My head rests on top of hers, and despite the topic, I enjoy this moment. "You just took things a bit easier and scaled back. Nothing wrong with that in the slightest. Everyone grieves differently, and that was your way of dealing with things as best as you could."

Moving around, she settles in with her cheek pressed on my shoulder. "Thank you. You know, you've been a huge help these past two weeks. I'm not sure I would have managed everything so well since the Nate debacle if it wasn't for you."

I squeeze her, inhaling her sweet scent. "There's nothing you need to thank me for. I'm always happy to help any way I can."

We stay silent for a while and my thoughts wander, this whole conversation with her eliciting some of my own regrets. "I should have been there more for you. I should have tried harder to reach out even when you kept pushing us away. I'm really sorry about that, Jules. I was an awful friend."

"What are you talking about?" She pulls out of my embrace, and I immediately miss the warmth of her body. "None of this is your fault, not in the least. There's nothing you could have done to make the situation easier for me, not when I didn't want that. I hated keeping my distance, but it hurt too much to see you guys. Your faces reminded me of my parents and how awesome life used to be.

"I couldn't avoid Ollie, at least not once he and my uncle practically forced me into family therapy with him, but I could escape you. If anyone has to apologize, it's me. No one should treat their friend this way, especially when they're only trying to help. But I didn't look out for *you*. I know how much my parents loved you and how much you loved them. You lost them and me too, and for that, I'm so, so sorry."

My stomach tightens at her words, and time seems to stop. This pain and guilt she carried around all these years makes my head spin, and I have to swallow past the lump in my throat. "You were trying to survive. Don't worry about me for even a second."

"No. You were just as important, and I should have been

there for you the same way I knew you'd be there if I really needed you. Just like you've always been. You never truly gave up on me, and I won't ever be able to tell you how much that means to me."

All I see on her face is trust, her eyes shining beneath the stars. I'm so mesmerized that all conscious thought flies out of my mind until there's nothing left but my yearning for this woman and the need to lean in and press my lips to hers.

Even though I initiated the kiss, intending to keep it light, Julia quickly takes over and becomes the aggressor.

She pulls me half on top of her, pressing me into all her gorgeous curves.

Both her mouth and body invite me to take what I've been longing for so much. Her touch, her smell, her whole being surrounds me, and I'm drowning in desire. Need. Want.

Pulling back, I kiss down her neck, spending some extra time at the sensitive spot under her jaw.

My body reacts to her instantly, my dick straining behind my zipper. I might lose my mind if I can't have her in the next few minutes, the sudden urgency making my movements sloppy as I trail my finger toward her breasts.

"Carter." My name leaves her lips in a breathy plea. "I've missed being with you like this so much. It feels like it's been years."

"Fuck, I know. I want you, Jules. Being around you without touching you has been pure torture for me."

At my words, she arches her back, thrusting her chest in the process. "I feel the same."

Our confessions are the last straw, and a moment later, we're a flurry of clothes.

When we're both naked, I pause and look at her body in the moonlight. She is, without a doubt, the most beautiful woman I've ever seen. Luscious curves, the softness of them driving me to the edge of insanity. I momentarily forget everything else, the sound of blood rushing in my ears the only thing I can hear.

When I line myself up at her entrance, I realize I'm still bare. Groaning in frustration, I sit back on my legs. "I don't have a condom."

Julia pushes herself up, wrapping her hands around my neck. "I'm okay without one if you are. I'm on birth control and clean."

"I am too." The words rush out in a quick breath. "Are you sure?"

She nods, and before I know it, I suck at her nipples and plunge deep inside her.

This.

I've missed this.

I can tell by the way she bites her lip that she's trying to be quiet, but a moan slips out of her mouth anyway. "Yes. This is exactly what I need."

I doubt anyone can see us in the darkness, but someone could definitely hear us. Which neither one of us seems to care about.

Our bodies work together like magic, causing pure ecstasy to pulse through my veins as I pump into her faster and faster.

Midway, we switch positions, and the sight of her on top of me is glorious. The way she pushes her hands on my chest as she switches between moving up and down and rocking back and forth drives me out-of-my-mind crazy.

I'm lost in her, there's no other way to describe it. She's all I can see, feel, and taste, making this experience as unbelievable as the other times with her.

My grip on her hips grows possessive, and something feels different this time. It's more intense than any other encounter I've had before, not just with her, but with anyone.

With both of us being so on edge, it doesn't take much longer for our orgasms to claim us, the shudders of pleasure rushing through me so strong, I see spots in my vision.

She collapses on top of me, and we're both quiet as I pull the blanket from the back of the lounge to drape over us, absentmindedly drawing circles on her back.

Lying here with her in my arms under the night sky takes this experience to a whole new level, because she fits so perfectly. The touch of her skin feels right, and hearing her soft breaths makes me want to hold her in my arms every day, if only to hear her breathe.

I can't remember the last time I've felt this content, like there's nothing missing, for once.

That's probably the reason why it takes me a few moments to realize she's talking to me and for the words to sink in.

"I'm going to move out soon."

his must be exactly what people mean when they talk about having an out-of-body experience.

Yes, the words came out of *my* mouth, but it's like my brain hasn't fully caught up yet.

Despite that, I have this burning sensation in my gut that tells me this is the right thing to do.

Even though it seems a bit crazy.

And most likely, it wasn't the best moment to blurt it out a minute postcoitally, but it's too late to take it back now.

Carter's still frozen under me, his body as tense as a board while he stares at me. A moment later, I start to untangle myself from him, sliding out from under the blanket to stand up.

"What are you doing?" Carter's voice is flat.

My movements lack energy as I try to find my clothes in the dark. "Getting dressed."

If I ever find my clothes that is, since I have no idea where the heck we threw them. For a moment, I consider leaving them out here until tomorrow, but I'm not sure if my brother will stop by in the morning or not.

I look at Carter's face, immediately regretting it when I notice his surly features. It was barely a minute ago that I left his embrace, and I already crave his touch and closeness again.

Which is exactly why I have to move out. With each passing day, this gets harder, and I don't want to get to a point where it becomes too much. Especially when we seem to lust after each other like this. It's only a matter of time before this goes south. Either my brother will find out or my stupid heart will get involved.

With my luck, probably both.

Might as well try and put some distance between us now, and hope like hell we'll eventually be able to go back to a normal relationship again.

I finally find both of our clothes and throw Carter's to him.

He grabs them, maybe a little too harshly. "Are you really going to move out? You just got here."

There's a rough edge to his voice, and it makes my stomach roll.

I can't tell if he's upset that I'm moving out or because I brought it up right after we had sex and it hurt his pride.

Can't really blame him for the latter. That definitely wasn't my best moment.

When I'm finally dressed, I feel collected to be able to look at him. "I don't know how to explain it, but I think it's the right thing to do. Whatever's going on with us scares me, and I think it might be good for me to live on my own for some time too. Maybe I won't like it, but I've never really tried, so I wouldn't know."

His lips press together in a grim line, all the elation and happiness from sex long gone. "I thought we were having a great time."

I clear my throat at his directness, glad it's harder to maintain eye contact in the dark. "I enjoy the time when we're together, but I also know our limitations, especially if we continue to keep this from Ollie. It's neither fair nor easy, and it makes me uneasy about the consequences. I think this"—I gesture back and forth between us—"will keep happening if we live under the same roof. It wouldn't stop until it went downhill and then all hell would break loose. You and your friendship are too important to risk for a few rolls in the hay."

Just imagining the event unfolding makes my heart hurt.

"Shit." Carter rubs his hands over his face, roughly, before shoving them through his already messy hair. "I've been making a mess of things, haven't I?"

I shake my head. "None of this is *your* fault. We're both adults, and we both wanted it. But I don't think it would be good for us to continue . . . this."

What I don't tell him is how scared I am of wanting more, of falling for him when he's made it clear that's the last thing he wants. The desire to be near him whenever he's around has already grown to heights I didn't expect, and I'm not even going to think about the smallest of butterfly babies that flutter around in my belly so often in his company.

Total no-no.

He doesn't look happy, but at least he's put his boxers and pants back on. Not that I can resist looking at the rest of his strong and toned body anyway. It seems like all sense of control between us has vanished, because I know I'm not the only one looking.

Trying a different approach, I soften my voice. "You're like family, Carter. I can't lose you over this fling." I have to catch myself from flinching at the words, but since I know his outlook on life and relationships, I'm realistic to know what this is.

"Don't call it that." He speaks through his teeth without looking at me.

Somehow his reply strikes a nerve with me, my voice having more bite than before too. "What else should I call it? I know who you are, and I've never *expected* anything more from you. You don't need to get butt hurt because I'm the one saying it out loud rather than thinking it."

I take a step closer to him but refrain from touching him, which is a lot harder than it should be. "If you're worried about me, I'm okay. I promise."

I am. I will be. Same thing.

He doesn't look convinced but nods.

It looks like he wants to say more, but doesn't.

When the silence becomes too much, I start balancing my weight awkwardly on the balls of my feet. "Well, I better get inside and try to get some sleep. Looks like I'll have a busy week ahead of me."

Carter studies my face, a pinched, tension-filled expression distorting his handsome features. "Let me know if you need help with anything."

I doubt it but don't want to start another argument. "Thank you. Goodnight."

"Night, Jules."

With a heavy heart, I turn around and walk to my room, an unwanted numbness spreading through my body, confirming that if I keep having sex with Carter, the hollow feeling would only get worse.

By some miracle, and spending more time online last night than actual sleeping, I have a few places to look at today. I thought it was going to take at least a few days, but after tossing and turning so much last night, knowing Carter was only a few doors down the hallway, I got desperate to check out what's available.

Since I didn't want to go by myself, and the only two other people in my life, Carter and Ollie, both don't qualify for this, I contacted Cora. Thankfully, Ollie didn't question my motives when I messaged him to ask for her number, mentioning wanting to meet up with her for coffee.

Smiling at Cora, I get comfortable in the seat across from her at the little coffee shop we settled on. "I hope it was okay I called. I know you've already had a busy morning working, but I didn't know who else to call."

She glances at me over the edge of her large coffee cup. "Are you kidding? I'm thrilled you did. I'm not exactly sure how much I can help you with the apartment search, but I'm more than happy to offer my assistance however I can." She's about to take another sip when she lowers the Styrofoam cup again. "Ollie knows about this though, right?"

I grimace and shake my head, a burst of guilt rushing through my system. "Not yet, but I'll tell him tonight, I promise. I haven't seen much of him, and I'd rather not tell him on the phone. It was somewhat of a spontaneous decision, but I know he won't be happy about it. Hopefully, he can understand I need to do this though."

She's silent for a moment, studying me in the quiet manner I've already gotten used to. "I know that's partially my fault, for taking up the little time he has outside of work, but I know he was looking forward to spending more time with you. But you need to do what's right for you, and your brother will get over it."

"If I only knew what the right thing was." I blow out a breath, staring out the window briefly. We're able to see part of the ocean from here despite the slightly gloomy weather today.

How fitting.

Cora had better luck with the weather earlier at her shoot when she and several other models experienced the sunrise on their paddle boards. The shoot was for a successful athletic clothing company, and I can't wait to see the finished product. I bet Cora's pictures will be perfect.

"Hey." Her hand reaches out across the small table, lightly squeezing my forearm. "You'll figure it out. You've had a lot of things to deal with over the past few weeks and years. Sometimes it takes some time for everything to fall in place and that's fine." She laughs, the sound light and melodic, and I'm unable to keep my own smile from appearing. She's so likable. "I hope it's not weird I know so much about you when you probably don't know a lot about me."

"No, it makes total sense. Like you said earlier, I haven't seen much of my brother."

Her nod is gentle, understanding. "I moved here last year from the East Coast, and it hasn't been as easy to meet new people as I thought it would be. I'd really like us to become friends if you want to."

"I'd like that a lot. Even though I've lived in this area for so long, it seems like I don't have any friends left. People have either moved away after high school or college, or they couldn't or didn't want to deal with our family drama."

The easiness is gone from her face, a somber expression in its place. "I've learned a while back that a lot of people don't know what to do when tragedy strikes. It's sad, but there's nothing you can do about it but move on. The good thing is you usually come out a lot stronger on the other side. Just remember that."

The heaviness in my chest feels a little lighter, and I can already tell that Cora's presence in my life is going to have a positive effect. "I will, thank you. I'm so happy my brother met you."

"Me too." She rubs her hands together. "Now, let's see those apartments you told me about. I'm curious."

I pull my laptop out of my purse, and we spend the next hour going over possible prospects, sorting out the ones that aren't good enough. Cora did this last year, and that seems like an advantage to me since she knows what to look for and what to avoid.

Maybe, just maybe, I'll actually make this work and get one step closer to the life I feel I so desperately need, especially with some distance from Carter, even if he doesn't agree with my decision. Even if I miss him with every fiber of my being, it's a necessary cost.

Chapter Twenty

CARTER

*J*ulia glares at her brother, her hands on her hips. "Ollie. Don't get your panties in a twist."

In return, he throws his hands in the air. "I'm not doing any such thing. Will you stop saying that?"

He's definitely worked up. They both are. It was supposed to be a quiet evening together at the house with the four of us enjoying a drink at the end of a long work day.

Instead, Cora and I stand to the side, while the two siblings have at each other after Julia told him she was moving out in the next few days into a temporary place while she's looking for a permanent place.

Oliver told Julia straight out that it makes no sense, and while I absolutely agree with him, I know attacking her the way he did, won't get them anywhere. They've done this exact same thing, with other topics, of course, a million times before.

Yet here we are. Once more. Different problem, same reaction.

I've always thought they're too similar in some aspects, knocking heads at every turn, especially when it comes to their pride. I'm ninety-nine point nine percent sure they won't be getting anywhere tonight.

"You're driving me nuts." Ollie clenches and unclenches his hands into fists, sending me a pleading look.

I immediately shake my head and hold up my hands. "Not going there and you know it." I've taken sides before when I was younger, and a lot more stupid, and I paid for it every single time. They both reconciled each time within a few hours or days, but whoever was mad at me, held the grudge for far longer than that.

"You said you're still looking for an apartment?" While I won't get in the middle of them, I can at least try and help.

Julia looks at me and nods. "Yes."

Before I can respond, Ollie cuts in. "Why can't you just stay with us until you find an apartment then? Why do you have to move out so suddenly?"

Her eyes flicker to me for a split second before she faces her brother, who's slowly starting to turn red. Poor dude.

This whole situation makes me feel guilty as hell. *I'm* the reason Julia's moving out so quickly. *I'm* the moron who basically drove her out of her own house, and boy, do I feel like shit about it.

"I have my reasons, Ollie. I want my own place." Her voice sounds strong and confident. "I need to be alone right now. I realized yesterday I've never truly been alone, and I think it would be really good for me. It's also still harder to be here than I thought."

Oliver's hands go limp at his sides at her admission. He still doesn't look happy but nods. "Okay."

She gives him a timid smile. "Thank you."

After putting his hands in his pockets, he lets out a big breath. "Let us at least help you find a good place. I don't want you ending up in some dump. I know a realtor I can call in the morning. Maybe she can help."

"Sounds good." Julia's giving in, even though I'm sure she'd rather do it her way.

It's something. I'm glad this didn't escalate.

Cora shifts next to me. "We can push our trip back too if you want, babe."

Ollie groans. "Crap, I didn't even think about that. It's been a long day."

Julia looks back and forth between them. "Oh, that's right. You're flying out to New York tomorrow afternoon to meet Cora's family."

They both nod.

"No way you're postponing that for me. I'm totally fine by myself. Promise." Julia clicks her tongue, and I have to bite the inside of my cheek to keep from bursting into laughter.

Despite the still slightly tense situation, and after what went down yesterday between us, all I can think about is how fucking cute she is.

And sexy.

If I don't get my body under control, this whole situation is going to get even more awkward in a few seconds. I clearly have some issues when it comes to Julia, my dick liking her a whole lot being one of them.

Oliver turns my way, instant boner-deflation. "Could you go look at some places with her?"

All eyes are on me, everyone waiting for an answer.

I try to keep a straight face and nod. "Sure."

"Oh, that's not necessary." Julia waves her hands around in front of her as if she's directing an incoming airplane to the gate.

I keep my voice low and gentle, not wanting to push her away. "I really don't mind, Jules."

Ollie pushes off the kitchen counter and walks over to Cora, taking her hand in his. "It would make me feel better to know CJ will be with you."

"Fine." Julia looks at the clock on the wall before getting a glass from the cupboard, filling it with water from the fridge. "I have a headache, so I'm gonna call it a night."

Cora and Ollie turn into a blur of motion at her words, Cora the first to go over to give her a hug before Ollie does too. "No worries. We're gonna head over to Cora's place. Get some sleep and feel better. You know how to reach me if you need anything."

Julia nods before waving her hand around the room one more time. "Night, everyone."

And then she's gone, the door to her room closing with an audible *click*.

Ollie comes over to me and claps my shoulder. "Thanks, man. I hate that I haven't been around much to help. The timing has been awful."

"It's nothing." I nod in the general vicinity of the front door. "You guys have a good night, and I'll see you at the office in the morning."

After another shoulder clap from Ollie, and a wave from Cora, they're gone, and I head to my room.

I stop in front of Julia's door, debating what to do, but then I see her light's out. The message couldn't be louder, so I head to my room, my footsteps shuffled, because it's not what I want.

I want to be with her, not separated by doors. I want to reassure her that we'll be okay. I want to offer to move out so she can stay in her own home, but Ollie's right. It's crazy at work, and I don't have time to find anything at the moment.

Mostly though, I want her in my arms where I can hold her close.

———

After dropping off Ollie and Cora at the airport, I decide to visit my mom on the way back. This underlying urge to see her has become stronger this last week, and I guess it's long overdue anyway. I rarely come here without her asking me to.

After parking the car at the curb, a few feet away from her bright green mailbox, I walk through the little white gate, spotting her in the middle of her flower beds. When she turns at the noise, the tired expression immediately transforms into a happy one, the smile on her face as warm as it always is when she sees me.

"Carter. What a pleasant surprise." The words are barely out of her mouth when her smile drops a little. "I didn't expect you. Is everything okay, honey?"

Of course, she thinks something's happened when I show up out of the blue. "Yes, Mom. I just thought I'd stop by to see you."

Not really the truth, but close enough. At my statement, she practically glows, giving the blazing sun some honest competition. Standing up, she takes off her garden gloves and brushes her dark-blonde hair out of her face.

Then she opens her arms wide, waiting for her welcome hug. "It's so good to see you. It's been too long."

"I know, Mom. Sorry I've been so busy." For some reason, I enjoy the embrace more today than I do during most of my visits.

"Doesn't matter, you're here now. Should we go inside?"

"Sure." I follow her inside the modest one-story family home. She moved a few towns away with her husband, Tom, when I went to college, and it's easy to tell how much she loves living here. "Is Tom home?"

"No, he went golfing with his brother."

"I see." He's without a doubt my favorite out of all of her husbands, and I'm glad they still seem to be going strong. I can't imagine being married at all, let alone five times. But he treats her well, and that's what I care about the most when it comes to my mom.

Once we're in the kitchen, she rummages around, washing her hands at the antique farmhouse sink before getting us some homemade lemonade from the fridge. We settle down at the round kitchen table, a place she's always preferred over the living room—probably because she likes to stay busy, multitasking by prepping or cooking food whenever she can.

After sitting across from me, she leans forward as far as the table will allow her, tilting her head to the side. "So . . . to what do I owe the pleasure?"

I give her a one-shoulder shrug. "Nothing specific really. Just thought it would be nice to visit."

"I always love seeing you, and I'm happy you stopped by." Folding her fingers atop the table, her gaze is solely focused on me. "So, how is everything? Are you still staying with Oliver?"

"I am." For some reason, I pause before rushing through the rest of the sentence. "Julia moved in about two weeks ago too."

My mom's whole face lights up at the mention of Julia's name. "That's wonderful. And a surprise. How's she doing?"

I occupy myself with my glass, wiping the condensation away with my finger. "Good. She broke up with that guy and is looking for a place of her own."

My mom nods. "She's such a sweet girl. You should bring her with you next time. I'd love to see her."

Because that wouldn't be awkward.

Plus, who knows how much my mom would read into things if she saw us together. "We'll see. Maybe."

We stay quiet for a moment while I continue to play with the glass. My mom's doing her silent mom game where she waits for me to speak, knowing that's the only way to get me talking.

"Mom, why have you wasted so much time getting married over and over again? You clearly don't believe in relationships that last."

She lets out the most wistful sigh I've ever heard, and my head snaps up.

For a moment, I'm worried I've offended her by my question, but she's actually smiling. Even though the smile might be more on the sad side.

She reaches across the table and touches my hand briefly. "Oh, sweetie. Is that what you think I've been doing?"

"Kind of seems like it." My voice is rough, and I wonder why the tightness in my chest won't loosen.

A dog howls in the distance as my mom stares at the orange tablecloth.

When her gaze lifts back to mine, her eyes are glossy. "I know I didn't always make the best decisions when it comes to love and definitely rushed into most of my marriages. I should have taken time to see how things developed first, but I've always been such a sucker for love. I was also trying so hard to give you a more stable home life that I unfortunately did the opposite. Repeatedly. You have to believe me though that I always did what I thought was best at that moment, for both of us, and I loved each one of them in my own way. And even though my first four marriages turned out to be mistakes, I don't regret the relationships. They prepared me for the best one."

"You don't even regret Dad? Even after he cheated on you and left us in the middle of the night without saying a single word?" My mother's the only reason I refrain from slamming my fist on the table. Instead, the venom collects in my voice as I push the words through gritted teeth.

In a weird twisted way, I love my dad. We sometimes talk on the phone, but I'll never forgive him for the way he treated my mom, even though he did apologize to her several years later.

At my comment, she laughs, and I wonder if I missed something.

"Your dad might be my favorite mistake of them all because he gave me *you*." She chuckles some more at the grimace I can't keep off my face. "Was your dad a crappy husband? Absolutely. Probably not the best dad either. But I still won't regret the time I had with him. You know, love and relationships can be incredibly tricky. I've always fallen in love too fast and clearly accepted marriage proposals too quickly. Most people are a lot smarter than I am when it comes to this love business. I've always thought too much with my heart and not enough with my brain. Thankfully, I'm done with that now."

"Why?"

"Because Tom is *it* for me, silly. No relationship has ever felt this right before. I've never felt so content or happy either. There was always something missing before, something that felt incomplete, but since that was all I knew, I believed it was normal. Turns out I was wrong. It was due to the wrong partners. Now, in hindsight, I believe you *know* when you've met the right partner, and you should *never* settle for less like I did so many times. Being in love with the person you're meant to be with, is single-handedly one of the best things that can happen."

We're both quiet for a moment while I try to absorb everything she said, her words replaying in my mind as images of Julia pop up in my brain. I let out a low groan, and my mom pats my arm reassuringly, probably mistaking it as a reaction to what she said.

"Honey, I can't ever tell you how sorry I am for screwing up your view of relationships, because it breaks my heart to see you alone. I want you to find your other half and experience how wonderful a great relationship can be. Life is so much better when you can share it with someone you love. It changes everything." She studies me for a moment. "I'm guessing there's a reason you're wondering about this now?"

I'm sure I look like a sullen teenager when I cross my arms over my chest and shrug. It's less because I don't want to tell her though and more about not knowing why I suddenly need this answered.

Her tone is gentle, the same way it gets whenever I'm hurt or she's worried. "You don't have to marry the next available girl that comes knocking on your door—actually, please don't do that—but maybe you can test out the waters? *Really* date someone and give a relationship a chance before you throw it out the window? If you decide it's not for you after all, then that's what it is. Just don't miss out on something special because of my mistakes. I don't want you to regret it later when it might be too late."

Her words hit me in a way I didn't expect them to. Am I worried about missing out on something special? Or it actually being too late for me at some point?

It awakens something inside me I can't identify. Something I've never felt before. It's strong and wild, just like my heartbeat right now.

"I'll think about it, Mom." I push my chair back and walk around the table, hugging her extra tight before I say my goodbyes.

I still can't get my head around the fact that she doesn't regret any of her marriages. How is that possible? I saw her heartbreak. I saw her tears. But every time, she bravely picked up the pieces of her failed marriages and started over. I hated watching her get hurt, especially knowing there was nothing I could do to help her heal.

But why did I come here now? Why have I finally found the courage to ask her rather than assume she regretted each and every relationship she's been in?

Julia.

She's the reason. Her husband checklist, her passion for

life, her strength, her ability to make me feel whole. Tomorrow, I'll spend time apartment hunting with a girl I can't stop thinking about. Tomorrow, I'll help her leave us.

Leave *me*.

And then Mom's words hit me again: Life is so much better when you can share it with someone you love. It changes everything.

It changes *everything*.

Chapter Twenty-One

JULIA

"What do you two think about this one?" Linda, our real estate agent says, looking at me and then Carter.

Even though she knows we aren't a couple, she keeps treating us like one. Or maybe she just thinks I'm incompetent. It might be my leggings and tank top outfit that throws her off, which couldn't be more opposite to her designer clothes that are only outshone by her sparkly jewelry.

If this doesn't show my failure at upgrading my wardrobe, I don't know what does. I did buy those dresses with Carter and wore some of them in Vegas and on dates, so I've maybe upgraded it by about ten percent. I'm sure that's considered a success, isn't it?

Linda's phone rings, and I'm relieved when she excuses herself to take the call. We listen to her high heels click across the hardwood floor until she steps outside and shuts the door behind her.

"I don't think she likes me very much." I blow up my

cheeks and slowly push the air out of my mouth. I'm definitely in a mood, which seems to amuse Carter, who laughs in response.

"Who cares if she likes you? You're apartment shopping, not friend shopping. She's only here as a favor to your brother, but she's been doing a good job so far, so don't complain."

At that, I groan. I hate being scolded in any way, but I guess he's got a point. Which makes it even worse, and I only manage a grumble. "Fine. She does seem to like you though."

He offers another bemused smile. "Maybe that's because I'm not scowling at her all the time."

I shake my head and feel the bun on top of my head loosen, a few strands falling out of it. "Nah. She had her eye on you before she even saw me." Which is typical, of course, because Carter is looking seriously hot in his navy slacks and gray button-up, the sleeves rolled up to his elbows. No tie, but the man doesn't need it to be the sexy executive. He did admit to dress to impress though, whereas I clearly missed the mark on that one.

Pushing his hands in his pockets, he levels me with an even stare. "I can leave if you're bothered by it."

"What?" I almost scream before switching to whisper-yelling. "Don't you dare leave me alone with her."

Thankfully, he laughs, the deep rumble of it immediately relaxing me.

"All right. Let's focus then. The faster we can find a place you like, the faster you can leave your new frenemy." He winks at me, and I give him a well-deserved eye-roll in return.

When his eyes don't leave mine immediately, I fight the desire to flee. Carter's acting a little strange today, and it's throwing me off. I prepared myself to hear lots of comments about wanting to move out, maybe some flirting since that seems to be his thing.

Instead, I've felt his intense gaze on me often, but it's not been in a sexual way. He isn't sending me any I-want-to-drag-you-into-the-next-room-and ravage-you looks, but looks that suggest I'm this new puzzle he's trying to figure out. Which makes even less sense. Because nothing has changed since I saw him last.

My effort to figure out what's different about Carter is interrupted when Linda comes back, her hips sashaying so rhythmically I expect music to blast from invisible speakers at any point. Apparently, that's more likely than the possibility that she naturally walks like this. Her focus immediately settles on Carter as it has been for most of the day, putting on her dazzling smile to show off her perfect teeth.

Ugh. I want this to be over.

"So, what are we thinking?" Her voice is falsely bright.

Pfft. *We*. As if she cares about me.

I remember Carter's words and put on a smile that matches hers. "*I* think this is my favorite so far, but there's still something missing. You said we still have one more on the list, right?"

For a moment, she looks taken aback by my friendly demeanor, and I'm pretty sure I just felt Carter shaking beside me, but I don't dare look at him.

Linda composes herself and nods. "Yes, we do. It's a little over your budget, but I think it's worth it." She hands me a sheet of paper, pointing at the price with her manicured finger. "Shall we look at it now, or would you rather do it on a different day?"

I'm still immersed in the details of the apartment when Carter responds for me. "Right now would be great. We'll head over and meet you there."

"I still can't believe I just applied for my first apartment. Did you hear what she said? If everything works out, I can move in at the end of the week." I clasp my cheeks in my hands, afraid my face will otherwise split in two from the huge grin I've had since we left the final apartment.

Thank goodness Oliver prepared me for the application process, just to be on the safe side, and I brought copies of everything I needed to apply right then and there.

Carter shrugs. "You liked it and went for it."

I'm bouncing from foot to foot, feeling like I'm high on life. "It's so beautiful, isn't it? I'll need to be creative with the space since it's a little smaller than what I had in mind, especially with all my work materials, but the big deck makes it worth it. I don't care if I'm forced to work on the floor for that. Too bad it doesn't have a direct ocean view but it's still fantastic."

"You'll figure it out, I'm sure. Ollie and I are there to help with whatever." We're almost back at his car when he suddenly stops. "Are you hungry? We haven't really had a break to eat today, and I'm starving."

I wasn't planning on spending any real alone time with him, but he's been looking at apartments with me for hours on end, so the least I can do is get him something to eat.

My hands fly to my stomach. "Yes. My treat."

Since we're only a few streets from the beach, we check out one of the little cafés that offers an ocean view.

It's perfect.

"I love it here." Taking in a deep breath, the salty air fills my nose, and my insides feel like they're vibrating. I'm pretty sure there isn't a cell in my body that hides my excitement at the moment. "I can't wait to live here."

"It's a great area." His reply is short and simple, but somehow it gives me hope that we might actually have a normal relationship again at some point.

It might take some time though. Going back to being friends with him is not going to happen in a day or two. Ignoring the longing to throw myself at him will take a little longer than that to go away.

Even right now, my nerve endings are firing because he's within grasp.

I try to focus on the hypnotic motions of the waves in the background, but even that isn't enough to ignore Carter's eyes on me.

Luckily, our food arrives soon after, and the silence becomes less awkward.

A groan escapes my mouth after the first bite. "This is *the* best egg salad sandwich I've ever had."

Carter gives me an amused grin but nods, looking pretty happy with his own food too.

I wipe the corners of my mouth with my napkin. "Sorry, food just makes me . . . happy."

Now he's chuckling. "No need to explain, Jules. Nothing wrong with enjoying your food."

When Carter's done, he wipes his mouth with a napkin

and leans back, his gaze focused on the ocean. "I went to see my mom yesterday."

I'm surprised about the sudden change in topic and almost choke on my bite. "You did?"

Their relationship isn't the strongest mother-son relationship out there, so I'm not sure what to think of it, especially that he brought it up. I don't think he'd do that if it wasn't for a reason. "How is she?"

He pulls his gaze away from the waves, focusing back on me. "She's good, really good actually. She's very happy with her current life, and things are still going well with Tom."

I'm finally done eating and take a sip of my water before I speak again, thinking over my words first. "That's awesome. You like him, don't you?"

He looks relaxed when he tips his head once. "I do. He's treating her like I think she should be treated, so that earns him all the points in my book."

I almost reach out to touch his hand but refrain. "That's wonderful. She deserves a good guy after all those losers." I flinch as my words register. "Sorry."

He waves his hands in a nonchalant manner. "Nothing to be sorry about. You're absolutely right. Some of them were better than others, I suppose, but they were definitely never good husband material." A chuckle comes out of his mouth, surprising me. "I'm sure, none of them would have met the requirements of your husband checklist."

I lean back and cross my arms over my chest. "Very funny. It is incredibly imperative to have this list fulfilled. It will guarantee my happiness."

"We'll see." His gaze bores into mine before he shakes his

head as if to clear cobwebs from his mind. "She asked about you when I told her you're back."

"Maybe I can go see her at some point. It would be fun to catch up. Plus, she always tells the best stories about your childhood."

"I think you mean the most embarrassing ones." He grimaces before dipping his chin.

Both his reply and his reaction make me chuckle. "Aren't those the best ones?"

"Maybe if it's about someone other than yourself."

"Fair enough, I can see your point." I sigh for a moment as memories flood my mind, my brain going back to my own childhood. "I always hated when my parents told embarrassing stories about me. Now, I wish more than anything they could tell some more. But I guess that's how life goes. We don't know what we have until we lose it. Sad but true. How great would it be if we could actually treasure the people in our lives the way they deserve to be treasured before it's too late?"

Carter leans across the table and takes my hand. "You're right, Jules. My mom said something similar. Told me not to wait around until it's too late and I lose something special." He's looking into my eyes as he says this, and a small shiver goes down my back. I'm thinking she said more than that going by his subdued demeanor today. But he sits back quickly, taking the comfort of his hand and connection with him.

After a few more minutes of reminiscing, I pay our check —much to Carter's complaint—and we decide to walk along the beach to see what else this small beach town has to offer.

It's only one town over from my family home, but for some reason, I've never been here.

On our walk back, we can't resist the little ice cream store, and decide to sit on one of the benches facing the ocean, watching the waves roll in as the sun slowly makes its descent. I close my eyes for a moment to fully enjoy the soothing sounds around us. The wind blows through my hair and the last rays of sun warm my skin.

"I think we should tell Ollie about us." Carter's words come out low and rushed, ripping me out of my peaceful moment like someone dropped a bucket of cold water on me.

I turn to stare at him in disbelief, hoping he's joking, but the expression on his face is dead serious.

What the hell?

I've thought of different ways this conversation could go, but I didn't end up with Julia's ice cream in my face in one of those scenarios.

"Oh my gosh, I'm so sorry. I swear I didn't do it on purpose." She covers her open mouth with her free hand, but I can see the laugh lines around her eyes twitching, right before her shoulders start shaking too. She's moments away from bursting into laughter.

Thankfully, they gave us some napkins at the ice cream shop, and I grab one to wipe my face as best as I can. That seems to do the trick for Julia, because she's suddenly bent over from laughing so hard. I let her have her moment, unable to keep my own grin at bay.

For now, I prefer this reaction over her yelling at me, but that could still be coming.

After putting her ice cream on a napkin, she grabs another one from the stack and pours some water from her bottle on it. "Come here." One of her hands is on my jaw to steady it while she wipes away the remnants of her ice cream attack from my face.

The contact doesn't last long, but the tingling sensation of her touch stays with me long after.

After throwing the napkins in the nearby trash can, she looks at me. "I really am sorry, Freddy. You know my reflexes are awful sometimes."

"I do know that, Daph, very well too. I'll never forget the moment I almost lost my crown jewels when we were teenagers." I flinch at the memory, making her laugh again.

A snort escapes her as she squints at me, her eyes lit with a twinkle of mischief. "You totally deserved that. Who in their right mind goes into a girl's bedroom in the middle of the night when she's sleeping?"

The ice cream incident lessened some of the distance between us, and I feel her soft breath on my face. The buzz from her previous touch lingers, making me even more aware of her.

It was crazy, absolutely fucking nuts, to think I could have sex with her and go back to normal afterward. Maybe I can plead momentary insanity? I definitely wasn't thinking straight, that's for sure.

I used to fantasize about this girl on an almost daily basis when I was younger. Back then, it was easy to write off as crazy teenage hormones, especially since she was around constantly. Now, that excuse doesn't work anymore.

Shit. I'm in so much trouble with this one. No other woman has ever driven me this insane or made me doubt my mind so much. My thoughts wander to Ollie and the consequences that might come from revealing our secret to him.

Julia pushes my shoulder. "Earth to Carter."

I will my brain to focus on our conversation and give her an apologetic smile. "The guys dared me to draw a mustache on your face. What was I supposed to do?"

Slapping a hand on her knee, she shakes her head. "Silly me. Here I thought saying no would have been an option."

"We were teenagers. If there's ever a time to do stupid things, it's that time."

"True." A flicker of a smile passes her lips. "Plus, you paid for your mistake."

"No kidding, Miss Nuts-Punch. I still have occasional phantom pain."

Her lips are still lifted at the corners, but after a moment, the smile doesn't reach her eyes anymore. Instead, the skin between her eyebrows furrows, pinched together in a tight line. "Does he really need to know?"

I know who she's talking about. It was just a matter of time before we came back to this dreaded topic. "I think so."

Leaning back, she links her hands behind her head and stares out at the lapping water. "Why now? Why at all?"

I sit back too, following her example and looking at the ocean. "My mom mentioned something yesterday that got me thinking. It was about missing out on something special and having regrets, something along those lines. One of the things I thought about was Ollie. *You* will always be his sister, no matter what, so I'm not too worried about your relationship with him. Not to mention that I'll be the bad guy in this anyway. But I think it would be so much worse if he found out later and maybe not even from us. He'd be so disappointed, and I'm not certain our friendship would survive that. I expect him to be livid regardless, but hopefully, he can still get over it at this point."

"Hmm." Her face is lowered so I can't read her expression well, but she looks despondent.

I move around, suddenly feeling restless. "And you know how much he values honesty. That's always been his number-one priority when it comes to not only his professional life but his private one as well."

Julia lets out a pained sigh before rubbing her face with her hands. "Ugh, I know. I don't like keeping this from him any more than you do, but at the same time, I don't want to drive a wedge between anyone either."

"I knew what we were doing, so I definitely can't feign ignorance or naivety."

"Neither can I." She studies me for a moment, her features tight in concentration. "Are you really sure about this?"

I nod, wanting her to know I'm serious about this. The conversation with my mom started a whole avalanche of thoughts I'm still trying to wade through, but dealing with Oliver first makes the most sense to me. Once that's done, I can move on to the next hurdle. I'm not a terrible human, and as long as Julia isn't hurt, Ollie can't be too upset. I didn't disrespect her in any way, nor would I. But he's fully aware of my views on long-term relationships.

It took me a while to accept that he was serious about Cora, so his position on me being the man for Jules won't even be on the spectrum. He flat-out laughed at Cora's suggestion that Jules and I were more than friends. Didn't give it a moment's thought. So, that's what I'm working with, and it's why I need to make changes. "I've thought about it a lot. I expect him to kick me out, but it's probably time for me to find my own place anyway. Being roommates was always a temporary solution."

Her eyes go wide. "Poor Ollie will be all alone again."

The fact she's worried about something like that makes me feel a little lighter, like the worst is over. At least when it comes to this conversation. "He's a big boy, Jules, and lived alone for years before we two homeless dorks came along. Plus, he's spending most of his time with Cora anyway. Maybe this will allow them to take the next step too, who knows?"

The bright smile is back on her face at the mention of Cora. "I'd like that. She's awesome, and I think they're really great together."

"I agree."

Since Ollie and Cora won't be back for two more days, we'll need to wait until then. Despite not looking forward to the confrontation, or what will happen afterward, I can't ignore the relief in my chest at the thought of having it out in the open.

No more hiding, and no more secrets.

It will allow me to move on, to get my jumbled thoughts in line to go after what I want. The gorgeous, quick-witted, and kind girl in front of me. Because I've finally worked out that I want more. Ollie will have to deal.

Chapter Twenty-Three

JULIA

The short distance from the parking lot to the little bistro feels like one hundred miles rather than one hundred feet. That might be due to my nerves though, since they're all over the place, to the point that I feel slightly nauseated. My brother and Cora flew back late last night, and both he and Carter thought it would be a great idea to meet here for lunch.

Normally I like it here, this cute little place in the middle of the Malibu downtown area a nice place for an escape.

But today is different.

So different.

Knowing Carter and Ollie are waiting for me—thanks to both letting me know via texts—and knowing what Carter is about to do, has done nothing but induce the desire to flee.

When I spot them at a table outside, I'm surprised to see Cora next to my brother. I was planning on sitting next to him to try and diffuse the situation a little bit at least, but that option is out the window now, and the only available seat is next to Carter.

After taking what feels like the hundredth deep breath since I left the house, I sit on the chair that Carter's already pulled out for me.

"Hey, guys." I lower myself onto the warm metal and turn to Cora. "I didn't know you were going to be here too. Good to see you."

She glances in Carter's direction before settling back on me with a welcoming smile. "I thought it would be nice to catch up with you two."

I'm still distracted by the fact that she's here when Carter wants to spill the beans. On second thought, he could be the reason Cora's here. Maybe he asked her to run interference for my brother. That might actually work.

But since she keeps crossing and uncrossing her legs, I have my answer.

My brother is the only one who seems normal, grinning at me. "So, show me the pictures of the new place. Carter said it looks like you'll be able to move there this week. That's amazing."

I flop back in my chair, trying to get my trembling hands under control. I'm not sure if I should be relieved we're not diving into the nitty-gritty right away, or nervous I have to endure this torture longer, knowing it *will* happen. "Of course. Let me show you."

A waitress comes to take our order. Once she's gone, I show Oliver and Cora the pictures of the apartment, telling them everything I can remember about the place. Carter is quiet throughout the whole exchange. Since it's not his apartment though, there's no reason to dwell on that fact. He's about to tell Ollie the truth so he won't risk his friendship with him, not because he realized he's madly in love with me and wants to profess it to the world.

Wow. Nice one, Jules. That went downhill pretty fast.

It's an old crush. Ignore all those silly feelings. You knew what you were doing, and now it's done. Over.

My brother seems satisfied with the apartment, which makes me happy, as he does know a lot about the real estate market.

After taking a drink of his water, he puts it back on the table with a loud clunk. "Oh, I totally forgot. We ran into one of Cora's friends at the airport." Both Cora and Carter stiffen. "He's looking for a date for a restaurant opening next month. I'm not sure if you're ready for that yet, but I thought I'd throw it out there. He seemed like a nice guy."

"Jules and I were together in Vegas."

Oh. My. Gosh.

It's eerily quiet—except for the sound of blood rushing in my ears—and I'm sure I'd hear if a needle hit the ground. Or maybe I'm sitting in my own soundproof bubble, because that's definitely what it feels like.

Oliver looks at Carter with a tilt of his head while I hold my breath. Cora doesn't seem to fare much better, her eyes as wide as they go.

"I know that, CJ. I was there when you guys got back." My brother shakes his head, his gaze clouding once he gets a look at everyone's expressions. "What's going on?"

Carter lets out a harsh breath, his voice low. "We spent the nights together, Ollie. In one room and one bed."

Holy. Shit.

I am literally yelling at him . . . inside my head. What on earth is he thinking?

Realization creeps across my brother's face, a flush quickly making its way up his neck and onto his whole face. I'm afraid he's going to jump across the table to strangle Carter, but the waitress appears with our food.

She takes in the scene at our table, the tension as thick as fog, the anger practically radiating off my brother's face, and her smile drops.

Yet, without a doubt, she is Carter's temporary lifesaver.

My brother's breaths come out short and almost violently, his nostrils flaring. If there was ever an epitome of an angry bull, that's him right now. *I* want to scoot back with my chair. Just until things have cooled down—provided they actually will.

Cora is the first to spring into action, placing her hand on my brother's arm, her voice soft and soothing. "Why don't you let him explain first?"

I use that moment to glance at Carter, shooting him an irritated look that's meant to silently convey "Really? That's how you choose to tell him?"

He only shrugs in response, and I have absolutely no clue what's going on in his head. If it wouldn't make things worse, I'd let him have a piece of my mind right now, that's for sure.

"Was this planned?" My brother's voice slices through the air, sounding almost venomous as his gaze is fixated on Carter.

So far, he's barely glanced at me, and I'm still unsure if that's good or bad.

Carter snorts beside me—he freaking *snorts*. What on earth is the matter with him? He leans forward in his chair as if he's actually trying to get into my brother's face. I'm starting to think he's lost his mind. "You're asking if I took her to Vegas to lure her into my bed?"

"It wouldn't be the first time you did something like that," Oliver practically spits across the table.

Carter leans forward even more, his posture and facial expression getting more aggressive by the second. "Be careful what you say right now."

With each passing second, I feel more nervous, shooting an anxious glance at Cora, who looks even more stressed than she did a few minutes ago.

"Why? Are you an item now?" His eyes go wide at the thought, and he seems to be holding his breath until Carter shakes his head next to me.

My brother throws his hands up in the air. "So why are you telling me this then? Why now? If this was a casual thing, do you fear she's going to come running to me because you've dumped her?"

Ouch. This arrow was probably meant for Carter, but it feels like it pierces me straight through the heart.

Carter leans back, slightly, and I take a deep breath.

His gaze is still steadily meeting my brother's. "It's not like that. I just didn't want to lie to you anymore and risk our friendship."

My brother lets out a humorless laugh. "You should have thought about that before you put your hands on my sister." His hand comes down on the table with a loud *smack*, making both Cora and me jump in our seats. "Damn it all to hell, CJ. This is exactly why I've always told you she's off-limits. What a fucking mess."

Did he just . . . Did I just hear him correctly?

Me . . . off-limits? For Carter?

"Excuse me?" The words are out of my mouth while I try to process what my brother just said.

His gaze flickers to me, and he blinks like he's forgotten I'm here. His gaze softens, but there's still enough residual anger in his eyes to make my blood boil. We both don't have much of a temper, but if someone pokes us hard enough, we react.

Heat rushes through my body, and I feel sweat form on my upper lip. My muscles are practically quivering beneath my skin to throw something at my brother—something off the table or maybe the table itself—but somewhere deep down inside me, I find the strength to resist.

Barely.

My voice is shaky when I speak, which makes me even angrier. "What do you mean I'm off-limits? Did you seriously tell Carter not to get involved with me?"

Ollie's jaw clenches and he tightens his hands into fists. "Of course I did. From the second I saw him checking you out when we were teenagers. You're my sister."

I inhale a sharp breath, my palms stinging from digging my fingernails into them, as Cora groans softly at my brother's admission.

Throughout every discussion I've had with Carter, I've wondered if that was the case, but hearing Ollie say it in such a nonchalant manner pisses me off even more. "What on earth does that have to do with anything? You have no right to tell anyone something like that. I'm not your property you can manage however you see fit."

His eyes look like they might pop out of his head, and his mouth is slightly agape. "Jules, I only want what's best for you."

"Oh yeah? And how do you know Carter isn't what's best for me?" I close my eyes when I realize what I just said.

Damn it. Can this get any worse?

Both men stare at me in shock. Cora, on the other hand, is trying to hide the grin that keeps threatening to spread across her face.

Just great.

But I'm *not* done yet. "He's your best friend, Ollie. Your damn best friend since you were little, so I know how highly you think of him. Why on earth wouldn't you want someone like that to be with me? It makes no sense." Words are starting to fail me as the ridiculousness of this whole situation starts to register. This isn't going anywhere. "You know what? Never mind. It's not like he's interested anyway."

And there it is. I just made it worse.

My chair scrapes loudly against the concrete when I push it back, almost toppling over. With angry tears in my eyes— maybe some embarrassed ones mixed in too—I get some money out of my purse and throw it on the table.

"I hope you're happy now." My voice sounds shrill, even to my own ears. Before either one of the guys can even think about getting up, I point my finger at them. "Don't follow me, don't call me, don't text me. I don't want to hear from either one of you for a while."

Then I turn around and stomp toward the parking lot, certain that every eye in the bistro and surrounding area is on me right now.

I definitely won't be coming back here any time soon.

What the hell just happened? Not only did Carter blurt out our misdemeanor without any warning, but he then confirmed we were just a fling, which makes me feel like shit.

Doesn't he have a clue what that would sound like to me? *Of course there's nothing going on between us, Ollie. She's your baby sister . . . who is off-limits.* Ollie told him I was off-limits? Carter was interested in me years ago? My head is spinning. It's too much.

What a freaking mess.

Chapter Twenty-Four

CARTER

*A*lmost a whole week has passed since I saw Julia at the bistro. It feels like it's been a lot longer, and the confrontation with Oliver has left more than just a sour taste in my mouth.

What an absolute clusterfuck.

I've wanted to go and see her every day since but wasn't sure that was the best idea after the way she left. Cora's the only one who's seen her, making sure we know that nothing has changed. Julia still doesn't want to see us. The two of them even did Julia's move by themselves—while I stayed at a hotel and Ollie at Cora's place. Thank goodness, the new apartment is mostly furnished, so there wasn't too much for them to do.

Otherwise, Oliver and I might have insisted on helping.

I know she needs space, and I've wanted to give it to her, but after a week of sleepless nights, I've decided it's been long enough.

Hence, I'm in front of her apartment door, hoping she'll let me in, or even just open it. Her car is in the parking lot, so she should be home. Exhaling a fortifying breath, I knock on the door.

After what feels like an hour, and several more knocks, she finally opens it. Then, she just stares at me. Not in confusion or anger, but with a completely unreadable expression.

Somehow that's even worse.

When the silence stretches between us, she crosses her arms over her chest, but I know better than to drop my gaze to her breasts.

That might earn me a nut-punch.

Something we both know I never ever want to live through again.

Clearing my throat, I try to get rid of the huge lump. "Can I come in?"

She releases a breath, and I realize how tired she looks. "What do you want, Carter?"

"I just want to talk. Please? I also brought some of that Chinese takeout you liked so much." I hold up the bags in my hands, and her gaze flickers down.

Wordlessly, she takes a step back and opens the door all the way. Relief floods me as I walk past her, trying not to react when she moves back far enough so we won't accidentally touch.

Shit.

My lungs constrict, making it hard to breathe, but I guess I deserve it.

The apartment is the same as I remember, yet different. Cream walls in the open living room-kitchen area, dark-brown wooden floor. On the other side of the room are double doors leading to a deck similar to the one at Ollie's house.

I walk over to the kitchen island to put down the bags before turning around to face her. "I like what you've done with the place."

I'm surprised what a difference a decorative touch can make—a purple blanket on the couch, a few pictures on the shelves along the TV wall, a vase full of flowers on the kitchen counter.

"Thanks. It's not perfect, but I like it." Her voice is steady, maybe a little flat, but she can't hide the spark in her eyes when she speaks.

Focusing her attention on the bags, she rummages through them, getting what looks like enough containers for both of us before walking to the couch. I follow like a lost puppy and sit next to her. I leave plenty of room between us, even though it feels weird and unnatural, but I'm trying to get back into her good graces. I need to.

I came here to make things right after all, not to make them worse. Hopefully, respecting her wishes will work to my advantage.

I haven't taken a bite, but I put the container on the small coffee table in front of us and turn to face Julia. "Listen. I came to apologize. I'm really sorry about what happened."

She swallows the food after chewing a few times, looking at me with her eyebrows raised.

My nerves are getting the best of me, and I wipe my hands on my shorts. I've never been nervous in front of Julia, or any other girl now that I think about it.

Nothing has ever mattered as much as this. "We both

suspected Ollie wouldn't react well, but I know I made things a lot worse the way I told him."

She puts her box down too, forcefully, a few pieces of rice flying out of the top. "You did. I don't understand why." Her voice isn't exactly hostile but not very friendly either.

I flinch. I've been berating myself all week over my behavior, trying to find a way to fix it. "I don't have a good explanation. Ollie started talking about you going on a date with a random guy he met at the airport, and the words just came out of my mouth. And then I couldn't stop. The urge for Ollie to know took over. I knew I'd started an avalanche, but at the same time, I was happy it was finally out in the open. It wasn't fair to you though, and for that, I'm truly sorry."

I send her a look I hope conveys my sincerity, foolishly hoping she'll forgive me just like that.

Her face is mostly still an empty mask. "As much as I wish we could turn back time, what's done is done. Cora said he wasn't done with you after I left."

I let out a humorless laugh. "Oh, no. He was just getting started. I'm pretty sure he used almost every curse word he knows and as expected kicked me out of the house. I don't think I've ever seen him this mad before."

"Not even when I broke his beloved one-of-a-kind surfboard that I rode down the stairs to the beach?" The barest hint of a smile forms; at least I hope I didn't imagine it.

Even though she's avoiding my gaze, I'm grateful she's bringing up something from our past. It brings familiarity with it, something not everyone would understand. Maybe it makes me slightly delusional, but it gives me hope we might be okay.

Focusing on her words, I chuckle. "Okay, maybe it didn't top *that*. I won't ever forget how red his face was when he saw his shredded board."

"I know. I really thought his head would explode." Her eyes finally meet mine as a small grin forms at the memory. "He didn't speak to me for almost a month."

"It was bad. Hopefully, it won't be as bad this time. He's not a stupid teenager anymore, plus he has Cora. I think it would have been a lot worse if she hadn't been there." I felt bad that Cora witnessed that shitshow. Had I known it was going to escalate so badly, I wouldn't have asked her to come. However, I can't deny I'm happy she was there.

She nods but stays quiet.

"Sorry I didn't tell you she'd be there. It was a last-minute idea, or I would have said something to you."

She stares at her hands, her voice thick with emotion. "You don't always need to explain everything to me. It's not like you have any sort of obligation toward me."

Can't say that didn't feel like a punch in the face. "Don't say that like we're strangers or mere acquaintances, Jules. That's the last thing we are."

One of her shoulders lifts a fraction. "You know what I mean. It's not like we're . . . together or anything."

Either I'm hallucinating, or there's a slight blush on her cheeks.

Seeing this reaction makes my heart beat faster, while my mind fights with itself over what to do. I came here to apologize, keeping everything else locked away for later.

Before my mind goes off on a crazy ride into Hopeland, I go back to the last topic, wanting to reassure her. "Don't worry about Ollie though. He'll come around, he always does."

"I know he will. I just hate having everything ripped apart like this." Her eyes snap up to mine, suddenly wide. "Oh crap. You guys work together. I didn't even think about that. I'm such an idiot. That completely slipped my mind. How are you managing? And where are you staying now?"

I bite my cheek from smiling at her cute rant and the way her eyes scan the room and the couch as if she's thinking about offering it to me. "I checked into a hotel for now, but I'm going to start looking for a place soon. Thankfully, we know a good realtor, don't we?"

Julia groans, stretching her legs out in front of me. "Oh, goodie."

My eyes automatically scan her tanned skin, the need to touch and explore almost impossible to resist.

Since lusting over her won't help my case, I try and focus on our conversation. "I'm not her biggest fan either, but she's good at her job and that's exactly what I need. I'm going to meet up with her in a few days. And about the work situation . . . it's not the best atmosphere at the moment, but we'll work through it. You know your brother. Thankfully, he's a professional who can keep this chaos out of the business."

Julia nods and picks her container back up, slowly poking at it with her fork. "That's good. I'm glad to hear that."

I mirror her, and we eat in silence. But I don't mind. I'm just happy she hasn't kicked me out yet.

Once we're done, I help her put away the trash and pack up the leftovers.

Then, we're back in Awkwardtown, staring at each other without knowing what to say.

I clear my throat. "I have a big presentation in the morning, so I better head back to the hotel."

"Oh."

Is that disappointment in her eyes?

My mind races when we walk to the door and she opens it—going back and forth over this evening, analyzing everything we said and her reactions. I walk past her but spin around at the threshold, making her almost bump into me.

"I lied. About what you said earlier." Once more, my mouth takes over, the words spilling out before I made a conscious decision about it.

Her eyebrows pull together as she stares up at me. "What? What did I say?"

The fluttery feeling in my stomach is so strong, I feel nauseous. Hoping to calm my nerves, I blow out a deep breath, Julia's eyes flickering to my mouth at the sound of it. "I want to take you out on a date. A real one."

She gasps as her wide eyes find mine. After swallowing loudly, her voice comes out in a whisper. "Carter, please don't. You don't *really* date."

I expected her to say something like that so I nod. Bending down, I keep my gaze steady on hers and my tone gentle. "With you, I want to try."

Her left hand grips the door a little tighter. "I don't know. What if this makes things even worse? I meant it before when I said I don't want to lose you."

I've asked myself the same questions, and I expected her to bring them up, but I'm still not sure how to explain my answer to her without sounding like a crazy person. But maybe that's what it takes. I've had a whole week to focus on

Mom's words to me about her past. How she grieves the way her marriages eroded my faith in anything long-term.

But there were two things that particularly resonated with me. There was always something missing before, something that felt incomplete. In the week without Julia, without any interaction whatsoever, that's what I felt. Incomplete. She's only been back in my life for a month, yet I've felt lost without her.

I want you to find your other half and experience how wonderful a great relationship can be. Life is so much better when you can share it with someone you love. It changes everything.

And I think I'm there.

So, if this is what it takes for me to show my heart, I'll do it. Because I don't want to lose her in any way either, so I get her question and concern. "What if it doesn't? I've been going over this since I had that conversation with my mom. I don't want to miss out on this chance with you. To have something real with you. I know I'm not the only one feeling this special connection between us. It's always been there, but it's grown into something so much more over the last month."

The indecision is as clear as day in her eyes, and I don't blame her. It's hard to wipe away the doubt she must feel after knowing me for so long. "Don't give me an answer right now. Just think about it, okay?"

She nods, and I take a step toward her, leaning in to place a soft kiss on her cheek. "You're gonna let me know?"

Her head bobs up and down again, and I chuckle at her obvious speechlessness. It leaves me with a lightness in my chest that I welcome. "Great. Have a good night, Jules."

"You too. And thanks for dinner."

"Anytime, Daphne. Anything for you." I lose the battle with myself and touch her cheek.

With a small smile on her face, she closes the door, but not before I hear her faint "Night, Freddie," making me grin like a total fool.

The soft breeze picks up my hair, stirring a loose strand around my cheek. The sun warms my face while I watch people on the boardwalk—talking, laughing, and playing. A couple is arguing close by, but I try my best to tune them out, wanting to focus on the positive around me.

No more dwelling on the past, getting frustrated over things I can't control, or chickening out of things because I'm afraid of them. It's time to live my life to the fullest. My new mantra.

"Jules?"

The familiar voice rips me out of my thoughts, and I'm surprised to see Carter approach in a slow jog, the butterflies in my stomach throwing him a welcome party.

His breaths come out quick and hard when he reaches me. "What are you doing here?"

Even though I heard him, I'm distracted when he takes a large gulp from the water bottle in his hand. Shielding my eyes from the sun, I watch his Adam's apple move with each swallow, utterly fascinated.

When he sees my hand on my forehead, he steps to the side, positioning himself to block the sun with his large frame. That also puts him closer to me, allowing me to get a good look at his shirtless body that's dripping with sweat.

Despite the heat, the hairs on my arms lift as I try to keep my cool at the sight of a half-naked Carter. "I know you usually run at the beach after work, so I thought I'd try my luck and see if I could catch you."

He studies my face, looking for answers to whatever questions are popping around in his head. He scans my body, finding my typical loungewear of capri leggings and a T-shirt. "Did you want to go running with me?"

I laugh at his question, because he couldn't be further off. "Nah. I started some workouts at home, but I think that's it for me right now. It saves me time, so I can focus on all the other million things I want to do. Work has been busier too this week with lots of new orders, so I'm pooped."

"More orders are awesome. Just make sure to take some breaks too." His smile is genuine and I smile back at him. "Looks like you've got the six figures in the bag."

I shrug, not wanting to jinx it, but I have the same thought. Or rather hope. "We'll see. I still have almost half a year to go, but so far, it looks pretty good, so I can't complain. I'll look into getting some help soon if the orders keep coming like that."

"That sounds like a good idea. Let me know if I can help."

Let me know if I can help. That's exactly what I expected Carter to say, because I know this man well. Nate never supported my *silly hobby*, and knowing Carter has my back, has always had my back, makes this discussion a little easier to digest.

Carter starts doing some stretches, and I'm failing miserably to keep my eyes on his face instead of his muscles moving and flexing. I mean, they're practically begging me to enjoy the show. No one can blame me.

Of course, he catches me staring and is unable to hide his smirk. He finally takes pity on me and sits down. "So, if you didn't want to run with me, why are you here?"

His question makes me fidgety, my gaze flickering down and momentarily stopping at his torso. Drops of sweat run down his chest and abs, and the sight is mesmerizing, to say the least, reminding me of how well this body works together with mine. He's the perfect mix of bulky and lean, enough muscles to be toned but not too much to risk a concussion when you run into him. I could stare at him all day long, which I guess I already do whenever I get the chance.

"Jules?" Carter's chuckle breaks through my haze, and I'm pretty sure someone could use me as a stoplight right now, because I must be that red.

"Yes, sorry." I play with my fingers to distract myself.

Out of the corner of my eye, I see him lean forward, bracing his elbows on his knees while he looks at the side of my face.

Waiting for me to say something.

Giving me the room and time I need. Something he's been trying so hard to do.

It's been three days since he stopped by my apartment, and he's been nothing but patient after dropping that "dating" bomb on me.

But I needed time to think.

Talking myself in and out of a million different *what ifs*, catching my bestie at a time where she wasn't asleep on the other side of the world to dissect this whole mess with her.

Cora has been lending me her ear whenever I've needed it too, keeping me updated on my brother as well. He seems to have moved on from angry to sulking, which I can totally live with.

When I peek at Carter, his features are soft, helping me feel centered.

Embracing change isn't always easy for me, but this expanding feeling in my chest whenever I'm around him, gives me the courage to take the next step. To say the words I know will change my life.

"Did you mean what you said the other day? When you came over?" My voice is merely a whisper in the wind, mixing with the calming waves of the ocean.

"Every single word." There's no hesitation when he replies, his voice strong and steady.

My gaze settles on his, my heart beating wildly in my chest. "You really want to give dating a try?"

"No. I don't want to give *dating* a try. At least not in general." His words sound final, like he doesn't want to leave any room for discussion. "Only with *you*."

I let out an anxious breath, a shiver running through my whole body. "Why?"

"You know exactly why. There's something between us. I feel it every time we're together, and I know you feel it too. It's special, incomparable to anything else. It's always been different with you, but I thought the reason was our long friendship. But having sex with you changed things. It intensified everything, shifting things, and making me want things I never thought I wanted." He sounds almost frustrated when he's done with his little speech.

All the while I stare at him like a moron, my mouth open, my eyes wide, completely unable to sift through the chaos in my brain. Even when I thought of the possibility of him saying yes, I never would have expected this admission. Confirming the same feelings that have been swirling around inside of me too, the ones that have been causing doubtful thought after doubtful thought and kept me up at night.

"And you want to explore that? Are you sure?" The need to be in this one hundred percent together is almost overwhelming.

"Positive."

We stare at each other as I go through the mental checklist I made for this conversation, momentarily moving to my husband checklist that's now taped to my fridge. Which might have been a bad move on my part since it reminds me of Carter every time I look at it, knowing how many boxes he ticks while still being off-limits.

Until now.

Maybe. Possibly.

The thought of that alone catapults me into a mix of euphoria and hysteria, and my brain can't seem to decide which path to ultimately take.

After closing my eyes for a moment, I tell myself I can freak out later when I'm alone. "What about Ollie?"

Since he's a sore subject, we have to talk about him. It's not like we can just ignore my brother, not that either of us really wants to.

Carter shrugs, his expression staying leveled. "He'll get over it, eventually. Even though he might have my balls first."

I flinch at the very probable possibility. But he's right, my brother will get over it, he just has to.

Leaning in, Carter's next words are a whisper on my skin. "But it'll be worth it. I just know it."

For a moment, I think he might kiss me, but he stays where he is, watching me curiously from a few inches away.

"So, Jules. Does that mean you're saying yes to going on a date with me?" His voice is low and pleasant, warming me from the inside out.

His blue eyes are filled with anticipation, excitement, and so much hope. I find comfort in his gaze the way I usually do and nod before I can change my mind.

"Really?" His eyes widen, his eyebrows shooting up an inch.

When he smiles widely, I laugh, because he looks like a little kid on Christmas. "Yes, really."

"Perfect. I'm glad. Wow." His grin is contagious, and I'm sure we look like morons to bystanders.

Then, his arms are around me, caging me in, and pulling me close to his chest.

"Ew." I chuckle, trying to push him away when he only tightens his grip. "You're all sweaty."

A moment later, I finally give up and lean into him, fully enjoying his embrace.

Nothing feels this good.

When he lets go of me, I hold up my hand between us. "But there's going to be a rule for our date."

He laughs before running his hand through his damp hair. "Of course there is. I wouldn't expect anything else from you." He winks at me, and I'm grinning like a fool, the lightness in my chest making me feel like I'm floating.

His fingers brush a strand of hair out of my face, gently pushing it behind my ear. "So, enlighten me, what is this rule?"

I scoot back on the bench to put some space between us, unable to think straight when he's this close. All I can think about are his lips on mine and his hands on my body, making me want to forget where we are and climb him instead. I can't deny how alluring and inviting that sounds, but if this is supposed to be a serious attempt at dating, I can't waste the chance by falling back on our attraction for each other right away.

Even though it pains me to do this, I hold up my index finger. "No making out or sex."

He opens his mouth, then closes it again. After closing his eyes, he clears his throat and nods. "Okay, I can deal with that."

I press my lips together at his obvious discomfort. "Are you sure?"

My heart sighs when he gives me one of his small smiles. It's his shy one he doesn't show often, and I've always thought it's cute as hell. The last thing anyone would ever think of Carter is being shy.

He rubs his chin and my eyes zoom in on his sexy stubble. "I wasn't expecting anything like this, but I understand why you're asking for it. I'm not going to lie and say it'll be easy, because my hands are already itching to touch you. But like I said before, it'll be worth it. And I can handle a few extra cold showers if necessary."

I might have shot myself majorly in the foot with my rule.

"Any other rules?" He arches one brow, patient as ever.

Shaking my head, I swallow loudly. "Not that I can think of, but I'll let you know."

"I bet you will." He crosses his arms over his chest, successfully distracting me once more. "Well, I have one rule too."

Now it's my turn to throw him a confused look. I didn't expect him to have one. "You do?"

"Yup." He looks like the epitome of casual, relaxing on the bench for the world to see. "None of those sexy little dresses we bought."

My chin drops, and he laughs at my expression.

"Sorry, Jules, but without my rule in place, I'm afraid I might not be able to agree to your rule." He tilts his head to the side as if to say "So what's it gonna be?"

I didn't miss the way his eyes raked over my body in appreciation in Vegas, but I thought that reaction was due to the sexual tension between us.

Determined to make this easier for both of us, I nod and stretch out my hand. "You've got yourself a deal."

His face lights up, the smile so captivating when we shake hands that I'm ready to melt into a puddle. "Perfect. I can't wait. I don't suppose you'll let me seal it with a kiss?"

I laugh, because he damn well knows that if we seal it with a kiss, there's no way we'll stop there. Especially when he uses his husky bedroom voice.

"Freddy, are you trying to get frisky with me?"

He bursts out laughing and shakes his head. "I'm guessing that's a no."

Regardless, because he's Carter, he leans in—I struggle to breathe—and gives me one of his gentle forehead kisses, one of my favorite things in the world.

Apart from the goof in front of me, that is. The goof I'm apparently now dating.

*J*ulia opens her apartment door before I even have a chance to knock, glaring at me with tired eyes. "I hate you. This is already the worst date ever."

I can't help but laugh at her expression, putting my hands over my heart. "Ouch. Good morning to you too, sunshine."

Her eyes narrow, but I still see the tiniest hint of a smile at the corner of her lips. "When you said date, I thought you were talking about dinner and maybe a movie. No one said anything about you standing in front of my door at six o'clock in the freaking morning to pick me up to go who knows where."

Grabbing her hand, I pull her into a tight hug, inhaling her sweet scent before I whisper into her ear, "I promise you'll like it."

When she agreed to a date yesterday, I spent all evening planning it, after walking her home first of course, basking in her presence as much as I could.

"I doubt that." She grumbles her complaints into my

chest, and I squeeze her one more time before pushing her back gently. "Come on, sleepyhead, let's go. We don't want to be late."

Her gaze flicks upward. "Late? How could we possibly be late to anything this early? Isn't half the world still asleep?"

I chuckle at her theatrics and reach to smooth out her frown. "Not everyone is a little nocturnal like you."

My hand moves to her cheek, and I gently brush my fingers over it. My heartbeat feels like it jumped into my throat as I watch her lean into my touch, right before she closes her eyes in pure contentment.

Shit. That feels good.

A soft breath escapes her pink lips, her mouth forming a small O, successfully waking up my dick too.

When she opens her eyes and looks at me, I inwardly groan, not having a clue how I'm supposed to keep my hands to myself today.

She holds up her own. "All right, you win. Let me go pee one more time and grab my bag so we can head out." She disappears into the hallway that leads to her bedroom and bathroom, but not before I can admire her round ass in the jean shorts she decided to wear—probably in an evil attempt to kill me today—almost missing her faint voice. "I put some water in to the fridge in case we need it."

"I'll get it." I close the door behind me and walk into the kitchen, getting the cold bottles out of the fridge. When I close the door, my eyes zoom in on the piece of paper, held up by what looks like a million little heart magnets.

Her husband checklist.

It's handwritten, meaning she actually took the time to

copy it from her phone after her awful date with Mr. Douche-canoe whose name I've already forgotten.

The fact that it's on her fridge, a place where she continuously sees it, doesn't escape my notice. Neither does the sensation of not being able to get enough oxygen. This is what Julia wants, what she's looking for.

A husband—her ultimate goal.

Despite the fact that the sheer thought of being someone's husband still gives me heart palpitations, there's also some flutters in my stomach now, shifting my focus slowly but steadily, and I can only hope they stir me into the right direction.

When I hear her footsteps, I spring into action and meet her at the door.

After locking it, she points her finger at me. "Can we get some breakfast somewhere? I'm starving."

"Yes, ma'am. I was planning on doing that anyway, grumpy butt." I put my arm around her shoulder and pull her into my side as we walk to the parking lot. When we reach my car, I kiss the top of her head before opening the car door for her.

Once she's settled, I rush around to my side and slip into the driver's seat. I'm eager to get us out of here, excited to get to our destination, especially since I know she'll love my surprise.

"You know, maybe my mood would be better if you told me where we're going." She gives me a pointed look, and I smirk at her.

"Nice try. Let's get you some caffeine and sugar. I'm sure you'll feel more human after that, or at least stop trying to bite my head off."

"Very funny." She sticks out her tongue as I drive out of the parking lot.

Half an hour later we're finally on the freeway, heading south. Julia's mood has improved after a large breakfast and an almost equally large coffee.

"So"—she brushes the windblown hair out of her face before closing her window—"where are we going?"

A chuckle escapes my lips. "Really? You think I'm that easy?"

I'm relieved to see a small smile. Happy Julia is so much easier to deal with than grumpy Julia.

She gives a half shrug. "It was worth a try."

"I guess so."

"By the way, I meant to ask you about Ollie." Just like that, her tone is more serious. "Have things improved for you guys? Has he started talking to you again?"

I shake my head, hating the heaviness in my chest every time I think about my best friend. "Not really. I mean, he has to talk to me, but it's always work related. Other than that, he usually leaves the room or ignores me."

"That sucks. It must be hard for you."

She sounds sad, and I take her hand, squeezing it lightly. "It hasn't been a lot of fun, but it'll be okay. You know your brother, he can be stubborn."

She sighs. "He's always been as stubborn as a mule. Some things never change."

Her fingers begin to play with mine, and I enjoy the comfort it brings me. It makes me feel like we're in this together.

"Carter, I'm sorry."

I peek over at her for a second, confused by her statement. "What are you talking about?"

"This whole mess with Ollie. If it wasn't for me, you guys wouldn't be having any issues right now."

If it wasn't for this busy traffic, I'd be pulling over right now, so I could *really* look at her, because I'm having trouble understanding where this is coming from all of a sudden. "I hope you're joking. What's going on with Ollie and me has nothing to do with you. I mean, yes, it's because of what *we* did, but *you* didn't do anything wrong. He just needs to wrap his head around it and get used to the idea of us being together."

She moves around in her seat, leaning across the middle console to rest her head on my shoulder.

The familiarity of having her this close, and being affectionate after I thought I screwed things up, makes my heart beat faster.

This.

This is what I've missed.

This is what I would have missed had I not finally understood Mom's advice about relationships.

It's *everything.*

"Thank you." Her voice is quiet next to my ear.

I turn my head to give her forehead a kiss. "Nothing to thank me for."

"I think there is. We're talking about your best friend here. You guys have been like brothers most of your lives. It makes me sad to know things aren't right with you at the moment."

We both know this situation is anything but ideal, but somehow I'm okay with that. Maybe it's some rite of passage that comes with these circumstances. "Don't worry your pretty little head about it. It'll be all right in the end, I promise. Why don't you close your eyes for a bit? I'll wake you up when we're there."

Just then, a big yawn comes from her mouth. "You really don't mind?"

I chuckle. "Not at all."

Having her this close has already made the trip so much better, even when she starts to softly snore into my ear a few minutes later.

We get to our destination without any major traffic jams, and I park the car as close to the entrance as possible.

I turn off the car and try to glance at her. "Wake up, sleepyhead."

Instead of waking up, Julia turns away from me and snuggles into her own seat.

"Typical." I laugh when she curls into a fetal position. No clue how she manages that with the seat belt on.

After getting out of the car, I walk over to her side and carefully open the door.

"Jules, wake up. We're here." I gently brush the hair out of her face and lean in to give the tip of her nose a kiss. It doesn't have the desired effect though, because she swats me away with her hand.

I study her for a moment. Now that her guard is down, she looks peaceful and a lot less stressed than she has the last few weeks. This looks more like the Julia I grew up with, the fun girl who couldn't laugh loud enough and loved life.

I know everyone changes as they grow up, but I never thought that special spark in her life would be dimmed. But I didn't expect her to go through the hardship she—and Oliver

—went through either. It sucked the life out of both of them for a while. Oliver just dealt with it better in the end, or maybe he didn't. Maybe he wouldn't have been so overprotective of Julia had their dad been around. We'll never know.

Trying again, I gently rub her arm, and she finally stirs. "Open your eyes, sweet girl. I promise you don't want to miss this."

A low groan escapes her lips, and it takes her another minute to finally look at me through her thick, dark lashes.

The corners of her mouth lift into a small smile when her eyes meet mine. "Hey."

"Hey yourself."

She sits up and gazes around. I see the exact moment when she realizes where we are. Her eyes widen and her mouth falls open. She squeals as she unbuckles her seatbelt in a hurry to push her face all the way into the windshield. "We're going to Disneyland?"

I nod when she looks at me. "Surprise."

Julia's always loved visiting the theme park, dragging her parents—and Ollie and me—here as often as she could, even when we were older.

Her eyes glaze over when she leaps out of the car and into my arms. Since I didn't expect it, she tips me off-balance, and we both fall onto the warm asphalt.

"This is already the best date ever." Her lips come down onto mine, and after a few moments, our kiss ends way too soon for my liking. "Thank you."

"No, thank *you*." My grin is probably as wide as hers as our excitement blends together. "I thought there wouldn't be any making out today?"

"Carter, you brought me to freaking Disneyland for our date. You deserve a big bonus for your efforts alone." Her smile is one of the largest I've ever seen, emptying my mind of all concerns and worries.

"It definitely has its advantages when you know your date as well as I know you." I wink at her.

Her eyes sparkle when she gives me one more kiss before getting up. "Can we go now?"

She bounces on her feet, making me laugh. "Of course. Let's go."

Chapter Twenty-Seven

JULIA

*M*y face hurts from smiling all day long, and I can't remember the last time I was this happy. Carter's officially the biggest trooper in history, going on whatever ride I pointed at, no matter if it was a thrill ride and I screamed his ear off, a slow ride where I felt like a kid again, or a water ride where we got soaked in three seconds flat.

I didn't realize how much I missed this place until we walked through the entrance. The familiarity was so overwhelming, I was sniffling for a few minutes. It was like my parents were there in spirit with me, the memories of them following me around and making this even more special.

I remember scoffing when my mom said that one day my own husband would take me to Disneyland, maybe with a few kids in tow. When I asked her what if my husband didn't like Disneyland, she looked at me and laughed. "Jules, you'll end up with a man just like your dad who'll do anything for the one he loves. You won't accept anything less, and the man you love won't give you any less."

Carter and I are brand new at this dating thing, but I still think they'd be happy for me . . . for us. Because Disneyland is the first place he's taken me to.

When Carter told me we'd have dinner at Goofy's kitchen where Mickey helps out as a chef, I jumped on him once more, not caring about the crowd around us.

No one has ever done anything this thoughtful for me.

No one.

Ever.

When the fireworks around us slowly come to an end, I let out a heavy sigh, sad when the video projections on the buildings start to disappear along with the music.

"Hey." Carter's voice is quiet compared to all the noise around us. "Come here." He wipes his thumbs across my cheeks and studies me. "I hope those are happy tears."

I swallow the lump in my throat. "I didn't even realize I was crying. Definitely happy tears though."

Under other circumstances, or more so with any other person, I'd be embarrassed about bawling like a little baby, but not with Carter. This isn't the first time I've noticed how much it helps we've known each other for so long. It puts me at ease like nothing else and has allowed me to be me, no holding back.

Dropping my head on his shoulder, I kiss his throat. "Seriously . . . this was the perfect ending to a perfect day. Thank you so much."

"You're so welcome." He pulls me closer into his chest, and I welcome the warmth of his body.

"I'm sad it's already over. I know we've been here all day,

but it feels like there's still so much to explore." I'm in my own bubble, barely noticing the commotion around us, everyone trying to get past us to make their way to the exit.

Carter pushes me gently away from him and turns me around so I face him. "It doesn't have to end yet if you don't want it to."

My thoughts freeze for a moment as I look at him. "What do you mean?"

"Well, I was kind of hoping for this reaction and reserved us a hotel room. That way we can come back tomorrow for another day."

There is so much I want to say, but the words are stuck in my throat as I gaze at him, unable to believe his offer.

When I keep mum, his eyes flicker away from me. "Only if you want to, of course. We can just hop in the car and head back home if you prefer that. No problem at all."

"Are you serious right now?" The words come out in a rush and a lot louder than I intended, and Carter laughs. I throw my arms around his neck and pull him as close as I can. His heart beats quickly against my own as I try to squeeze his much bigger body as best as I can.

A burst of giggles stirs in my belly, mingling with a thousand butterflies. "I'd absolutely love to stay another day. Are you sure you want to go through all of this craziness again tomorrow?"

He breathes out an easy laugh, tickling the sensitive skin under my ear, before pulling me back and holding me at arm's length. "Are you kidding me? Today was awesome."

Since I didn't think this was Carter's definition of a fun day, I raise my eyebrows in question.

He pokes me in the ribs, and I giggle again. "Really. You

had fun, so I had fun. It's as simple as that." He holds his arm out for me, and I wrap my own arm around him, snuggling into his body. "Let's get the car and drive to the hotel to check in."

"Wait a second." I halt mid-step, making him stop too. "Is that why you asked me to bring another set of clothes with me, in case I got dirty?"

His chuckle is low, his eyes sparkling mischievously. "Maybe?"

"Well played. I'll give you that. Even though I wouldn't have cared about wearing the same clothes again if it meant we could stay another day in the happiest place on earth."

"I know, silly. Now let's go." He pulls me back into the walking crowd as my heart is ready to burst into a million pieces out of pure joy.

Disney's Grand Californian Hotel is just around the corner, and the concierge at the check-in desk informs us they even have their own entrance to the adventure park.

I'm in heaven.

Even more when we get to the suite, which doesn't just have top-notch amenities, but is also decorated with all sorts of Disney details. It's stinking cute, and I can't help myself from taking pictures of everything.

I'm still taking it all in when Carter gives me a kiss on the cheek. "I'm going to take a shower."

The spray turns on a moment later in the bathroom while I gaze out the window into the night and the few lights that are still on in the park. Even after spending all day out there, feeling like a child once more—carefree, loved, and simply happy—I still have a hard time wrapping my head around the fact that Carter brought me here.

To the place he knows means so much to me.

The same place I begged both him and my brother to go to every year, even when it wasn't "cool" anymore.

You won't accept anything less, and the man you love won't give you any less. How I wish my mom was here to laugh and cry with.

Noise coming from the bathroom pulls me out of my thoughts, leaving only one thing on my mind.

Carter.

The man who went out of his way to make this date as special as it could possibly be, earning about a million extra points in my book with his thoughtfulness.

My gaze flies to the bathroom door that's not closed completely. I imagine Carter in the spacious shower, the hot water cascading down his beautiful body . . . If it wasn't for my own stupid rule, I'd—

I made the dang rule, so I might as well break it.

My clothes are off in two point five seconds, and I sneak into the bathroom as quietly as I can.

Carter's sculpted back faces me, and I'm a little giddy he hasn't seen me yet. That bubble quickly bursts as the glass door lets out the longest squeak in history when I close it behind me.

His head snaps around so fast, I'm worried he might have hurt it before my name falls from his lips.

I grimace and wave at him. "Hi there."

A laugh breaks from his chest as I shake my head at my awkwardness.

At least, he finds it amusing.

When his gaze finds mine again, it's so heated, I feel it in every single cell of my body.

Even more so when he takes my hand to pull me closer. "What are you doing, Jules? Are you naughty?"

I tilt my head to the side and stare up at him, a hum vibrating in my throat. "What if I am?"

His smirk might be the sexiest thing I've ever seen. "I wish I could say I'd be all noble and leave you to your shower before we make a mistake, but you're too much of a temptation, and I want you too much. Only if you're sure though. If you're not, say the word, and I'm out of here."

"Never." I don't give him a chance to say another word when I drop to my knees and take matters into my own hands so to speak. And mouth. Soon, I'm relishing in Carter's groans and his fingers in my hair until he gets impatient and pulls me back up.

Holding my chin securely in his hand, he looks down at me, his pupils so dark, the blue is barely noticeable. "You're a little vixen, you know that? Putting your mouth on me like this. What am I going to do with you?"

I open my mouth to reply, when he closes the distance between us and captures my lower lip with his teeth before sucking it deeply into his mouth, eliciting a low moan from me. All conscious thoughts fly from my brain when Carter devours my mouth with an intensity that makes me feel like I'm floating.

When his hard length pokes at my belly, I wrap one leg around his hip, silently urging him to give us both what we long for so badly. As he grabs me under my butt, I wrap my other leg tightly around his body too, barely having enough time to take a breath before he drives into me.

He's relentless as we both chase our high, the intensity between us passionate and a little scary.

When my legs go weak, I have the distant thought that it might not be from this encounter that's so incredibly sexy, I want to savor this memory for the rest of my life. The way he looks at me, the strong eye contact he holds, the yearning on his face so intense it's almost overwhelming. Touching me in a way that's more powerful than anything I've ever experienced before.

"Now, Jules." His words barely make it past his gritted teeth as the orgasm rips through me with such a force, I almost expect us both to land on the floor in one big mushy pile.

Instead, Carter holds on to me, gently pushing me against the cold wall before leaning his forehead on mine as we both listen to our harsh breathing slow down.

"Best shower ever." Carter's voice sounds hoarse, his exhales tickling my chin.

The only thing I manage to do is hum in agreement, utterly spent.

"Let's get cleaned up."

Puckering my lips, I barely reach his nose to give it a small kiss. "I'm not sure I can move."

Carter chuckles, slowly easing out of me while I untangle my legs from him, stretching out my legs until my toes reach the tile.

His hands are around my waist, still supporting me while I wait for the feeling to come back into my legs. "You okay?"

"I will be in a minute I think."

Where's that built-in shower bench when you need it?

Once I'm certain I can stand on my own, we take turns washing our hair and bodies, Carter never missing a chance to run his fingers down my body or patting my butt. When we're done, we wrap up in fluffy robes and lie on the king-sized bed.

I stare at the ceiling and groan. "I don't want to move again."

"Not even for room service?" Carter's face appears in my vision, a sly smile on his face as he leans down for a kiss.

"Well . . . if you ask me like that, I'm sure I could move a little." I giggle, something I've done more today than in the last few years combined.

He brushes a wet strand of hair out of my face and wiggles his eyebrows. "So . . . does that mean there are no rules for tonight?" He smirks at me and wiggles his eyebrows.

I'm trying hard to look contemplative but fail miserably and chuckle instead. "I guess you can say that. You're very hard to resist on a normal day, but then you take me to my favorite place in the whole world? I'd say that deserved a rule-breaking of the highest form."

He studies me for a moment. "I hope you know I'd never expect anything from you in return. I'd never want you to do something out of some form of obligation."

I sit up at his words and shake my head. "Oh goodness, no. You know I would never do anything because I think it's expected of me."

"Just wanted to make sure we're on the same page. I wouldn't want to pressure you like that." The corners of his mouth lift in a smirk. "Now come back down here." He pulls on my arm, and I lie back beside him.

We look at each other, and I wrinkle my nose. "You know, I didn't really like my own rule anyway, but I thought it would be important for us."

Taking one of my hands, he brings it to his mouth for a

soft kiss. "No point in denying how much I hated the rule from the second you said it, but I understand why you did it. And that's exactly the reason why nothing else is going to happen tonight, even though I already know it's going to be pure torture for me. I'll probably need a really cold shower in the morning. By myself this time. No more sneaking up on me like you did earlier."

Just the thought of our shower session makes my body tingle in places I thought wouldn't tingle for a while. "I know you liked my little surprise as much as I did."

"Are you kidding me? I loved every minute of it."

My face grows hot at his words. "I'm glad. I enjoyed it too. A lot."

His hands capture my cheeks, and he gives me one of the softest kisses anyone has ever given me. It's a kiss that leaves me breathless, the emotions behind it nearly overwhelming me again like in the shower.

Something has changed, every little touch, look, or gesture affecting me in a way that makes me feel safe but also a little anxious. If his wide eyes are anything to go by, he's just as overwhelmed as I am.

After another long moment of wordlessly staring at each other, I blow out a puff of air and give him a shaky smile. "Should we take a look at the menu?"

He gives me a once-over, and I playfully slap his arm. "Will you stop it already?"

"Sorry. I'll be good now, I promise." He gets the menu from his nightstand but gives me a serious look before handing it to me. "Just know that this is important to me, more important than having sex. I want to give *us* a real chance."

His words stun me for a moment before I manage to swallow my feelings that threaten to bubble over. This day has turned me into an emotional mess. Lifting one of my hands, I gently run it over his stubbled cheek. "I feel the same, which is the reason I came up with this silly rule, not that *I* was able to follow it for long."

The smile on his face is slow and sexy, once more not helping the situation one bit.

"Would you stop looking at me like that already?" I throw my hands in the air and hop off the bed, motioning with my hand for him to give me the menu.

Carter laughs, but gives in to my request.

We order what seems like half the menu and enjoy our quiet night in, breaking my rule once more.

Again, my fault.

Chapter Twenty-Eight

CARTER

*S*aying our first date was a success might be the understatement of the year.

No, scratch that.

Understatement of the century.

We had another fun-filled day before heading back to Malibu. It's impossible to deny how things have changed in one week. We spend as much time together as work allows, and I'm enjoying this new routine of meeting up at her place after a long day of work, not to mention relaxing together on the weekend.

That means I spend most of my time at Julia's place, and she keeps pointing out how much money I'm wasting on my hotel room. Of course, she's got a point, but I'm planning on rectifying that as soon as I can.

After all the crap I gave Ollie about doing this exact same thing with Cora and how boring it must be, I finally get it. I can't imagine there being anything more relaxing than winding down together with a good meal, a great movie, and of course, some mind-blowing sex.

"Carter. What are you still doing in bed?" Julia walks into the room with a towel wrapped around her body and another one around her hair, her eyes wide when she sees me.

I don't say anything back and shrug. My eyes travel up and down her body, taking in the tanned skin and curves. Curves I wouldn't mind devouring once more, still not satiated after the sex we had when I got back early from work.

It was weird to go to work this morning after spending all weekend with her. Not in a bad way, just different. But then, I got my first taste of that last week after our Disneyland trip.

When I'm with her, real life almost disappears, and I wonder if I'll ever get enough of this woman.

"Stop ogling and get ready. Neither the sex nor the catnap was planned, and my brother won't be happy if we're late for dinner. It's a miracle he invited us at all, so we probably don't want to push our luck just yet." Gazing out the window for a moment, a deep frown etches her forehead before she snorts. "Even though I'm almost certain this is Cora's doing. Ollie is way too much of a butthead to come around this quickly by himself."

Things have been going well with us since our first official date—even though I definitely don't consider that the start of *us*, it probably began way earlier than I even realize—but this fight with her brother is harder on her than she admits. I'm not happy about it either, but I'm also not concerned about it. But then it's her brother and not mine.

Although, I guess that's not strictly true. I do get it. One of the things their dad impressed upon Ollie was how to care for Julia, how to not only love her but respect her, even though she was younger. And the feeling is mutual.

Yes, they fought. Still fight. But there's always been a much deeper devotion between them. And I know that's what Jules worries about the most. That their fierce connection will be lost. But it won't be. Ollie won't allow that to happen, and that's what I'm trusting in.

I get out of bed and walk to where she's rummaging through her dresser. My footsteps are quiet, swallowed up by the plush cream carpet. Her body shivers when I come up behind her. "Stop worrying about it so much. It's all good. In the end, it doesn't really matter if Cora's behind it or not. The most important thing is that he agreed to do it, and we get to spend some time with him. Both of us, *together*. I'll be right there beside you the whole time. All right?"

She straightens and I put my arms around her, kissing her bare shoulder, wanting to reassure her. If I could, I'd take all the problems and worries away from her.

Right here. Right now. *Forever.*

Thankfully, she relaxes and leans her head back on my chest. "I just want things to go back to normal. I hate having two separate camps with you guys. It makes me feel like I'm choosing between the two of you, and I don't like it. Not one bit."

I squeeze her, nuzzling her neck, loving the fact that I know this soothes her. "No one is making you choose between us. It won't ever come to anything like that, I promise."

I hate seeing her like this, especially knowing I'm part of the reason. I'm half of the problem. If it wasn't for me, she wouldn't have any issues with her brother. The thought alone makes my stomach churn.

Julia puts her hands on mine, brushing her thumb over my skin. "Hey. Don't you start worrying now too."

Shaking my head, I let out a breath, making her shiver as it hits her exposed skin. To distract both of us, I lower my head and start trailing soft kisses up and down the curve of her neck. I inhale deeply, loving her fresh scent that reminds me of a tropical beach vacation.

Maybe we should take one of those once we have some downtime. I don't think I've ever thought of going on a vacation with a woman before, but it feels right. Imagining it makes me . . . happy. Like pretty much everything concerning Julia does.

Her pulse quickens under my lips, and knowing I'm the one doing this to her is a major ego boost.

"Carter." My name falls from her lips in a breathy whisper, making me push even farther into her, sucking on her skin a little harder. "We need to stop."

Her words don't sound convincing, but sadly, my mind chooses to intervene too, forcing the rational part of my brain to take over. With a frustrated groan, I let go of her neck and take a small step back.

The same frustration and desperation is mirrored in Julia's eyes when she gazes at me over her shoulder. "Rain check?"

After a resigned nod, I give her cheek a kiss and squeeze her butt, making her squeal. "I'll be good now, I promise."

I hold up my hands and move away so we can both get ready.

Oliver opens the door and stares at us for a moment before springing into action. "Hey, guys. Come on in."

The words come out slightly grumbled, but at least, he traded the frown for a small smile.

Progress.

"Hey, Ollie. It's so good to see you." Julia goes in for a quick hug that looks a bit unnatural for them, but it's better than the glare he's shooting me over her shoulder.

For now, I'm happy he remains calm at the sight of his sister and me together. "Thanks so much for inviting us."

Another grumble from Oliver as we stand in the doorway in awkward silence.

It's a little odd being at the house when he kicked me out three weeks ago.

"Are you guys planning on staying out there all night? Come on in already." Cora's voice comes from somewhere inside the house. Judging by the smell permeating the air, my guess is the kitchen.

Since I was usually the one cooking here, I doubt Oliver has donned an apron for us.

I put my hand on Julia's lower back and give her a gentle push so we can finally go inside. She takes the lead, and Ollie walks silently next to me, immediately joining Cora's side when we get to the kitchen.

Cora greets us with a big smile. "I hope you're hungry. I might have gone a little overboard. But what can I say, I love cooking." She shrugs and chuckles.

Julia walks over to the sink and washes her hands. "Is there anything we can help you with? Anything else to prep?"

I follow Julia's lead and wash my hands too. "It smells great."

Cora shakes her head. "Not really. It's all done, but thank you. We just need to put the food on the table if you want to help with that."

I look at all the dishes she points at and laugh. "You weren't exaggerating, were you? Have you been in the kitchen all day?"

"Carter's right. You didn't have to make all of this for us." Julia squeezes Cora's arm and chuckles. "It looks awesome though. I can't wait to dig in."

Cora's smile could light up the whole room. "I wasn't sure what everyone felt like, so I made different pizzas, salads, appetizers, and desserts. Ollie helped a lot too though when he got home, so I can't take all the credit." She sends him an adoring look that he returns.

For a moment, I wonder if that's the same way Julia and I look at each other.

Oliver bends down to kiss Cora's cheek. "I just cut a few things here and there, babe. You can hardly give me any credit for that."

My gaze flickers to Julia, who's beaming at the sight of the couple in front of us, without a doubt happy to see them together like this. I'm happy for him too though. They really are a great couple.

Cora gives Ollie a quick kiss before clapping her hands. "Shall we? Everyone grab something so we can get started."

With four people, it doesn't take us long until we're seated. Even though the dining table can easily seat six to eight people, the food still barely fits.

We all dig in, and I can't stop gazing at Julia. She's clearly enjoying the food, continuously closing her eyes to savor the flavors.

I might watch her eat all night if she keeps going like this.

Grabbing her water, she takes a drink before setting the glass back down. "Cora, this is so good. You'll have to give me the recipes for everything. I can't decide what I like best."

"I'm so glad you like it. I'd be happy to give you the recipes. Most of it is super easy. I really like to cook, but I'm also super lazy, so I prefer easy dishes that don't take forever to make." Cora chuckles and looks at us, waving her hands in our direction. "Enough about me though. Did you guys do anything fun recently?" She looks at Julia and winks.

We haven't talked a lot about Cora, so I'm not sure if she knows what we've been up to or not.

Julia gives her a delightful smile in response. "We did actually. Carter took me on a date to Disneyland last weekend and we ended up staying for two days."

Oliver's fork stops midway to his mouth as he gapes at us. It takes him a few moments to regain his composure before he clears his throat. "Wow. That's . . . great. You stayed there the whole weekend?" His eyes flicker to me before focusing back on his sister.

Julia, of course, can't hide her absolute joy and exuberance, gracing us with the same goofy smile she gets every time she thinks about the trip. "Ollie, it was soooo amazing. We did everything you can possibly imagine, went on a lot of the old rides, and tried the new ones too. Carter didn't complain once. It was awesome. Perfect really."

Thankfully, he gives her a genuine smile in return, allowing them to share a moment. I take this as a good sign, hoping things will get better from here on—at least for the two of them. Ollie's behavior tonight makes it seem like Julia was right, and it was mainly Cora's doing that brought us together tonight.

Ultimately, it doesn't really matter though as long as it helps smooth things over so everything can change for the better. It also makes me incredibly grateful to Cora for trying to fix our relationships. It doesn't have to be her problem, but she's made it hers too. Such a good deed. She's such a great counterbalance to Ollie's somewhat inflexible nature. It makes me wonder if Julia and I complement each other similarly.

"How's the house-hunting going?" Cora's eyes are fixed on me.

I choke on the drink I just took and feel everyone's gaze on me. *Way to go, Carter. It's just a simple question.* "I'll catch up this week with everything. The hotel is obviously only temporary."

Cora shoots Oliver a look when I mention the hotel, but he avoids her gaze and stays silent.

We polish off an impressive amount of food, while Cora carries most of the conversation for the night, even though I admit that Ollie's tried. When they refuse any help from us to clean up, Julia and I get ready to leave.

The goodbye seems a little less awkward than the welcome, and Oliver even gives me a small smile and a nod. That's more than I've gotten from him since I dropped the bomb about his sister and me, so I take it.

He really does like to hold his grudges.

But I'm sure things will be back to normal soon.

Chapter Twenty-Nine

JULIA

"*H*ow do you feel about tonight? Do you think it went well?" My words hit the darkness of my bedroom, knowing Carter isn't asleep yet. He's behind me, his arm tightly wrapped around my middle.

He exhales, his breath tickling my skin. "I think so."

Neither one of us approached the topic as we drove back to my apartment, following our night routine before slipping into my queen-sized bed—which won't be big enough for the two of us forever.

Even though we're alone in the room—in the whole apartment—we both whisper. I wonder if it has something to do with the late time of the day, the blackness surrounding us except for the nightlight shining through the door from the hallway. I was so used to having an en-suite bathroom that I ran into something more than once when I had to use the bathroom in the middle of the night. So, nightlight in the hallway it is.

Carter moves his hand away from my stomach but keeps it loosely on my waist. "You don't think it went well?"

I turn around to face him, focusing on whatever I can make out in the darkness. Then, I think about his question and sigh. "I've been thinking about it ever since we left Ollie's house, but I'm still not sure. I don't think it went terribly, but I had hoped it would be better than it was. Maybe it's just me, and I'm a little off today."

Carter brushes his hand across my cheek, his voice calm. "Give it some time. I'm sure it'll be like old times before you know it. He's seen us together now and didn't lose it, so I think that means we're over the worst. And I'll take that for now. It's definitely a good first step."

"You're right. It really did go well when you look at it that way. I guess it was stupid of me to expect things to just go back to normal."

His hand stills. "Hey, there's nothing wrong or stupid about that at all. You just want your relationship with your brother to be okay again, as anyone would. I want it too, but I've also butted heads with him more often than you have, so I'm used to him needing a while to cool off. Forcing it never really works."

I lean into his hand, loving how the warmth of his skin seeps into my own.

Just then, his phone lights up on his nightstand, and Carter sits up to look at it, a small smile pulling at his lips at whatever he's reading. He types something before groaning. "Dang battery. I better get the charger. Do you need anything from the kitchen?"

"Some water would be nice, thank you." The words come out a bit rough, and Carter nods.

"Of course. Be right back."

Usually, I watch his retreating back, but this gnawing

feeling has me glancing at his phone on the bed instead. The way he smiled at whatever he was reading . . . it was that same shy smile he so seldom shows. And usually he leaves his phone in the kitchen at night, but tonight he wanted to keep it on him. Different what-if scenarios shoot through my head, one more unwelcome than the next, each making me feel sick to my stomach.

Goodness, I'm not even sure where these thoughts are coming from right now. This whole evening has thrown me off.

Just then, the screen lights up again, the words clear for me to see on the lock screen. **Can't wait to show you what I got. See you in the morning.**

The screen is dark again by the time Carter comes back and hands me a glass.

"You okay?" The concern in his voice is unmistakable, but suddenly, my brain's a total mess, going so fast I can barely make out a thought.

The words of the message blink like a neon sign in my mind, weaseling their way into my head. Into my heart. Even though I know this is irrational, I'm unable to keep the seed of doubt from planting.

Suddenly, I feel like I can't get enough oxygen, a foreign pressure weighing on my chest.

"Do you want to talk about it?" Carter touches my shoulder, and I find every ounce of control not to flinch.

"Not really." I don't want to tell him about the irrational jealousy and fear I'm still trying to fight, trying to convince myself it was nothing. He probably thinks this is still about my brother anyway.

Carter brushes over my hair. "You know you can talk to me about anything, right?"

I nod, even though I'm not positive he can see me. "I know."

I'm sure he isn't happy about my answer, but he doesn't push.

And that's exactly what I need, which is hard when we're together in bed.

We're quiet for a moment before he speaks again, "Let's go to sleep. Maybe that will help."

"Sounds good." After a moment, my doubts win. "Are we still meeting for lunch tomorrow, or will you be too busy with appointments?"

"Nope, we're still good. It should be an easy day, and I'll be at the office all morning."

"Okay."

And then I'm numb.

Because he just lied to me.

Why did he just lie to me?

Maybe I should have asked him straight out, but instead, I try to trick my brain into thinking that nothing has changed.

I close my eyes.

Everything will be okay.

Except that the man who hates to lie and values honesty just lied to me.

"Thanks for coming, CJ." Oliver gets both of our surfboards out of his truck and hands mine to me.

"You know there isn't a better way to start the day." The words come out automatically like they always do, but I suddenly wonder if they're still true. Lately, things have evolved around Julia a lot more, and I've really enjoyed waking up next to her in the morning.

I've spent the occasional night with a woman, but breakfast was usually the latest I could make myself stay. For starters, I'm not the biggest cuddler, and overnight stays always seem to equal exactly that. And then it's almost as if the expectations change by the hour too. The longer I stay, the more the woman thinks I'm into her.

Everything is the opposite with Julia, and I can't seem to spend enough time with her. It's always been like that though. Since she's my friend, I'm used to spending time with her. That makes it completely normal and natural that I'd enjoy being with her a lot more than a random woman, right?

"Are you gonna stand there like an idiot all morning?

We're gonna miss the sunrise." Oliver pushes my wetsuit into my chest and starts walking toward the water with his board, already clad in his wetsuit. "Hurry up."

I put it on with lightning speed, grab my board, and run after him. The water welcomes me despite its chilly temperature, sending a quick shiver through my body. At least it clears my head at the same time, and my focus is solely back on the ocean and my best friend, who's a few feet ahead of me. I paddle after him, welcoming the soft wind in my face as I catch up with him.

I couldn't believe my eyes this morning when I woke up to go to the bathroom and found a text message from Ollie on my phone. **Can't sleep. Morning session?**

Since the universe seemed to be on our side—I mean, what were the odds of me waking up a few minutes after he sent me a text?—I left a message for Jules, got changed, and hopped into my car to meet him at the beach. Ollie brought my gear since it's still stored at his house.

When we're out far enough, we quietly sit on our boards and watch the sun slowly come up in the east. Witnessing the sky change colors never gets old, no matter how many times I've seen it before. It's never quite the same either, the colors painting a different picture every time.

Somehow, it always serves as a reminder for how simple and beautiful life can be.

If we only let it.

"We have to clear the air about Jules." Oliver's voice sounds calm, his gaze still on the sky.

The tension drains from my body, the fact that he sounds almost normal filling me with optimism. "I know."

I'm not sure what he hears in my voice, but he turns his gaze on me, studying me.

He scrubs a hand over his face, his voice gruff. "I'm sorry I've been such an ass. I hope you can understand why it hit me so hard."

This is so typical of him, apologizing for his behavior, even though he's still not completely over the conflict. He's one of the few people I know who are capable of doing that. It's quite impressive really. I usually have to be completely over the problem before I can see straight enough to even consider an apology.

Exhaling loudly, I hold on to the board as a bigger wave comes our way. "I totally get it, so there's nothing to apologize for. I would have been disappointed if you hadn't lost it."

"Really?"

"Yes, man. She's your family, and I definitely don't have a good record when it comes to women. Not to mention that I've never been interested in a relationship. Shit. I wouldn't trust myself either. But this is Jules. Everything's different with her."

Oliver points a finger at me, his face drawn into a serious expression. "That's good, I guess. Just don't play around with her. If you think this isn't going anywhere, just tell her right now. I'm sure she'd be pissed, rightfully so, but at least you wouldn't drag it out and break her heart. That way, I also wouldn't have to hurt you for breaking her heart. I'd hate to do that. So please, do me a favor and figure out your shit."

I hold out my hands in front of me. "Hey. We're talking about Jules here. I don't want to hurt her either, you know that. And I really don't want to screw things up. But don't rip my head off every single time I make a mistake, because I'm sure they'll happen. No one is perfect, and I'm beginning to understand that no relationship is either."

His eyes leave my face in the middle of my little speech, and he's looking out over the water again. Several good waves have already passed us, but neither one of us makes a move to take any of them.

"So." I clear my throat, trying to move the topic away from me, hoping it will allow things to be more normal. "How are things going with Cora? You guys have been extra tight the last few weeks."

The answer is written all over his face and the self-satisfied grin that's spreading. "Man, she's great, isn't she? Do you think it's too early to ask her to move in with me? We've been spending most of our free time together anyway."

His voice is soft when he talks about her, but it really doesn't surprise me. These two seem to be a perfect match from everything I've seen.

"You're asking *me* that?" Pressing my hand over my heart, I chuckle. From the way Ollie joins me, he must have realized how ironic his question is, even more so after the conversation we just had about his sister. I'm definitely the last person to ask for relationship advice.

And yet, I actually feel a sense of relief, or maybe gratitude, that he's asking. He trusts me. And that feels fucking awesome.

"I guess I am." He shrugs. "Speaking of moving. Sorry for kicking you out of the house."

I wave off his words. "No hard feelings, man. You gave me the push I needed to get my ass moving."

"Thanks." He looks relieved.

I'm desperate to tell someone about my plans, but

thankfully, Ollie's distracting me enough to keep me from obsessing over my secret.

He claps his hands. "Now back to Cora. Humor me. What do you think? Too much too fast?"

I grin at his persistence to talk about her, his feelings for her clear as day. Giving his question some serious thought, I focus on the water. The cold is slowly penetrating my body through the exposed pieces of skin, and I start moving around on my board, wanting to get my circulation going.

My mom's conversation is at the forefront of my mind once more. "You know, I actually don't think there is too early, too fast, or too long. Whatever feels right whenever, I guess. I mean, look at my mom. She *finally* seems happy after those awful losers. She suggested trying things and not giving up hope seems to be an essential part of making things work. At least those are my two cents, but what do I know?"

"Seems to me like you know more than you realize." His words sound genuine, and I'm surprised at his praise. "I think I'll ask her. I'm tired of the constant back and forth, and since her place isn't very big, we're usually at my place now all the time. I'm in love with her, and I like having her around. It somehow just makes sense, I guess."

Life is so much better when you can share it with someone you love. It changes everything. Seems Mom was right. Ollie's dating habits weren't that different to mine before he met Cora.

"Sounds like you've got your answer right there." I grin and hold out my fist to him that he bumps with his.

Thankfully.

For a moment, we smile at each other like the idiots we are while the sun rises higher in the sky.

I tip my head in his direction. "But seriously, I think she's good for you. And it's obvious how much you love her. So I'm with you. Looks like it's time to grow up, huh? Time to trade in that bachelor life for something else?"

"It sure looks like it, doesn't it?" He rubs his hands together and turns his board around. "Enough with this girl talk. Are we gonna do this now or what?"

I copy his actions. "You bet. Let's ride those waves."

We surf for about an hour before heading back to the truck. Usually, surfing helps clear my mind.

Our conversation plays on a loop as I head back to the hotel to get ready. As I thought, Ollie and I are sorted, and it's time to get on with my next plan.

Chapter Thirty-One

JULIA

The restaurant is almost bursting at the seams when I get there. When did Tuesday lunch hour become this popular? Carter texted me about ten minutes ago that he got here early and grabbed us a table.

The hostess skillfully walks me through the array of tables inside and out back. Before she even turns into his direction, I see my lunch date sitting at a corner table.

I point toward him. "I see him, thank you."

She nods and leaves, but not before sending an appreciate gaze in Carter's direction, making my stomach churn.

No, Julia. Don't do this again.

I've been having more self-talks in the last fourteen hours or so than I care to admit, unable to forget that mysterious text message Carter got from an unknown number, right before he lied about his plans for today.

I want to give him the benefit of a doubt, but my thoughts have been circulating around the situation over and over again. Waking up by myself this morning, instead of Carter's arms, only worsened my mood.

Being this irrational isn't like me, and it drives me bonkers that I can't get a grip.

At this point, I'm unable to focus on much else, my mind racing to find an answer it's happy with.

More than once, I considered cancelling our lunch date, but I couldn't bring myself to go through with it. Maybe I can work up the courage to ask him straight out, even though the sheer possibilities of outcomes are enough to make me slightly hysterical.

Being exhausted after last night isn't helping, so maybe I'll take a nap when I get home.

When I reach the table, Carter's thankfully preoccupied with his phone and doesn't see me, giving me another moment to pull myself together.

Dressed in black suit pants and a gray button-down, he looks immaculate like always. The matching suit jacket hangs on the back of his chair, and I wonder for about the millionth time how guys manage to wear full suits in the summer. I'd melt in about two minutes.

His hair looks more disheveled than it usually does, and I wonder if he's been running his hands through it a lot this morning, or maybe someone el—

No, no, no. Not going there.

And I know in my heart of hearts that I have no reason to doubt Carter. He's always been a man of his word, and even if he's a flirt, I doubt he'd cheat.

I know this irrational thought stems more from learning that Nate had been testing the waters with another woman before we broke up. I only found out the other day when he sent me a random text to let me know he was dating again. He didn't want me to find out from someone else, which at the time I thought was kind. Thoughtful even. Honestly, I hadn't cared. He even admitted that he'd seen her for a while before we broke up. And again, it hadn't bothered me. I was so not in love with Nate.

But after the unnamed text and then Carter's lie, I began to recall similar behavior in Nate. He had started carrying his phone everywhere with him, and I'd often found him smiling at a text, refusing to say why. He'd come home later than usual on occasion, but I'd never suspected a thing. Now, I know just how naïve I was.

But this is Carter. This is the man who pleaded for me to give us a chance, and logic, gosh, my heart is telling me to stop seeing things where there aren't things to see, but I'm struggling.

He finally looks up, the scowl on his face turning into the smile I love so much when he notices me. "Oh, hey."

"Hi." I wave at him awkwardly, trying my absolute hardest to push these crazy thoughts away.

Carter gets out of his chair and pulls me into a hug. "It's so good to see you."

"Bad day?" My question comes out muffled since I'm pressed into his shoulder, enjoying the moment of closeness despite errant thoughts.

"You can say that." He pushes me back to look at me. "But it's much better now."

Leaning down, he brushes my lips gently with his, and I'm immediately lost in him.

I'm about to wrap my hands around his neck when he breaks the kiss, chuckling.

"This might not be the best place to make out, Jules." He takes my hand and gives my cheek a gentle kiss.

When I peek over his shoulder, several eyes are already on us. How embarrassing. Heat rushes into my cheeks, and I press my lips together. "Sorry. I'm a bit out of it today."

He tilts his head and grows still, observing me. "Everything okay?"

I pull away from him to sit down, Carter mirroring me as I take a large sip of the water on the table. "Yeah, I guess. Actually, I don't know. I haven't been sleeping very well this week, and I think it's messing with my brain. I forgot about some orders, so I'm stressed about how I'll get everything done in time while also trying to keep up with the new orders that keep coming in."

His brow wrinkles. "Is there anything I can do to help? Why didn't you say anything? I didn't know you had trouble sleeping."

I know he wouldn't understand if I told him my reasons. He already has enough on his plate without worrying about me on top of everything. I don't want to be a burden to him.

A warm breeze gently stirs the tablecloth, and I brush my hand over it before shaking my head. "I just need to get more organized and seriously weigh my options about hiring someone to help. Even if it's not for the jewelry-making itself, having someone take the business side off my hands would allow me to focus on the production."

Carter nods, probably happy about business talk. "Absolutely. I'm sure I have some good contacts if you want them."

This time, the smile comes a little easier. "That would be awesome, thank you."

He waves me off and stretches his arm across the table to take one of my hands. "Anything for my girl."

"Your girl?" I repeat his words in a trance as I blankly stare at his face, my insides clenching in a troublesome way.

His smile falls a little at my expression, turning into something else, something more serious. "You've always been my number-one girl. Do you not like it when I call you that?" There's an edge to his tone, and I don't like it.

"What? Yes. I mean, no." A few strands of my hair come out of my ponytail when I shake my head almost violently. "It's cute."

I don't watch his reaction as our waiter chooses that moment to come to our table, taking our orders.

The rest of lunch goes by quickly and mostly consists of small talk. It's a little painful and awkward, so I keep my gaze on my food as much as I can—a veggie burger with fries—even though I'm not really hungry.

As we get ready to leave, Carter fills me in on what happened with my brother.

My lips automatically part in a grin, and I feel like this is the best thing I've heard all day. "I'm so happy he came around and you guys talked it all through."

Carter takes my hand as we walk out of the restaurant. "Me too. There might still be a few awkward moments here and there, but I think the worst is over."

"I agree." My gaze is on my feet, and I'm almost itchy to get back home. Maybe I'm getting sick. I truly need to take that nap. I think knowing it's coming helped get me through this lunch. The news about my brother made it worth it though. "You should have told me earlier. This is huge."

"I know, sorry. I guess I was preoccupied with this meeting I had this morning." He shrugs, and his comment makes me stop halfway to the parking lot.

Is he talking about what I think he's talking about?

"What meeting?" The words are out of my mouth before I can stop them, my heart beating loudly in my chest.

He looks away from me, fidgeting with my hand. "Oh, it's nothing. Just some meeting."

My stomach churns. Crap, I'm going to be sick.

I pull my hand from his and take a step back, needing some room to breathe.

Carter's voice is low when he bends down. "Jules, what on earth's going on? I know something's been on your mind, and it's killing me to see you this unhappy."

When I feel like I can breathe after a few deep inhales, I straighten as much as I can, telling myself to stop being such a wuss.

With my hands on my hips, I keep my voice down, still aware enough of my surroundings to know there could be dozens of eyes on us. "It's just about you and me and . . . us. Everything. I'm confused, and unsure, and angry too. So angry all of a sudden, and I hate it."

His eyebrows draw together and he tilts his head to the side. "You don't like where this is going?"

"That's exactly my problem, because I do. Maybe too much. We've been spending so much time together, and you're sweet, and kind, and I'm falling for you more and more every day. It's so intense, it scares me sometimes." The words just keep coming out of my mouth while Carter's staring at me with wide eyes. "And then there's this whole thing about that text message you got last night and lied about. It started all these thoughts in my head, these scenarios of how this could end badly, and I don't know how to stop it. It's driving me insane and . . . and it's just too much."

Carter stiffens, a panicked expression flittering across his handsome features. "Shit. This wasn't supposed to happen like this. You weren't supposed to find out."

My brain finally catches up with my mouth, not only realizing what I admitted to him, but also how he responded.

My heart feels like someone took a hammer to it, and for a moment I feel like my body isn't working anymore, like everything continues to live around me while I die on the inside.

Carter takes a step toward me.

He reaches for me, but I flinch away. "Let's talk about this."

The last bit of self-preservation kicks in, and I turn around to run to the parking lot across the street.

My focus is on my car, my safe zone. I need to get myself together before I can deal with Carter. My head feels too foggy, the heartbeat in my ears so loud, I can barely hear him yelling.

"Jules, watch out. No."

The sound of screeching tires is the only thing I hear as something hits the side of my body. Pain shoots through me as I tumble onto the hard asphalt.

"Shit. Jules." Carter is suddenly above me, frantic. I've

never seen him like this, the color drained from his face as he turns and yells, "Call nine one one."

Dark spots flash in my vision, and my whole world turns black.

"Where is she?"

I hear Oliver before I see him, his voice identical to the panic I feel deep inside my bones. When he comes to a halt at the front desk, he looks like he's five seconds away from a breakdown.

Not that I can blame him. I had to sit down too when I felt like I couldn't stand anymore without losing it.

When he's done talking to the clerk, his gaze searches the waiting area on the other side of the room until it lands on me.

He heads my way, turning a few heads when he starts yelling at me, "What the hell happened?"

His face is white, completely drained of any color, his eyes frantically moving back and forth between mine when he collapses in the chair next to me.

I open my mouth but nothing comes out.

"CJ, talk to me." He grips my shoulder with a shaky hand, pleading with his eyes.

My head moves left and right on autopilot. I don't feel in

control of my body in general. "I don't know. One minute we're talking, and the next she's running into the street and straight into a car. It all happened so fast, and she wasn't facing me, so I didn't see her face before she collapsed on the ground in a heap."

I barely choke out the words before pressing a fist to my lips, just thinking about what happened, of Julia lying lifeless on the street, makes a wave of nausea roll through me.

He gives me some room, slumping deeper into his chair like something knocked all the air out of his body.

It seems like my brain got a jump start, the words suddenly pouring out of my mouth. "There was all this blood on her head and on the ground. She must have hit it when she fell. And she didn't respond to anything."

Oliver runs his hands over his face, his shoulders dropping. "What did they say? How bad is it?"

"I don't know . . . I just don't know." I exhale a long breath, my own terror bubbling up. I don't think I've fully processed what happened yet.

A million questions fly through my head in a constant loop. Not to mention the many ways today could have gone differently. What I could have said differently. Reacted differently.

Pain funnels into my heart. I can't stop reliving those few minutes that changed my life.

Fear clenches like a tight fist around my chest, and I'm unable to shake it off, no matter how hard I try. "By the time I reached her, she'd already passed out, and the paramedics couldn't tell me anything when they got there. They kept talking about needing to do more tests. I'm not sure if she ever gained full consciousness—they didn't let me ride in the back with her—and once we got here, they wheeled her off right away and told me to wait."

"Shit." His hands go up to his face again, rubbing at his eyes. "Why would she run into the street anyway?"

His eyes are red-rimmed as his gaze bores into mine, waiting for an answer.

I swallow loudly, rubbing my hands up and down my pants. "I . . . I'm still not really sure what happened either. We met for lunch at the Hawaiian Grill. She was a little off but said she hadn't been sleeping well. When we walked to the parking lot, she suddenly started talking about being confused and angry and something about falling for me, and some other stuff."

He groans. "Shit."

"I know. That's what I said."

Ollie's face turns into a sour mask, and I'm afraid he might either attack me or spit in my face. "Your answer was *shit?*"

I cross my arms over my chest before letting them drop again, drumming my fingers on my legs. "Well, yes. But it wasn't about the falling for me part. She said something else . . . and it hadn't even registered what she'd said before. But before I could explain anything, she'd already taken off . . . Fuck."

Oliver's nostrils flare like an angry bull, and I instinctively lean back in my chair, not that it really puts much distance between us.

Before anything else can transpire, a nurse walks over, coming straight for us. "Are you both here for Julia Bradford?"

She's tall with a huge mop of brown hair on top of her

head. I immediately recognize her as one of the nurses that took Julia from the EMTs. She looks tired, like she's been here for more than just a couple hours already.

"Yes." We both shoot up at the same time, a tendril of panic seizing my chest.

"How is she?" Oliver asks.

"She's stable and in her room. I can take you to her if you want. Dr. Miles will be with you shortly to update you on her condition." That's all she gives us before she spins around, expecting us to follow her. Which we do, of course. We're trotting after her like two loyal dogs, not letting her out of our sight.

After going through the security door, it's only a short walk down the hall, Julia's is one of the first rooms after the nurses' station. My breath speeds up when the nurse reaches for the doorknob, blocking our view for a few more seconds until both Oliver and I get our first glimpse of Julia, a collective gasp echoing around the room.

There's only one bed in the room, and Julia looks tiny in it. She's pale, with white gauze wrapped around her head. Several machines beep, cables running from it, the parts attached to her body disappearing under the sheets.

The nurse gives both of us a nod that I tell myself is supposed to be reassuring. "She's sleeping right now, but use the nurse call button if you need anything. The doctor will be with you shortly." Then she leaves, shutting the door quietly behind her.

Almost simultaneously, we both move closer to the bed, quietly staring at her until there's a knock on the door. A lanky man walks in, wearing the typical doctor outfit of dark blue scrubs with a white lab coat. We walk over to him, both of us shaking his extended hand.

"I'm Doctor Miles."

"How's my sister?" Ollie sends the doctor a darting gaze, his voice a little shaky.

The doctor looks at the chart in his hand, writing something on it before closing it. "She's doing okay considering the circumstances. She's been in and out of consciousness, still in shock, which is normal. We did the FAST exam when she came in—our sonography test that allows us to check for serious abdominal injuries—so we know there aren't any internal bleeds. All signs for a mild concussion are there, but all in all very promising. Some bed rest, fluids, and a mild pain reliever should allow her body to pull through this rather fast. Her head wound looked a lot worse than it was, which is common for head injuries. She was lucky nothing worse happened, and miraculously, the baby is doing well too. We were able to find a strong heartbeat."

He looks at us with a small smile on his face, obviously happy to give us the good news.

When neither Ollie nor I react with anything but stunned silence, he tilts his head and furrows his eyebrows. "I take it you didn't know about the pregnancy?"

The question earns him simultaneous headshakes from my best friend and me. Our gazes meet, and even though I didn't think it was possible, he has even less color in his face now than he did before. As if on reflex, I shake my head again, silently conveying I really had no clue.

Oliver looks back at the doctor and clears his throat, his

voice shaky. "Do you know how far along she is?" Then he turns to me and asks on a shaky breath, "Is it yours?"

Fuck. Three words. *Is it yours?*

Is it mine?

The enormity of what he's implying hits me like a freight train straight into the chest. The possibility of Julia's ex being the father didn't even cross my mind. It takes everything in me to keep the nausea at bay.

The doctor checks the chart again, his right index finger quietly moving across the paper. "It's hard to be sure at this point without additional tests, but it looks like she might be around seven weeks. She'll need to see a gynecologist to ensure the baby's all right, but at this point it looks promising. We're going to run some more labs to make sure she goes home with everything she needs."

I faintly hear Oliver thanking the doctor before he leaves the room.

The room isn't huge, and it only takes me a few steps to walk from one side to the other, which I do. Repeatedly.

Back and forth.

Back and forth.

When the walls close in on me, and I almost blindly grab for something to steady me, I can feel the freak-out build in my chest. "I was just getting used to the idea of being in a relationship, but a baby. Fuck."

Ollie grabs me and pushes me into a chair. "Sit down before you faint, asshat. You look as white as a sheet. You're lucky Jules was just in an accident, or I'd beat the crap out of you."

He grabs his hair and looks like he's ready to pull it out.

"A baby. Shit. I'm gonna be an uncle." He chuckles, but I'm too out of it to be able to tell if it's a happy one or not.

Julia's pregnant.

She's having a baby.

My baby.

I'm going to be a father.

Chapter Thirty-Three
JULIA

My brain feels fuzzy when I wake up, my head throbbing like a marching band is parading in it. At least this time, the extreme disorientation is gone, and I know where I am.

I woke up for the first time a few hours ago in the ER before passing out again, tired beyond measure—but not until a nurse and doctor saw me to tell me what happened.

This time, I also know I'm not alone even before I open my eyes. I take a deep breath, knowing the familiar scent all too well. But having the confirmation right in front of me when I finally manage to peel open my eyes is a million times better.

Carter.

He's in a chair next to the bed, staring at me. His hair is a mess, the expression on his face pained. He blinks several times before jumping out of the chair to get closer.

"Hey." His voice is raspy, like he hasn't used it in a while. I wonder if it sounded off to him too when he clears his throat almost immediately.

I hold out my hand to him, and he grasps it desperately between both of his. "Hey."

My eyes drift behind him for a moment before focusing back on him.

"Ollie will be right back. He went outside for some fresh air and to call Cora."

Then he looks at me again like he can't believe I'm awake. His hands shake around mine, and he swallows several times before letting out a soft curse. "Don't you ever do anything like that to me again, you hear me? You scared the ever-loving shit out of me, and I'm not sure I'll ever recover from this."

When I notice his shiny eyes, tears well behind my eyelids too, and I want nothing more than to give him a big hug. I'm not sure how possible that is with the IV and blood pressure reader attached to me.

The lump in my throat is hard to get past, but somehow I manage. "I'm so sorry."

The first hot tear runs down my cheek, and Carter manages to give me the most gentle and careful hug anyone has ever given me.

"Tell me if it hurts, okay? The last thing I want to do is cause you even more pain." His words are a soft whisper next to my ear, and I nod into his shoulder, sniffling nonstop until I manage to calm down.

"Luckily, the pain isn't too bad, at least until I move. The hip pain and headache are the worst, but it's manageable." The car that hit me wasn't driving very fast, so I was very lucky and "only" have a mild concussion and some nasty bruises and scrapes, but at least, nothing's broken, or worse.

I move around to adjust my position but quickly regret it

when the movement pulls on my IV. "I can't wait until I'm free of these tubes and needles."

He sits back in the chair that's pushed to the bed as close as possible without letting go of my hand.

"I can imagine. They're never fun." After sighing heavily, he regards me with a cloudy gaze. "The doctor told Ollie they'll keep you overnight for observation, but you should be able to go home tomorrow."

"Yes. Lots of bed rest, fluids, and mild pain meds if I need them."

His eyes shut for a moment at my response. "I'm so happy they don't have to keep you for longer."

I look at our intertwined hands. It feels so good to have him here. When I woke up earlier, all I wanted was to see his face so I could apologize to him. To imagine that this happened because of my behavior is beyond embarrassing. Heat creeps into my face as I stare at the ceiling. "I'm so sorry I ran away like that. We wouldn't be here if it wasn't for my stupidity."

"No, no, no. I don't want to hear a peep about that, or for you to even think about it. All that matters is that you recover as quickly as possible. You have to focus on yourself right now and on getting better. Not to mention . . . you know." His gaze flickers to my midsection, and I draw in a sharp breath.

Right before my eyes tear up again as I remember the doctor telling me about the news.

I'm pregnant.

I'm still in denial, because it doesn't feel real. At all. They showed me ultrasound pictures though, proving there's actually a human growing inside of me.

"The baby." My voice is barely audible, my other hand automatically going to my belly, IV be damned.

He nods, his eyes trained on my stomach. "We'll figure it all out, no need to stress about anything. You hear me?" Our eyes meet, the sincerity in his easy to detect. "I'll take care of you, both of you. I promise."

His mouth opens again like he wants to say more, but after the shortest knock in history, the door opens, and my brother rushes in with a frantic look on his face, and I wonder if Carter somehow messaged him.

"Jules." He rushes over to the bed and stands awkwardly at the foot of it. With the table and the machines on one side and Carter on the other side, he has no direct access to me.

Carter reluctantly lets go of my hand, but steps away immediately, making room for my brother.

He pats Ollie on the shoulder. "Here, man, sit down. I'll go find us some coffee."

"Thanks, CJ."

I'm beyond relieved the two of them still seem to be doing well, even after the baby news. The doctor told me he'd informed them, but I had no idea how they took it, and I was honestly half-expecting to see at least one of them with a black eye.

Carter gives us a small smile and heads out the door, my brother immediately jumping to my bedside.

He grabs my hand, and as much as I love my brother, it makes me long for Carter's touch again. It's just not the same. Thankfully, he only squeezes it once before letting go.

Flopping back in the chair, he looks at me with tears in his eyes. "How are you feeling?"

I lift my shoulder in a small shrug. "Okay, I think. Tired

and bruised, but nothing unmanageable to be honest. They gave me some pain medication that's safe for me to take, and it seems to be helping."

He lets out a harsh breath before leaning back and clasping his hands behind his neck. "I can't tell you how glad I am to hear that."

The expression on his face is pure agony when he rubs his eyes with the base of his palms, causing my chest to tighten in a way where even rubbing doesn't make it go away. I've thought about how incredibly hard this must have been on him.

Since we've never been close to the rest of our family—despite the fact that my dad used to work with my uncle—it's always just been us. First us four, and after the accident, only us two. He must have been out of his mind when he got the message about my accident.

"It's okay, Ollie. I'm okay," I try to reassure him, not wanting to see this anguish on his face anymore.

He lifts his head, wiping away the remnants of his tears before taking several deep breaths. "I know, I know. It just all seems so surreal. Not just the accident but the other news too."

"You mean that I'm pregnant? You can say it, you know. You guys are both acting like it's a forbidden thing to talk about or something." I can't help but grimace, and out of nowhere, a chuckle escapes my mouth. It feels really good for a moment, until my head starts pounding, but I manage to keep the flinch to myself.

Thankfully, smiling doesn't hurt. "Looks like we're getting a new family member."

He brushes one of his hands through his hair and scratches the back of his neck. "I know, huh? Crazy."

"Crazy indeed, Uncle Ollie."

He smiles when I say that, and so do I. "I'll be the best uncle ever."

"I have no doubt about that." The words come out tenderly, exactly the way I mean them.

There are still about a million things I'm uncertain of right now, and I know they haven't simply disappeared because of the accident. I'm not sure I'm ready for what's to come, but I do know I have a new priority.

A new reason to keep focused and keep well, both emotionally and physically. No matter what happens, whether I'm with Carter or have to return to the family home, I'm going to love this baby with all of my heart.

The hospital hallway smells as uninviting as it did yesterday, but at least the staff here seem top-notch. They kept Jules overnight as promised, and I know she's thrilled to get out of here. I'm the lucky one who gets to pick her up.

Rounding the corner of her room, I immediately spot her by the window. She's nestled into the corner with her arms crossed in front of her chest and her head leaning against the wall. I come to a stop, watching her in this quiet moment before she sees me.

The desire to be still and let the relief sink in that she's okay—truly okay—hits me as hard as when I first saw her after the accident, even though it feels like I've aged ten years. Seeing for myself she's okay, definitely relaxes me.

"Are you ready to go?" I keep my voice low so I won't startle her, but one of her hands still flies to her chest.

Her eyes flicker to the clock above the door. "Sorry, I wasn't expecting you yet. I must have lost track of time. Let me get my things, so we can head out. If you don't mind waiting, I'm a bit slow right now."

She's been doing this, acting like she's an inconvenience, like the only reason I'm here is because she was in an accident, *and* because she's having a baby. *My* baby. Since I didn't want to cause her any more stress, I haven't said anything.

We haven't really talked about what happened either.

Ollie thought I was crazy not to bring it up, but she doesn't have to deal with everything at once and can work through one issue at a time. After all, she was in a fairly major accident, was hurt badly, and found out she's pregnant.

Every one of those things would be enough for most people to work through at any given time.

Since I'm not planning on going anywhere, I'll wait until she's ready to talk about us, the baby, and whatever else is going on in her beautiful mind. For now, it's enough for me to be able to see she's okay, and to spend as much time with her as possible.

When she's ready, I plan on sweeping her off her feet the way she deserves—both figuratively and literally.

Walking over to her, I put both of my hands on her arms and wait for her to look up at me. "Jules, it's me. Of course, I'll wait for you. Stop driving yourself nuts with all those crazy thoughts flying around in that pretty head of yours."

She brushes a strand of her dark hair out of her face but it falls straight back down. I lift my hand to push it back softly, safely tucking it behind her ear.

"Thank you." She touches the bandage that's wrapped around her head without looking at me, and I wonder if she feels self-conscious about it or if something else is going on.

I've been having a hard time reading her. It's almost like she's trying as hard as she can to block out her feelings, and I hate it.

When she's done, I grab the small bag from the bed and hold out my hand to her.

Thankfully, she takes it. "One of the nurses is waiting with a wheelchair, so let's get out of here. Hospitals freak me out."

I shudder, and one corner of her mouth lifts a little. I swallow the urge to fall to my knees and beg for things to go back to the way they were before this shitshow happened, or rather the way they were before that awkward evening before, but that would only make the situation worse without being helpful.

Patience seems to be the only way to go.

On second thought, I can't be patient about one thing. I stop her before we get to the door. "One sec, Jules. I know this has been incredibly hard for you, and I don't want to add any more stress, but I can't live another second without talking about that text message you saw. The one I lied about."

A fresh round of regret slices through my heart, feeling like it's cutting me open from the inside, displayed in my shaky voice.

Tears well in Julia's eyes at my words, and I've never hated myself more than right now, knowing I've caused her such pain.

Cupping her cheeks as gently as I can, I lower my head to be on her eye level. "Jules. That text was from Linda, the real estate agent. She was looking for houses for me and found one. We met up yesterday morning. The only reason I lied about it was because I wanted it to be a surprise."

Julia closes her eyes, tears spilling over from behind her closed lids as a quiet whimper escapes her mouth. My limbs tremble at the sight. Seeing her like this pains me more than I ever thought anything could.

My voice is weak, the words barely audible when I try to plead with her. "I'm so, so sorry, baby. This is all my fault. I should have just told you the truth. None of this—"

Her hand goes up to cover my mouth as she shakes her head once. "No, don't say it. It's not your fault." She blows out her cheeks, inhaling and exhaling deeply before opening her eyes. Her beautiful brown eyes are still covered in a thick layer of tears, almost glittering as she stares at me. "Your reply to me . . . before the accident . . ."

"It was all about the surprise, about the house. Nothing else, I swear." I lower my head to hers as gently as I can, trying not to put any pressure on hers but unable to stay away. "It was so stupid. I shouldn't have said it like that."

There hasn't been a minute since the accident where I haven't berated myself for what I did, the guilt eating at me until it was almost unbearable.

One of her hands comes up to cover one of mine. "You couldn't have predicted my reaction, Carter. Or the unfortunate timing of the car driving down the street when I decided to run blindly across it. You have nothing to blame yourself for, but thanks for telling me about the message. I should have just asked you, but I was so in my head, not to mention irrational. Since it's so unlike me, I blame it on the early pregnancy hormones, but that's a topic for another day."

A noise in the hallway reminds of where we are.

She blinks. "Let's leave, okay?"

Her posture looks a little straighter, her gaze a little stronger—and I hope I'm not imagining it, but also a little less sad—as she wipes away the remnants of her tears.

Just then one of the nurses stops in front of the door with a wheelchair in front of her. "Hop in, Miss Julia."

There's still so much I want to say but it has to wait until later. For now, I'm happy she can go home, even allowing me to hold her hand. It gives me a glimmer of hope that things might turn out okay.

Julia winces at every bump and corner, and I want to drive at a snail's pace, having pissed off more than one person on the road already. "The doctor told us to make sure you take it very easy, especially since you aren't allowed to take any strong pain medication, which means the pain will stick around for a bit longer. Everyone's there to help you."

She huffs. "Yeah, it's really fine."

On the outside, she seems okay, but we all know better. The way her forehead creases when she thinks no one is watching, how she breathes harder whenever she moves around, or the way she constantly wrings her hands.

Her answer doesn't surprise me in the least. Oliver and Julia are very similar when it comes to pride and accepting help.

Time for my plan to come into action. "Well, I actually wanted to ask you something."

That gets her attention, and she looks at me. "What is it?"

"Well, as you now know I found a house, but since there

are a few things that need to be done first, it will take some time until I can move in."

"It's awesome you found something so fast, and I can't wait to see it. If you want to show it to me . . . of course." Her voice is sweet, and I bask in the sound of it.

"Absolutely. I think you'll like it. Well, I hope you will." I stare at her for a moment, swallowing at the contrast of her tired eyes and her long, dark hair shimmering in the sunlight.

When we stop at a red light, I turn toward her. "Anyway, I was wondering if you'd mind if I bunk with you until my place is done? I'll sleep on the couch, so I won't disturb your sleep. That way I can be there for you too. You know, just in case you need help." I blurt out the words before biting the inside of my cheek, not wanting to ruin this whole plan.

She doesn't say anything for a while, only chewing on her lip.

It feels like hours later when she gives me a small smile. "I know what you're doing, and I really appreciate it, but I really don't need any help. But you're welcome to stay with me until your place is done. I told you before, you're wasting a ton of money on that hotel room."

I give a shaky laugh, grateful she agreed. That's all I wanted. "And as so often, you were absolutely right. Do you want to stop at the Chinese place to pick up some food?"

"Sure. Why not." Her response is immediate, and the small smile remains on her face, which I savor.

It also reminds me of the doctor's advice, to take things one day at a time, which I'm more than willing to do. All I want is for her to be safe and happy, and staying with her is going to be the best chance I have at making sure of that.

We stop to get the takeout and end up getting enough

food to feed a whole football team, but at least that means we'll have plenty of leftovers. When we reach Julia's apartment, she insists on taking one of the food bags while I go to the trunk to remove both of our bags.

She looks from my hands to my face before she smirks. "Seems like someone was a little presumptuous, huh?"

My own smirk at her playful question turns into a huge grin in no time. "I like to call it optimistic and prepared."

"Fair enough."

I almost miss her soft chuckle as she walks away, leaving me to stare after her like an idiot.

After a moment, she looks back at me over her shoulder. "Come on, doofus. You know I have no problem eating most of this stuff by myself."

And there she is. My girl. Throwing out commands in that sassy and adorable way of hers. Grabbing the rest of the food, I quickly catch up with her.

We're going to be fine. More than fine. Awesome.

*T*his pain sucks.

It's funny how you think you've experienced pain until you go through something a lot worse. Then you'd much rather experience the previous kind of pain again since comparably, that suddenly seems like a walk in the park.

But hey, there's always childbirth waiting for me now too.

Needless to say, my mood hasn't been the best since the accident last week.

Even though everyone's been trying their best to help and cheer me up, most days I feel utterly unmotivated and just want to hide in bed all day. The aches and pains, the constant fatigue, and surprise, surprise, this newfound nausea that doesn't seem to go away.

The only good thing is that my head finally feels a little better, and despite feeling like I want to puke my guts out, I actually don't.

The sun shines through my bedroom window, which is usually a good motivator to get me out of bed, but it doesn't seem to help today.

"Suck it up, Jules." I push my hair out of my face, and take a few calming breaths.

I lie there for a moment longer, staring at the ceiling and wondering what Carter's doing out there. I told him to go back to work, but of course, he hasn't. Ollie is one hundred percent behind him on this, so I gave up after a few days of trying. I'm not sure why he wants to stay here with me since it must be incredibly boring for him. All I do is nap, eat, and watch TV in bed. That's pretty much it. Carter's making sure of that.

He's still sleeping on the couch, which was a little awkward at the beginning. On one side, I wanted to ask him to come to bed with me, but on the other side, I wanted to be alone and appreciate him understanding that.

I'm also pretty certain Carter's right about the reasons why sharing a bed right now isn't the best idea. Even in our sleep we gravitate toward each other, and I feel crappy enough as it is. No need to push my luck.

I'm also not completely sure where things stand with us as a couple. He's still affectionate toward me but hasn't brought up my kind of love confession I screwed up majorly, and I'm incredibly grateful for that.

For now, I'm happy with this avoidance game we're playing, at least until I feel a little more like myself.

Hopefully, the pain will start to ease up soon so I can get a good night's sleep and stop feeling like crap.

After a long, warm shower—that takes about ten times longer with me moving like a turtle, not to mention Carter checking in on me to see if I'm okay, pretty much every single time—I feel more human. I'm actually ready to leave my room, ready to face the day, and quite possibly, my new roommate-slash-maybe boyfriend-slash-definite baby daddy.

What a mess.

"There you are." Carter's cheery voice greets me before I've even fully stepped over my threshold. He's walking toward me, a big smile on his face until he looks me up and down, inspecting every inch of me as if he can see what's going on under my clothes. "How are you feeling? Is the pain any better?"

"Not really. Getting hit by a car from one side and then falling onto the ground with the other one wasn't a good combination."

He flinches, a worried expression marring his face. "I can only imagine. I wish I could take away the pain."

I know he would in a heartbeat, because he's that good a person. He always has been. Even when we were kids and my brother once had a scare about possibly needing a new kidney, Carter was right there, offering one of his. Luckily, it turned out to be a false alarm, and all organs could stay with their owners.

I look him straight in the eye to make sure he's really getting my message. "It's not your fault this happened, and I'll get better soon. It's just bruising, and I'm lucky nothing worse happened." I let out a deep breath, happy to have gotten that off my chest. Because I truly am grateful, even though I'm not performing any happy dances.

After studying me for another moment, he nods. "Fine. One more thing, and then I'll zip it. Please promise me you'll let me know if it gets too much so I can help, okay?"

His gaze is alert and his jaw set, and I know there's no point in arguing with him, not that I want to.

I'm actually happy to give him this. "Promise."

"Thank you." The smile he gives me makes my heart skip maybe a tiny bit faster.

Squeezing my hand, he gently pulls on it. "Come on. There's something I wanted to show you. It's nothing major though. I'm probably too excited about it."

We come to a stop at the dining room table where he points excitedly at the contents covering every possible surface. Dozens of my business shipping boxes are lined up, filled with bags of my jewelry.

"Did you . . . did you get my jewelry ready for me to send out?" My mouth hangs open at the mere thought of anyone doing such a thing for me, but especially Carter, since it's clearly not his thing.

I press my fingers to my smiling lips, warmth tingling in my limbs.

Carter pulls me closer, pointing at every little bag and box as if I didn't already see them. "You mentioned you were really behind with your orders, so I found your finished orders, packed them ready to be shipped, and I printed out your new orders too, so you can get started on them as soon as you're up for it."

Tears spring into my eyes at the thoughtfulness, but I wipe at the corners of my eyes before they spill over. "You really didn't have to do this, but I appreciate it more than I can tell you. Thank you."

He waves me off in the nonchalant way that's typical for Carter. "Don't mention it. I'm just happy I could help. I left everything unsealed, so you can double-check them before we tape it up. And then I can drop them off at the post office."

I open my mouth to say something, but he's on a roll, still babbling away. "And I'm also meeting up with the brother of a good client of ours in the next few days. He's in his last year of business school and looking for a job to make some extra money. He sounds like a good fit, so I thought I could check him out and see if he'd be a good fit for you. You're going to need even more help with the business now, and I want to make sure you get someone good. That way you could completely focus on making the jewelry without having to worry about the business side of things."

I go up on my toes—one of the only parts of my body that doesn't hurt—and press a soft kiss to his cheek. "Thank you. It would be nice to find someone like that."

My simple gesture must have thrown him for a loop because he's still blinking at me, so I do a one-eighty and change the subject. "So, I was thinking about something. You really don't have to if it's too much, but . . . do you want to come to the baby doctor with me tomorrow?"

That does the trick, his whole face immediately changing at my question. There's a shimmer in his eyes I've never seen before, but it's gone when he blinks.

Then he gives me one of his smiles that makes my heart beat a little faster. "Tell me when and where, and I'll be there."

Chapter Thirty-Six

CARTER

The car trip to the doctor is filled with silence, as we're both stuck in our own heads with the impending visit.

On the one hand, I truly enjoy being in Julia's company, even without talking. Just being around her gives me this overall feeling of weightlessness nothing else has ever given me before.

On the other hand, there are still about a million things we should talk about, and I'm definitely getting antsier the more time passes. There's no doubt how I feel about her or what I want. If anything, the accident made it all clear as day.

The thought of losing her has been enough to give me nightmares.

Talk about understanding what a blessing in disguise means.

I'm not sure a hit straight to *my* head would have been able to help me see things clearer.

Now, I just need to make sure Julia understands that too.

When she's ready.

Or when I lose the last of my restraint and confess my love for her.

"We're almost there." The navigation system informs me we only have one turn left. "Are you nervous?"

Since we're still on the highway, she's enjoying the ocean view until I have to take the next turn. I keep my eyes on the road but feel her gaze turning to me. "A little, but the doctor came highly recommended by the hospital. That makes it better."

Her voice is soft but steady, just like mine. That makes me hopeful she feels as certain and positive about things as I do, or at least starting to get there. "I agree. I'm glad you got that recommendation. We only want the best for the baby."

Our baby.

I don't say "our baby" since we still haven't talked about the fact we're actually going to be parents. Together. To our child.

Shit. We need to talk about this soon before I explode.

Julia only nods in response, and I park the car in front of the white, nondescript building when we arrive a minute later. Thankfully, it doesn't seem very busy, and we're checked in and sitting in the waiting room in no time. It probably helps that we're here so early in the morning. Julia's always flexible with her job anyway, and nothing and no one can get me back to work until I'm absolutely sure she's okay, even if she refuses my help most of the time anyway.

I couldn't handle the thought of leaving her by herself.

Ollie wants to take care of her too, but Julia said his overbearing nature would be too much at the moment. She knows he means well, and I know exactly what she means. Even though I'm having a super hard time giving her the room and quiet she so obviously longs for, I know my best friend wouldn't be able to do the same. He'd hover and be in her face like it's nobody's business.

So, Ollie and I made the necessary arrangements that has allowed me to work remotely as much as possible.

"I think we're up next." Julia's next to me on the small loveseat, nervously twisting her fingers.

"Are you sure you want me to come in with you?" I don't think she knows how badly I want to go with her.

"Of course I do. You have just as much right to be there as I do. It's your baby too." The last words come out in a whisper, and all I want to do is pull her into the biggest hug.

Before I can reply, a young nurse opens a door on the other side of the room. "Julia Bradford?"

We both get up, and I put my left hand on her lower back, hoping to give her some comfort since her nerves are clearly shot. She's probably redone her ponytail about ten times since we got here, and she might add some holes to her jeans if she rubs them any more with her hands.

After taking Julia's vitals and asking some standard questions about the pregnancy and our family histories, the nurse leaves us alone in the examination room.

Thankfully, we don't have to wait long until the doctor comes in. I was a little unsure if I'd be happy with a male doctor when Julia told me about him, but Dr. Yamatochi is a small guy with a big personality, and I like him immediately. Julia seems to feel the same if the smile on her face is anything to go by. He definitely has a way with patients, even when he talks about risks, complications, and everything else than can happen or that we have to watch out for.

"Well, let's take a look at the baby, shall we?" Dr. Yamatochi claps his hands together.

Since I was sitting in the visitor chair on the other side of the room, I get up to stand next to the examination table, putting my hand on Julia's to give it a light squeeze. My chest fills with warmth when she not only returns the gesture but also holds on to my hand like it's her new lifeline.

The doctor squeezes some gel onto Julia's exposed stomach and starts moving the ultrasound wand around for a few seconds before stopping. "There it is."

I stare at the screen, unable to see much more than a little blip. The doctor does his thing, taking measurements before pushing a few buttons on the machine, until the room fills with the most beautiful sound I've ever heard.

The baby's rhythmic heartbeat.

"A strong heartbeat at one hundred and sixty-five beats per minute. With the dates you've given us and the measurements of the embryo, you should be right around eight weeks, seven weeks and six days to be exact. And everything looks great. Let's get some more blood tests done, and then we'll see you back in four weeks." He gives us another reassuring smile as he hands Julia the ultrasound picture he printed out.

The picture has captured my full interest, and I barely notice when the doctor leaves the room.

I momentarily forget about everything except the little body in the picture. It's still too early to make out much, but it's easy to see the head and the rest of the body.

It's absolutely incredible.

"Wow." Julia lets go of my hand, bringing it up to cover her mouth instead as she stares at the little printout.

"Wow indeed." I gulp, my mouth suddenly dry, as I somehow manage to help Julia off the table, watching her as she fixes her clothes and gathers her things.

It's like I'm surrounded in a bubble, stuck in my head where my thoughts are busy bouncing around like little rubber balls.

How is this my life?

Two months ago, I was living the life of a bachelor, and now, I have the love of my life beside me and a little person soon to enter the picture. Surreal.

I lift my head when Jules walks to the door, looking back over her shoulder. Her grin softens into a genuine smile as she utters the words I know will forever change my life. "Are you coming, Daddy?"

"*T*hat's it." The words rush out of my mouth as I put my fork down on my plate with a loud *clink*. Carter looks up at me from across the table, a forkful of pasta halfway to his mouth.

It's been two busy days since the doctor's visit, and we still haven't talked about anything baby related, or us.

I've been trying to catch up with work—getting all those boxes shipped out with Carter's help and starting on new orders, slowly of course—while Carter has been out a few times for renovation-related appointments.

When he's here, he mostly spends his time on the computer, closing it every time I come close enough to catch a glimpse of the screen.

He told me it's house stuff, and he doesn't want to spoil the surprise, but enough is enough. The curiosity has been killing me, only adding to the things we've been pushing under the rug.

The baby. Us.

"I know you've been giving me room and space since the

accident because you mean well. I understand you want to make my life easier and avoid adding any stress. And I really appreciate all of that, but not talking about what happened is starting to stress me out more than everything else." My voice is laced with frustration, but I also feel relief.

So much better.

To my surprise, Carter chuckles. "I was wondering how long you'd make it."

My eyes turn into slits as I glare at him. "You knew this was going to happen?"

"Not for sure, but I thought it might. Now we know you're really ready to talk about everything. I know how important it is for your recovery to get as much rest as possible, not just because of the baby but also because of *your* injuries. I know you're pretending to feel better than you do." His gaze moves to the floor, his voice gentle.

My throat feels suddenly dry and swollen, and I close my eyes for a moment. "I'm just a baby about the bruises."

Getting up, he grabs his chair and moves it around the table to sit right next to me, personal space be gone. I turn to face him when he grabs my hand. "You're not a baby, Jules. It hurts, end of story. Everyone would be in pain when half of their body is covered in bruises and they can't take strong medication. I'm here for you because I want to be. I want to help as much as I can. And you can always talk to me about this stuff, anything, you know that."

My hands tremble as I nod, mad at myself that I didn't say anything before. "I know you are, and there's so much I want to talk to you about, but I just never know where to start."

I've wanted to bring it up several times since we got home

from the hospital last week, but I always end up chickening out.

For some reason, I'm terrified he's going to get up and leave once we actually have "the talk."

"How about we take it one topic at a time and start with the biggest elephant in the room? That little nugget in your belly." He lifts one of his hands toward my stomach but pulls it back at the last moment as if he isn't sure he's allowed to touch me that way. His gaze is gentle though when it snaps back to mine.

"Okay. I can do that." I've been catching myself in the same situation since I found out I'm pregnant—my hand hovering over my belly or actually touching it. Which is a funny thing considering I don't look or feel very pregnant yet —besides the consistent nausea and growing boobs. Also, the baby is only the size of a raspberry, which makes this whole experience even crazier.

When I realize I just disappeared in my own head again, I focus back on Carter's face. "Well, what are your thoughts on the pregnancy?"

"Did you know you were pregnant before the accident?"

We both ask our questions at the same time and chuckle.

I decide to go first, shaking my head—thankfully sans headache now. "I had no idea, I swear. Otherwise, I would have told you right away. I was just as shocked as I imagine you were when you found out."

Carter gives me a small smile, but it doesn't reach his eyes. "I wouldn't have blamed you considering how I always used to talk about never wanting children." He sighs heavily. "But to answer your question, it's still a little hard to wrap my head around it, but at the same time, I'm also excited. I catch myself thinking about how it will be, holding my baby in my arms, or later on, playing sports together. All kinds of things. It . . . it feels *right*."

My heart pounds rapidly as I carefully listen to each of his words, even more so when he starts rubbing his thumb over the sensitive skin of my palm.

His voice is gentle and light, mirroring his smile. "There isn't anyone better I can imagine having a baby with than you. You'll be the best mom out there."

Unexpected tears sting my eyes, and I rub them away before they can spill onto my cheeks. "Thank you. I can't even tell you how happy I am that you feel that way. I think that was the biggest reason I waited until now to ask. I was so scared you were only here out of obligation or guilt."

He shakes his head before brushing his fingers over my cheek so tenderly, I feel it all the way to my heart. "You still haven't gotten it, have you? I'm here for you, for you *and* the baby, because I want to be, not for any other reason."

Swallowing has become a real task as he grabs the sides of my chair and pulls until it bumps into his.

My legs are caged in by his, and the yearning in his eyes is so intense, it registers deep in my bones. I can't decide on what sensation to focus on first. The butterflies in my belly, or my racing pulse. No matter which one, it's intense to the point of making me dizzy.

"My beautiful and stubborn Julia. I love you with a magnitude that rivals the thrills of the ocean. This time with you has shown me that relationships aren't perfect, but they can be incredibly fulfilling when you open your heart to them."

The buzzing in my ears is loud, the tears spilling down

my cheeks faster than Carter can wipe them away. For a moment, I wonder if I'm dreaming, putting my hand over my heart when it feels like it might break out of my chest at any second.

I grab Carter's hand to put it in the spot mine just was. "Feel this."

"Your boobs? They feel nice. Have they grown?" He wiggles his eyebrows and I laugh.

I laugh before I cry some more, tears soaking Carter's shirt when he pulls me in for a hug.

When I've finally calmed down, I grab the napkin, trying to wipe my face as best as I can before gazing at Carter again.

He's still in the same spot, the same position, waiting for me. For my reaction.

My words.

My love.

This beautiful man, who etched his way into my heart long before I even understood what love is. The way he read me adventure stories in the fort my parents built for us even though Ollie thought it was lame, or the way he taught me how to surf when my brother's patience had long dissolved into thin air.

A small part of me aches that it took us this long to get to this point, but I'm not sure we would have been able to make it work before now, without these tragedies that lined the way to something so beautiful.

"I love you, and I hate that you're sleeping on the couch." I sniffle, swallowing hard as I'm still trying to wrap my head around what's happening.

"You say when, and I won't ever leave your side again."

"When." Tears fill my eyes again, and I point at them. "I swear, it's the hormones."

He chuckles, leaning in for a kiss that has desire burning in my belly even though Carter's keeping it light.

I groan, ninety-nine point nine percent certain, he probably won't touch me until I'm completely healed. Unless I can convince him otherwise. At least I'll enjoy trying.

Chapter Thirty-Eight

CARTER

THREE WEEKS LATER

"Jules, please open the door so I can help you." I let my head hit the bathroom door once more, hating to feel this helpless.

"Go away. I'll come out when I'm done. I don't need you standing right on the other side of the door listening to me throw up. That just makes it worse." Her voice is gravelly, and she barely gets the words out before another bout of heaving hits her, and I finally take a step back from the door.

"You win. I'm gone." I take a few more steps and lean against the wall, staring a hole into the bathroom door. No matter what she says, I'm not going far.

It's been three weeks since we had our little baby talk, and I don't think I've ever been this happy or content before. It's not always easy, especially when Julia's pregnancy hormones visit, but now that we know the reason behind her mood swings, it's a lot easier to handle them.

Now, it's basically like it has been before the accident.

No, never mind, we still haven't had sex yet.

Much to Julia's dismay, and the few choice words she likes to throw my way whenever I tell her we can't yet.

Everything looks great with the baby, but the bruises have only started to fade this last week. I couldn't handle the thought of hurting her any more.

She doesn't know it yet, but tonight I'm planning to make up for all the lost time, with great detail to attention, having missed our physical intimacy as much as she has.

"I hate this." The toilet flushes while Julia mutters aloud to herself. The faucet turns on before the buzzing sound of her toothbrush filters through the door.

I push off the wall when she finally comes out a few minutes later, taking in her pale complexion. "You don't feel well. Let's do this another day."

Holding up her hands, she shakes her head. "No way. You've been teasing me with that house for weeks now, and I want to have my surprise. As much as I dislike this whole sickness thing, it might not go away anytime soon. So we might as well do it now. It's as good as any other day." She shrugs and walks out of the room, and I follow her into the kitchen. "Let me just grab my water bottle and a few snacks, and I'm ready to go."

I catch up with her as she opens the fridge. "Are you sure?"

"Yes. Now stop asking me, or you'll drive both of us crazy."

I salute her and grab my own things, so we can leave when she's ready. "I'll be waiting by the front door then." I catch her small smile before she disappears behind the fridge door again.

A moment later, I stop in my tracks when she calls my name, drawing it out like it has a million syllables. I press my lips together to keep from groaning, hoping it isn't what I fear it is.

Turning around, I give her an innocent look. "What is it?"

She points at the fridge door before looking at me. "Did you take some of the magnets off? It looks different?"

I bite the inside of my cheek so hard, I might have drawn blood, trying as hard as I can to not think about what I did, because she reads me like a book most of the time. "Nope. Didn't touch the magnets."

"Huh." Julia shrugs before walking over to me, thankfully completely oblivious.

Thank you, pregnancy brain.

Less than half an hour later, we pull off the main road onto one of the small side streets filled with houses. The properties aren't huge, but still decent sized, especially for this area.

Julia's eyes are wide as she stares at me. "Wait a second. Did you seriously buy a house right by the ocean?"

I barely manage to keep the smile off my face. "Stop being so nosy already. Just wait and see."

She huffs out a breath, then looks back out her window in silence.

A few hundred feet down the road, I slow down and get a little remote control out of the middle console, holding it toward the upcoming property.

"You're kidding. You scored a house with a freaking gate?" Julia's gaze snaps in my direction, her voice an octave higher than usual.

This time, I lose my battle and a triumphant grin spreads across my face.

Then I nod, feeling good all over again about my purchase. "It was one of those 'being in the right place at the right time' moments. When I called our special realtor friend Linda, she'd just received the papers for this new house. It belonged to an older couple wanting to sell as fast as possible because they were moving to the East Coast. She said it needed some things done but that it was a killer deal. And boy, was she right. I put in my offer, and they accepted it right away. The rest is history so to speak."

"That's awesome." The smile she gives me is her truly happy one, the one I love seeing the most, and it makes the taxing and exhausting work worth it.

Shifting around in her seat, she faces me, leaning across the middle console. "Soooo . . . Did I miss you getting rich somehow?"

Her comment makes me laugh, once again screaming familiarity to me in a way I know I'd never have with another woman.

It's one of the things I cherish the most in our relationship. "Well, I don't usually shout it from the rooftops, but let's just say, I've been pretty lucky with some investments over the years."

She slaps my arm playfully and chuckles. "No way. Good for you. And here you were rooming with my brother."

"Nothing has changed really." I lift one shoulder in a shrug. "It's just nice to have the security, to know the money is in my bank account if I need it. And now I've got a great investment with this house too."

Her focus turns back on the house in front of us, a decent-sized, two-story beachfront house. "Well, looks like you did a good job."

The house isn't a mansion, especially compared to a lot of other houses in Southern California, but it fits in without standing out. The most important thing is I like it a lot and hope Jules will too. Otherwise, I might have a problem. "Shall we?"

We get out of the car, and Julia goes toward the front door when I catch her arm. "Let's go around the house. I want to show you the back first."

"Okay." She looks confused but doesn't comment any further.

I lead her along the side path of the house to the back. Julia stops when the ocean comes into view in the distance.

The property is on the cliffside, overlooking the ocean with two decks on the back of the house. The top one is my favorite. It's larger than the one at Ollie's house, and I thought of Jules the second I stepped out on it for the first time, and how much she'd love it.

When she remains silent, I walk up behind her, wrapping my arms around her middle, and enjoying her body pressed against mine. Nestling my head into the curve of her shoulder, I whisper into her ear, "Do you like it?"

She puts her hands on mine, atop her belly, and squeezes them. "Are you kidding me? This is so beautiful. I can't believe it's yours. I love it." She cranes her neck, looking around past the property lines. "Seriously though, Carter. I'm so happy you were able to snatch up this beauty. Is there a path that goes down to the beach somewhere?"

I turn her a little to the right and motion toward the gate. "Just over there."

"How perfect." She rocks on the soles of her feet, barely refraining from bouncing. "I'm so excited for you."

"Us, Jules. Us." Before she can respond, I take her hand, and pull her back to the front of the house. "Let me show you the inside."

"Carter. Wait. We have to . . . You can't just . . ." Her eyes sparkle in the sunlight when I turn around, and I'm mesmerized by her beauty.

Pulling her body flush with mine, I capture her lips in a searing kiss that leaves both of us breathing heavily. "Can we talk about this later?"

Her cheeks are flushed, and her eyes slightly glazed over when she nods. "All right."

I chuckle.

Works. Every. Time.

I press my lips to hers one more time before leading her inside our home.

Fuck, does that sound perfect.

Chapter Thirty-Nine

JULIA

The first thing I notice when we walk into the house is the fresh paint smell. My pregnancy has intensified my sense of smell tenfold, so it's a good thing I've always liked the smell of paint. It's weird, but at least it's better than enjoying the smell of gasoline. That was my brother's thing when we were little.

"Wow." I look around the impressive room in awe, immediately liking the open floor plan that's flooded with natural light. The hardwood floors contrast beautifully with the light-gray walls, the exposed white wooden ceiling beams, absolutely stunning. When we walk farther into the kitchen, I can't help myself and walk over to the big wall of windows overlooking the ocean. Even though we just stood outside looking at the view, I doubt I'll ever get enough of it.

Carter is quiet as he leads me around, showing me the chef's kitchen with top-of-the-line appliances and a beautiful breakfast bar. His eyes are on me the entire time, surely about to combust if I don't share my thoughts with him soon.

Once we're done downstairs, he leads me up the staircase

to the second level. It's decorated in the same simple style as the downstairs, with lots of light and neutral colors. It suits this house well though, especially with the ocean view as a backdrop, not to mention Carter too since he's never been big on materialistic or flashy things.

After showing me a beautiful master bedroom and guest room, both with chic and elegant bathrooms—including steam showers—he stops in front of a closed door.

When I look at him, he doesn't open the door right away, my quickening breath betraying my nervousness. "What is it?"

He chews on his lip before giving me a shy smile. After a moment of consideration, he seems to make up his mind, taking a step aside to make room for me. "Why don't you see for yourself?"

After shooting him a questioning look, I reach out for the door handle, not sure what to expect. I push the door open all the way before my hand flies to my mouth at the sight in front of me.

A nursery.

Carter has a freaking room for our baby in his new house.

Looking back at him, I'm not surprised to feel my eyes burning. He gives me a small smile and puts a reassuring hand on my back. I look at him for another moment before my eyes flicker back to the room. It's the cutest room I've ever seen.

The walls are painted in a neutral beige, with a white crib and changing table on one side. Since the room is right next to the master bedroom, it has the same ocean view, and it couldn't be more perfect.

His voice is soft behind me. "I thought . . . if you'd like, maybe we could decorate it together once we know what the baby is?"

My heart feels as if it's swelling, the warm feeling in my chest expanding endlessly. "I'd absolutely love that."

When Carter's arms encircle my waist, I turn around, eager to see his handsome face. My mind plays a loop of happy memories, all including Carter, bringing me a sense of calm and contentment.

When he runs his nose along my jaw, I immediately start fidgeting, the heat pooling in my belly so strong, I whimper. "Carter."

"Yes, baby."

"I can't wait any longer."

He pulls back, staring into my eyes so intensely, I feel like he's staring straight into my soul. "Tell me you'll move in with me."

The needy fog in my brain bursts like a bubble. "What?"

"I bought this house for us, for you and me, and our baby." He kisses me. "Say yes."

He said *our* house earlier, or something like that, but I was so distracted by the view that I wasn't sure I heard him correctly.

Seems like I did.

I open and close my mouth several times before tilting my head. "For real?"

My gaze wanders over to the open door of the master bedroom he showed me before. Without overthinking it, I walk to it again, standing in the doorway, staring at the massive four-poster bed with the breathtaking panoramic view next to it.

Carter takes my hand and pulls me inside, sitting on the

edge of the bed with me perched on one of his thighs. "So, what do you think?"

My head does a quick bobble as my mouth spreads into an almost painful grin. "Absolutely, yes. It's all so beautiful and perfect."

"Like you." His gaze does me in, and I tackle him, pushing him back on the mattress, ignoring my slightly achy limbs.

I need to have him right now before I go completely insane. Thankfully, he doesn't protest this time, helping me push down his pants far enough to free his hard length. By some miracle, I chose a dress today, and I don't hesitate before pulling it up to my waist. My underwear is next, pushed to the side in one quick swipe, so I can finally, *finally*, sink down on him in one swift move, taking exactly what I've longed for so much.

And gosh, it feels so good to have him inside of me again. He fills me perfectly, like he does every single time.

"Fuck. Give a guy a warning before you give him a heart attack." His face contorts in pleasure, showing me he's been as desperate for this as I have.

Our fingers rub and stroke, squeeze each curve, exploring everything we've missed so much. It's quick and frantic.

Every touch, every kiss, every little moan and groan, feels as incredible as before, but somehow also more special.

Having everything out in the open—our relationship and our feelings for each other—turns this into so much for than *just* sex. When my release hits me, I close my eyes and hold on to Carter with a steel-like grip. It's that intense.

My eyes grow hot as I bite back tears when I realize that having sex with someone you truly love turns it into something magical, solidifying this connection between us on a completely different level.

His gaze is on me as he pulses inside me, the words "I love you" leaving his lips on a sharp exhale as he pulls me down on his chest.

I enjoy his nearness more than I could have ever imagined. He caresses my back until both of our heartbeats have returned to normal, and all I can think about is how he's *my person*. The one I want to share all my dirty little secrets with, and the one I want to look at first thing in the morning and last thing at night.

His breath tickles my ear, his cheek pressed against mine. "And here I was planning on taking my sweet time with you tonight to make up for all the lost time."

"Good. I'm looking forward to it." I give him a cheeky grin, and he laughs. "I love you."

His answering kiss is soft, no tongue or teeth, but still leaves me with warm and happy feelings galore. "I love *you*."

He pats me on the butt and chuckles. "Now get off me. There's still a surprise waiting for you."

That has me sitting up, my eyes wide. "The nursery wasn't it? There's more?"

His eyes sparkle with mischief. "Well, I guess that was half of it. But I have another half surprise for you."

"Hold that thought." I hold up a finger and clean up in the bathroom quickly before heading back to him. "Alrighty, let's see it."

Carter grins and holds out his hand, which I take without hesitation. He leads me back downstairs and off to a little corridor with three more doors I missed earlier. The first one is Carter's office, the second one a small bathroom.

After shooting me an anticipatory glance, he once more steps aside, letting go of my hand. "This one's for you. Open it."

To say I'm nervous is an understatement. My hands are shaking when I finally open the door a moment later.

My heart does extra thumps when I get my first good look at the room, and I'm not sure how much more it can take today.

Holy shit.

"This is all for *me*?"

Carter chuckles before giving me a small push. "Yes, it is. Go check it out already."

atching Julia inspect her studio, as I like to call it, is absolutely priceless. She has the biggest smile on her face as she walks around the room, brushing her fingers along the walls of shelves and the huge craft table.

After a ton of online research, I purchased pegboards, baskets, and about six hundred other forms of storage, which she's inspecting in detail.

Seeing her this happy makes every single minute I spent on Pinterest and in craft stores worth it.

Once she's had her fill, she walks back to me, wrapping her hands around my neck and going up on her toes. "This is the best surprise ever. I've never seen a craft room this awesome. I couldn't ask for more and have no idea how I'm ever going to be able to thank you for everything."

Her eyes are so expressive, shining so brightly, and I could get lost in them forever. "I'm glad you like it. Just let me know if something's missing, and we'll get it for you. Anything."

After pressing my mouth to her soft lips, I reach for her hand. "Come with me."

We walk through the kitchen and out the back door onto the deck. With the beautiful blue sky, and the ocean sounds playing softly in the background, I search her face for the last glimmer of hope I need.

The soft wind around us calms me as I take a deep breath. The simple act of fresh, salty air filling my lungs gives me the courage to do what I've planned on doing.

Out of my back pocket, I take the folded piece of paper that's been burning a hole in my pants for the past few hours. After unfolding it, I scan it once more before turning it around so Julia can see it too.

She regards me carefully, clearly no clue what's going on until realization dawns on her face and she points at the paper. "Wait. Is that— I knew something was missing from the fridge."

Her eyes snap back to mine as I nod, releasing a breath at the same moment I tear the paper in half.

Her husband checklist.

"I know I will never be everything you put on here."

Rip.

"But let me assure you I will try my hardest to be *everything* you need."

Rip.

Her gaze flickers back and forth between my face and the paper in my hand, or the little that's left of it. "Carter. What's going on?"

I go down on one knee and pull a small box from my front pocket.

The wood is hard under my knee, not that it would

matter if sharp rocks dug into my skin right now. Nothing would deter me from making this moment happen.

Her mouth falls open as she blinks rapidly at me before putting a shaky hand on my shoulder.

The skin on my face feels tight as my stomach clenches and churns, the butterflies multiplying by the second.

A tingle runs up my spine as I get my breathing under control. "Julia Bradford, you've been driving me crazy for most of my life. You've always been my favorite girl, no matter if you had mud all over you, threw ice cream in my face, or cried all over me when you realized you'd never get an invitation to Hogwarts. Those special memories make me love you even more, and you're everything I could possibly want. I know it might seem quick, but if the accident has taught me one thing, it's that things can change in a split second. I treasure you beyond words and want you by my side for the rest of my life. Will you marry me?"

Tears silently slide down her face, but they can't overshadow the beaming smile that's spreading across her face. "Yes, silly. I love you so much. Yes, yes, yes. Of course, I will."

"Really?" Even though I was obviously hoping for that response, my brain's still trying to process this moment.

I get up quickly and caress her cheeks.

Then there's kisses. Lots and lots of kisses.

Julia is the first to pull back, a mischievous glint in her eyes. "So . . . Do you actually have a ring in that box?"

I laugh when I realize I've never gotten that far, the ring box still unopened in my hand.

Winking at her, I hold out my hand. "Why don't you check?"

Pulling back the lid of the box, a simple platinum band comes into view, paired with a beautiful princess-cut diamond.

I wanted to go extravagant on the ring, but Cora—thank goodness for that woman and all her help—reminded me to think about if Julia is the flashy kind of girl.

She clutches her chest with her left hand before I take it gently into mine to put the ring on. She turns her hand this way and that, throwing little rainbow rays all around us. "It's so beautiful."

"*You're* beautiful." I let her admire her new jewelry for a moment before stealing another long kiss. "And we can make it a long engagement if you'd rather wait for the baby first. Totally up to you. Whatever you want goes."

With her eyes dancing, and her voice bubbly, she leans her head on my chest, allowing her to listen to my out-of-control heartbeat. "We'll figure it out."

We stay like this for a long time, our future surrounding us, slowly swaying to the breeze that wants to be recognized, just like our love did.

Just like Mom said, love does change everything.

And now, I'll have that forever.

EPILOGUE

Julia

ALMOST TWO YEARS LATER

There is a soft knock at the door before my brother pokes in his head. "They're all ready for you guys." He gives me a reassuring smile but his gaze doesn't linger long on me, quickly flickering past me to his wife, Cora, and their baby squirming in her arms. The grin on his face is starting to look painful. "Look at all of you. My three favorite girls in one room. And all so beautiful."

Unable to resist, he slips in and shuts the door behind him, walking over to his leading ladies, smothering both with gentle kisses. Oliver and Cora surprised us all when they eloped on their tropical vacation just a couple months after Carter and I got engaged. Not even a few weeks later they announced they were expecting too.

At that point, I was already in my last trimester, but it was fun to share the last bit of my pregnancy with Cora.

What's even better is to have the cousins so close in age. They already love each other like crazy.

"Are you ready to throw some flowers for Aunt Jules?" Cora looks at Emmi, her sweet almost one-year-old cooing and throwing her little arms up in response.

We knew it would probably be chaotic and maybe even messy to include the two little ones in our wedding, but we wouldn't have had it any other way. Everyone's been looking forward to our wedding, even though Carter might have been a teeny bit frustrated that it took us almost two years to get to this point, but I didn't want this to be more stressful than it had to be.

There was simply so much going on with healing after my accident and moving into the house. Then our baby boy was born and we wanted to wait until he was a little older and we had settled into our roles as parents.

"Well, I'm ready for sure." I get up from my chair and smooth down my dress. Growing up, I always thought I'd choose a puffy princess dress. Instead, I immediately fell in love with my simple lace dress. The second I saw it at the bridal store, I knew this was it.

It's ivory, fitted through the bodice and hips, and covered in vintage-inspired lace with an open back. It reminded me of my mom's dress, is absolutely stunning, and most of all, it makes me feel beautiful on this special day, so I hope Carter will like it too.

"You look utterly gorgeous." My brother walks over to me and puts a hand on my shoulder. "Mom and Dad would be so proud of you." His voice is thick with emotion, and if the excessive swallowing is anything to go by, he's trying to keep it together for me.

"Thank you." I take a deep breath and close my eyes before looking back at him, still trying hard not to cry.

Cora comes up to us and gives us a hug, squishing Emmi between us. "Stop being all sentimental, or we're all gonna cry. Since that's not an option right now, I better head out. I'm sure people are starting to get antsy. See you guys on the other side." She gives me one more reassuring squeeze and heads out, leaving us alone.

"Let's do this." I grab my brother's arm and pull, making him chuckle.

"*Now* you want to hurry? You've made poor CJ wait all this time, and *now* you're the one trying to pull *me* out of the room?"

I laugh nervously, still feeling a little guilty for the long engagement, but that's why we're here. To fix that. "Exactly. It's been long enough, and I'm more than ready to finally make it official."

"Fair enough." He pats my hand for a second and nods. "Let's get this show started then."

And off we go to meet my husband-to-be at the end of the aisle.

Carter

My nerves were shot long before they started playing Mendelssohn's Wedding March. Just when I think I might pass out, my best friend opens the back door of our house, holding Julia on his arm.

Finally.

My Julia.

She looks magnificent, as always. Her long dress gently flowing in the breeze, hugging her body in all the right places. I've learned to be patient over the last two years. Before waiting for this day to happen, I spent months waiting for our child to be born. It was easily the most agonizing experience I've ever had. Even though I'm so close to my goal, I feel more impatient than ever, mere seconds away from sprinting down the makeshift aisle on our deck, so I can throw my bride-to-be over my shoulder to get this over with.

"Almost there, Carter. Don't lose it now." Cora chuckles as she passes me, taking her place on Julia's side in front of the flower arch. Emmi is in her arms, playing with a few remaining rose petals she kept from her flower girl job.

I give Cora a tight-lipped nod and focus on the aisle, noticing that Oliver and Julia aren't in sync with the music at all.

Wait. Is Julia pulling her brother?

A chuckle escapes my lips, and my mom shoots me a curious look. That Julia seems just as impatient as I am lifts a weight off my shoulders, allowing me to finally relax, especially since they reach me at that point too.

"Hi." She's in front of me, a little bit out of breath.

So fucking beautiful.

"Hi yourself." I grab her hands, unable to keep from touching her a moment longer. I take a step closer and bend to kiss her, which results in a few chuckles from the audience.

I stare into her pretty brown eyes and forget everything around me. Even though I hear someone talking, I'm in a daze, and almost miss my moment to say "I do," but Ollie comes to the rescue and nudges me from behind, whispering the words.

Julia grins at me, saying her "I do" less than a minute later. My mom comes up to us with Hayden perched on her hip. He's holding the little pillow with our rings in his arms, squishing it to his chest like it's his new favorite toy.

"Dada." He gives me a drooly smile, showing off the few teeth that finally broke through before his first birthday a few months ago.

"Thanks, big guy." Seeing my boy causes me to look around the small crowd of friends and family that came to celebrate this special day with us.

Making today even more perfect.

Julia and I exchange rings, before we're finally declared husband and wife.

After a way too short kiss, Hayden seems to feel the excitement around us, starting to cheer and bounce in my mom's arms before leaping into ours.

Julia and I hug him tight between us, and everything my mom said finally makes sense. The journey might have been littered with mistakes, but ultimately love directed us to where we were meant to be.

This is what I've been waiting for all these years, for this special connection—my special someones—to fill my heart and make me feel utterly complete.

AUTHOR NOTE

Thank you so much for reading my words!

If you enjoyed *The Husband Checklist*, it would mean the world to me if you could leave a review. Word of mouth and reviews go a long way, and I'd appreciate it so very much.

For more books and bonus scenes, please visit my website www.jasminmiller.com

ACKNOWLEDGMENTS

I had such a blast writing The Husband Checklist. Carter and Julia were incredibly fun and sexy but also threw a ton of emotions at me. I hope I was able to tell their story the way they wanted me to. As always, a group of fantastic people played a huge role in getting there.

A huge thanks to my husband, as always. Nothing would ever be possible if it wasn't for his constant love and support. The patience this man shows me daily, especially with anything book-related, is beyond admirable. He's basically an angel and deserves the biggest gold star for that alone. He and our little monsters are the reason I'm chasing after this dream. (And to get these crazy voices out of my head, but that's a whole other issue. lol) My heart beats the loudest for all four of them. Forever.

Suze, this might have been our craziest ride so far, and you were there to catch me throughout all of it. Thank you so incredibly much for always being there to help and for giving me the metaphorical slap in the face when I need it. As crazy as it sounds, I'll always love you for that. But I know you get it.

Alicia, thanks so much for always being there for me and for helping out any way you can! I adore you so hard!

Karen, Melissa, Kristen, Stephie, Jackie, and Shayne. You ladies helped so much with your feedback, and I'm so grateful to have found you. Your love and support make my heart so happy. You're absolutely amazing. Thanks for everything. Shayne, double thanks for the extra set of final eyes.

Marion, I'm having a hard time finding the right words to say thanks to you. You blew the magic dust into this edit I needed so badly. The story is so much better because of you. Thank you from the bottom of my heart!

As always, Judy, I'm finding joy in correcting all the mistakes you find. So grateful for your fantastic proofreading skills.

Najla, you're my cover queen, and I can't thank you enough for creating this gorgeous cover (and the beautiful graphics) for me. You and your work are amazing!

My lovely ARC and promo teams. I have so much love for every single one of you for helping me with reviews, creating beautiful pictures and posts, and for spreading the love about my stories. You guys are all very special, and it wouldn't be as fun or awesome without you. Thank you for loving on my words and for supporting me. It means the absolute world to me.

Awesome Peeps, you're exactly that (awesome!!) and so much more. Beyond awesome!! I can always count on you to put a smile on my face, and that is worth more than I could ever put into words. Thank youuuuuuu!!

My readers. Goodness. Anyone who's ever picked up one of my books. You're all like magical creatures to me. That you give my stories a chance is indescribable and fills me with so much gratitude, I might explode into a glittering rainbow at some point. ;)

You're all rock stars to me, and I wish I could give every one of you a big hug. 🩶🩶🩶

ABOUT THE AUTHOR

Jasmin Miller is a professional lover of books and cake (preferably together) as well as a fangirl extraordinaire. She loves to read and write about anything romantic and never misses a chance to swoon over characters. Originally from Germany, she now lives in the western US with her husband and three little humans that keep her busy day and night.

If you liked *The Husband Checklist* and would like to know more about her and her books, please sign up for her newsletter on her website. She'd love to connect with you.

www.jasminmiller.com
jasminmillerbooks@gmail.com
Facebook.com/jasminmillerwrites
Instagram.com/jasminmiller
Twitter.com/JasminMiller_
Facebook.com/groups/jasminmillerpeeps